Don't you

PUCKING

DARE

Sheridan Anne

Don't You Pucking Dare - Kings of Denver (Book 4)

Anne, Sheridan

Kings of Denver (Book 4) Don't You Pucking Dare

Cover Design: Sheridan Anne

Editing: Fox Proof Edits

Formatting: Sheridan Anne

Beta: Holly Swain-Harvey & Kat Uluave

DISCLAIMER

Don't You Pucking Dare was previously published as Tank - Kings of Denver (Book 4) 2018-2022.

The content of Don't You Pucking Dare remains the same with new edits and tightening up of each chapter. The story within has not changed. Simply received a facelift plus new interior formatting, title, and cover.

PROLOGUE

SOPHIE

My eyes spring open into the early morning haze, my stomach clenching with unease. "Ahhhhhhh, fuckkkkkkk," I groan, throwing the blankets back and scrambling out of bed butt naked, no time to find any clothes. I clamp my hand over my mouth, terror rocking through my veins.

My feet slam against the carpet as I race to the bathroom. *I'm not gonna make it. I'm not gonna make it.* "Babe," Tank grunts behind me, as I hear the familiar sound of the big guy throwing himself out of bed. "What's wrong?"

If I stop to reply, I'll end up blowing chunks all through our bedroom, and despite this man being my husband and the love of my life, there are some things a woman simply must keep to herself. Instead, I race through to the bathroom, the tiles cold under my feet as

1

I slam the door between us, the loud thud echoing through the silence.

Knowing my big caveman is bound to attempt to follow, I hastily lock the door behind me, my fingers scrambling over the little button and wasting precious seconds I simply don't have.

Confident I'm free to hurl in peace, I take the final steps to the toilet and drop to my knees, hastily gripping the toilet seat and pulling it up. Finally, I hang my head over the rim just in time to violently throw up, emptying the contents of my stomach into the toilet.

"Babe?" Tank rushes out, looming over me as he rushes in to grab my hair, pulling it away from my face.

Horror blasts through me, realizing I mustn't have locked the door properly. "Get out," I cry, trying to shove him away. This man has seen me at my highest highs and every one of my lowest lows, but this is where I draw the line.

Tank scoffs, completely disregarding my need for privacy as he manages to get the hairband off my wrist. He wrangles my hair up into a messy bun, then once he's certain it's not going to fall out, he gets up and finds a washcloth. I hear the water running and within seconds, Tank is right back at my side, handing me the wet washcloth while I rest my forehead against the cold porcelain of the toilet.

After two more chunk-blowing episodes, I'm finally able to get up off the bathroom floor, and without hesitation, I fall straight into Tank's big arms. He wraps me in his embrace, one hand gently holding the back of my head against his chest as his other snakes around my body, claiming as much of my body as possible. "Feeling better?" he murmurs as I listen to the heavy thumping of his heartbeat through his chest, my eyes closing, already completely exhausted with the day and it's not even 7 a.m.

Closing my eyes, I take a few calming breaths, and as my stomach finally begins to settle, I nod against his wide chest. "Yeah, actually. Heaps better," I tell him, feeling a newfound energy pulsing through my veins.

Tank drops a soft kiss to the top of my head and releases me as I step out of his warm arms and turn toward the vanity. My brows furrow, not understanding what the hell just happened. How strange to go from violently throwing up to feeling perfectly fine.

Stepping up to the vanity, I smirk at Tank's attempt at putting my hair up. It's an absolute mess, and if I was outside in nature, I'd have the birds confusing it for their nests. I appreciate it all the same though.

Pulling open the drawer, determined to brush my teeth and get my clammy ass through a shower, I start digging around for everything I need when my fingers brush across the small packet of tampons. My whole body tenses, something gnawing within me.

I start doing the math while shaking my head.

No, I couldn't be . . . Could I?

"Babe?" Tank questions, sensing my alarm. He steps right up behind me, taking my hips as he stares at me through the bathroom mirror, his eyes wide. "What's wrong?"

"I, umm . . ." I swallow hard before locking my gaze on his through the mirror, knowing damn well he's not going to like this. But there's only one way to know for sure, and I'm not about to do that with him gaping at me. "I'm gonna need you to get out."

"What?" he breathes, gripping onto my hips tighter. I know exactly what's coming next.

Turning into him, I shove my hand against his chest and shove him back toward the door. "Two minutes," I tell him as he gapes down at me, not even budging a little.

"Babe," he mutters. "What the fuck is going on? Is something wrong?"

I shake my head. "Everything's fine. I just need two minutes," I tell him. Then using all my strength, I push and prod at him until I can finally get the door shut between us. But let's be real, the man is an absolute monster. If he really wanted to stay and find out what's on my mind, he could have done it easily. Hell, he could overpower me just by breathing in my direction, which tells me that he's giving me this moment of privacy. I couldn't be more grateful.

Knowing there's a clock ticking down on his patience, I dash back to the vanity and shove my hand back into the drawer. Pulling out the box of pregnancy tests that we keep for those *just in case* moments, I empty the whole packet out on the counter and grab all four of the bastards.

"Babe?" Tank questions through the door as I make myself comfortable on the toilet—a toilet that's definitely seeing more action than any other morning. "What the hell is going on in there?"

After popping the lids on all four of the tests, I position them between my legs in one hand and take a shaky breath. I mean, why only pee on one when I can pee on them all, right?

Nervousness pulses through me and I have to force myself to

concentrate on what I'm doing. *Calm down, Sophie. It's just a little pee. You do this all the time. Relax your hooch and let the river run wild and free.* I repeat my mantra over and over again, trying to get my body to relax just enough to get this over and done with.

Feeling my body finally starting to relax, I make sure I'm not about to pee all over my hands when I hear the big bastard on the other side of the door. "Babe?" Tank demands, sounding as though his mouth is right up against the wood.

And just like that, the river runs dry.

"Shut up," I yell back at him, frustration starting to consume me. "You're ruining my concentration."

"Concentration? What the hell do you need to concentrate on in the bathroom?" he questions.

"Argh," I groan, almost dropping one of the tests into the toilet. "Be quiet."

Tank lets out a frustrated groan before I hear him back up from the bathroom door and flop down on the bed. But if I were a betting woman, I'd say he's sitting as close to the edge as possible, ready to pounce on me the second I open the door.

With Tank out of the way and the pressure to perform fading from existence, I'm able to get this show on the road and relax enough to relieve myself. Trying to peer down between my legs, I make sure I've got my aim right, but the slight movement throws me way off course, and I end up peeing all over my hand. "Ahhh, gross," I groan, mortified with myself. I mean, shit. Who would have thought peeing on a few sticks would be so hard?

The second I can, I spring up from the toilet and hurry across to the vanity. After laying down a few tissues on the counter, I place the tests on top of them before scrubbing my hands silly, terrified of looking down at the tests beside me.

"Were you seriously just trying to pee?" Tank asks from the other side of the door, clearly not able to remain on the bed for long.

"Yes," I mutter, rolling my eyes.

"Then why the hell did I get pushed out?" he demands. "I've seen you pee millions of times, and you know . . . it's never really taken this long before."

"Oh. My. God. Tank. Would you shut up? I'm still concentrating," I tell him as the first little line begins to appear on the tests, making the anxiety burn through me. My hands shake and I start to pace.

Just a little while longer.

"Babe, let me in."

"No."

"I swear, I'm knocking this door down in three seconds," he rumbles.

A second line starts to appear on all four of the tests, and my eyes bug out of my head. I lean down, gripping one of the tests and gawk at it as the second line becomes stronger, more defined. I scramble for the box, double-checking the results. "Wait, wait, wait," I yell over my shoulder as Tank begins counting down, my gaze locked on the little pictures on the side of the box. My hands shake so violently I can barely make out the words.

"Three."

Fuck.

"Two."

One line. Not pregnant. Two lines . . . pregnant.

Holy shit.

"One."

I spin around, turning toward the door as tears of joy spring to my eyes, but it's too late. The door is ripped right off its hinges and tossed toward our bed, my husband storming through the empty doorframe. His sharp gaze sails over my face with deep concern, my tears throwing him off. "What's the matter?" he rushes out, taking my hips and pulling me in close, his gaze holding me captive.

Shaking my head, I take a step back, putting just enough space between us to bring my hands up. Catching the movement, his gaze drops, clearly very confused by what the hell is going on. "I . . . I don't understand. What's this?" he questions, taking the test from my hand and glancing over it.

A smile stretches over my lips, already so in love with this little alien growing inside of me. "You're going to be a daddy," I tell him, my voice breaking over the lump in my throat. The raw happiness is like nothing I've ever known.

His face goes white, gaping at me for just a moment. "Are you serious?" he questions, his gaze falling back to the test. Tank studies it closely, grabbing the box and checking over the results, his heart in his eyes. "Holy fuck."

"Yeah," I laugh, watching as a wide smile spreads across his face.

His eyes sparkle with undeniable happiness, and not a second later, he throws the test and the box over his shoulder before lifting me off the ground, pulling me into him. "Fuck, yeah," he roars, before crushing his lips to mine in a deep, loving kiss.

I laugh, unable to pull myself away as I lock my legs around his waist, holding onto him with everything I am. "I haven't brushed my teeth yet."

Tank strides out of the bathroom, his hand gripping my ass as he takes me right back to bed. "I don't give a shit," he says against my lips. "We're going to be parents."

"No," I tell him, feeling him hardening against my stomach. "We're going to be great parents."

CHAPTER 1

SOPHIE

The heavy bang of the front door echoes through the house as I maniacally try to put the finishing touches on my story, preparing to send it to my editor. I've been working on this for weeks now and I can't wait another second to finally be able to say that it's done. The fact that it's taken this long has already been driving me insane.

"Babe, where are you?" Tank calls through the house, as I hear the familiar sound of him kicking off his shoes and dumping his heavy hockey bag in the entryway.

I roll my eyes, knowing there's no way in hell that he would have lined his shoes up neatly next to mine, a conversation we've had many times over. "I'm in my office," I yell back, a smile playing on my lips.

Even after all this time, I still get a rush when he comes home to me. Just the sound of him coming through our door is a gift in itself.

The thought has me groaning at myself. Who would have known, back in my skank days, that this would have been my life? The idea of settling down with a man and becoming his wife never crossed my mind. Not until Tank. And now, I'm here saying shit like *the sound of him coming home is a gift*. Ugh, what the fuck is wrong with me? These stupid pregnancy hormones have been fucking with me non-stop.

Tank barges into my home office and he pauses by the door, groaning with hunger as he takes me in. Knowing he's coming for me, I only have a second to hit send on my email to my editor before his hands are on my body. He pulls me out of my chair before turning me to sit on the edge of my desk and stepping in between my legs. "Fuck, Soph. You've got to give a man some warning when you're planning to work in your birthday suit."

I shrug my shoulders, my hand slipping up the front of his shirt and brushing over his body, the feel of his tight abs beneath my fingers giving me life. "It was hot today."

Tank's eyes sparkle and become hooded as he cradles my stomach, the same way he does every time he sees me. "How's this little guy doing?" he asks, leaning in and pressing a gentle kiss to my lips.

The second Tank talks, our son starts kicking as though there's some kind of house party going on in my guts. I'm only five months along, so I'm not to the point where it's uncomfortable, just a slight fluttering from within. "He's good," I smile. "I think he likes the sound of your voice."

"Of course he does. I'm his daddy," Tank says, his fingers roaming over my stomach. "How was work? Did you finish your story?"

"Sure did," I tell him. "Only just hit send as you walked in. I'm starving though. Lunch wasn't nearly enough. I was about to go and get myself something else to eat, but seeing as you're home . . . Perhaps we could go out for an early dinner?"

Tank lets out a sigh. He's become such a homebody since we found out I was pregnant. It's as if he doesn't want to share this moment with the rest of the world, which I guess I understand. It's rumored that his coach is looking at him to take on the role of captain this season, so the press have been a little wild on him lately, but it comes with the territory. It's something we've had to get used to ever since he signed with the NHL. "You know I like it when you cook dinner in your underwear, with that sexy little bump showing."

"I thought you hated my cooking?" I ask, lifting my chin and smirking up at him.

"I do. It's terrible," he says. "But watching you strut around, barefoot and pregnant . . . Mmmm, it does something to me."

My tongue rolls over my bottom lip, the hunger in his eyes making me wet. "Really? Now?" I question with a hooded stare, desire pulsing through my veins.

"Mmhmm."

Tank moves in even closer. I feel his erection right up against my core, and I groan as he starts to grind, both of us hungry now. Since the moment I fell pregnant, my sex drive has been out of this world, which means I'm regularly exhausting my man. I'm constantly all over him, but he hasn't complained yet, more than satisfying me every single time.

His lips come down on mine as I quickly rid him of his shirt, putting his sculpted body on display. He's so fucking stunning, mouth-wateringly delicious. He blew me away the day I first met him in the Denver University campus gym, and now, years later, it's only gotten better.

My hands move to the top of his pants and after making quick work of them, his lips drop lower to the sensitive skin below my ear. I groan, tilting my head and opening up for him as my fingers curl around his huge, thick cock, desperate to feel that familiar stretch when he pushes inside me.

He's so big, I can barely fit my fingers around him, but I give him my all anyway. A man like Tank deserves nothing less. My hand pumps up and down, my thumb curling over his tip just the way he likes it as he reaches down between us and presses his fingers to my needy clit.

My body jolts with pleasure as he rubs small circles and a soft moan tears from the back of my throat. He keeps going, teasing me until I'm right on the edge, and only then does he lower his fingers and slowly push them deep inside my cunt. "Oh, fuck," I pant, tipping my head forward to his shoulder, but he's not having a bar of it. He twines his free hand into my hair and pulls my head back to kiss me deeply.

His fingers curl inside me, massaging my walls as my eyes roll in my head, undeniable pleasure pulsing through my body.

His touch is everything. So fucking delicious and raw. And over time, it's only gotten better.

Knowing my body better than I know it myself, Tank pulls back, freeing his fingers from within me and a soft, broken breath escapes me. But he's right there again, his hand around my back, scooting me right to the edge of the desk. He lines his thick cock up with my entrance and thrusts deep inside me.

"Oh, God," I groan, gripping onto his strong shoulder as he stretches my pussy wide, filling me to the brim.

Tank grunts and stills inside me, needing a moment to gather himself before pulling back. He fucks me hard, finally relieving the ache that's been there since he left for training this morning. He works my clit, rubbing tight circles as I hold on for dear life, panting and groaning until we come together, our highs rocking through us.

That's the one thing I've always been able to count on with Tank. When I need it, he's always ready for me. Doesn't matter if it's at home, in bed, or at the ice rink during the break before the final period of the championship game. He's *always* ready.

As we come down and catch our breath, I notice that my desk has been cleared, papers everywhere while my laptop has found a new home upside down on the ground. Tank helps me off the desk, and I pick up the laptop, checking for damage before setting it back on the desk.

"How'd the rest of your story go?" Tank questions as he goes around the room, picking up my scattered papers.

"So good," I boast, glancing at him as a wide, cheesy grin stretches across my face, more than proud of my investigation. "Turns out the asshole did murder the guy."

"What?" Tank questions, his head snapping up as he gapes at me. "I thought the whole point of him asking you to cover his story was to clear his name."

"Yep," I say, popping the *p*. "Turns out he's not only a liar, but a murderer, too."

"Shit, Soph," he sighs, something tightening behind his eyes that puts me on edge. We've had this conversation a million times before, so I know exactly what's about to come out of his mouth. "Should you really be chasing these types of stories while you're pregnant?"

I give him a big, beaming smile, one I know he can't resist. "I'm an investigative journalist. It's what I do. It's in my nature to seek out these stories and put bad guys away. And besides," I add. "I didn't chase this story. It fell right into my lap."

Tank presses his lips into a tight line. "Did you put the bad guy away?"

My smile morphs into a wicked smirk. "No, I have him tied up in our bedroom to use as our BDSM sex slave," I deadpan before rolling my eyes. "Of course I put him away. I went to the cops this morning and handed in the evidence. They were kind of annoyed that I was sticking my nose in places it didn't belong again, but I'm pretty sure they were just jealous that I got the information before they did. Which, naturally, I pointed out. But then they admitted they were grateful because they've been trying to pin this asshole for months."

Tank rolls his eyes and lets out a small huff. "You know I don't like it."

"I know," I say, stepping into his arms and looking up at his handsome face, those familiar butterflies swarming with every touch he gives me. "But you know the deal. I love what I do and I didn't spend four years in college to be your full-time housewife. I want to work. It makes me feel as though I'm making a difference in the world. So, I can either have your approval and in return I'll be completely open with you so you know exactly where I'll be at all times and with who. Or, I can do it behind your back and you'll be in the dark. Either way, I'm not stopping," I tell him, reaching up on my toes to plant a kiss on his lips. "Take your pick, *big guy*."

"Don't use that against me," he warns.

"I don't know what you're talking about," I lie, knowing he loves it when I call him big guy. It reminds him of the day we met.

He groans, spanking my ass as I pass him. "You're so fucking stubborn."

"And you're a pushover," I laugh, turning around and walking backward just so I can catch the grin on his face. "I wonder how you'll handle it when this baby comes out with my attitude."

"Nah, there's no way," he says, shaking his head in denial. "My kid is going to be an angel. He'll have those fucking gorgeous blue eyes of yours, but he'll have my patience and perfect behavior."

"You wish, big guy." I scoff at just how naive he is, and as if seeing that as a challenge, he rushes me and scoops me into his strong arms, whipping me up off the ground. He turns and starts heading for the door when my hand whips out, gripping onto the frame to stop him. "Wait, I need my laptop," I rush out.

Tank turns on his heel, stalks back toward the desk and bends, so I can collect it without falling out of his arms. I place it down gently on my bump and enjoy the ride as Tank takes us out to the living room. He sits down on our couch, and I make myself comfortable in his lap. "Here, I wanted to show you this," I say as I find the webpage I was looking at earlier today, feeling an excited flutter deep in my womb and smiling at the feel of my son inside me.

Bringing up the webpage, I turn the laptop so that Tank can see. "Pretty damn awesome, isn't it?" I grin, my gaze scanning over the stunning stroller I'd found earlier this morning.

"Um, I guess," he says with a shrug, having absolutely no idea about baby stuff. "I told you to just buy the stuff you want. You don't need my approval for it."

"I already did buy it, you big moron. I just wanted to show you," I say proudly, before pointing out something on the screen. "Look, it has cup holders."

Tank grins at my excitement while he winds his hands around my body and lets them rest on my bump. I don't think he even knows he's doing it, but since the day we found out, anytime I'm near him, his hands always find my stomach. It's as if it's his way of protecting what's ours.

Joy springs to life in his eyes when the baby begins to kick, and I know with everything that I am, Tank is going to be an incredible father to our little boy. Our son isn't even born yet and he already loves him unconditionally.

"What are your plans tomorrow?" he asks after the baby has settled down, his hand still hovering over my stomach as I lean into his shoulder.

"Dani and I are having our girls' day, remember?" I remind him. "You told Miller you'd watch little Mia with him."

His eyes widen in fear. "Shit, that's tomorrow?" he questions. "That's . . . shit, that's close. What am I supposed to do with her?"

I laugh, picturing the two morons with that little girl and all the trouble they could potentially get into. "Whatever you do, just keep in mind that she's only three months old. She's fragile. You can't use her as a football like you did with Jaxon's son the other week."

"Bullshit," he scoffs. "That kid loved it."

"He's nearly one, of course he loved it. But Mia is barely out of the newborn stage. So something tells me that's not going to go down in the same way," I inform him. "Besides, I'm pretty sure Dani will castrate you if you even think about it."

He scoffs, though the sparkle in his eyes suggests he's more than prepared to face Dani's wrath if it makes Mia happy. "It's not Dani I have to worry about,' he tells me. "Miller will put me in the ground if anything happens to that baby on my watch."

"Oh, I know he would," I laugh.

Tank smirks and I roll my eyes before the words have even come out, knowing that whatever it is it's bound to be something ridiculous. "Let him come for me," Tank laughs. "He couldn't touch me even if he tried."

I groan, shaking my head as Tank's eyes soften, his fingers trailing up my body and to my chin, raising it enough to capture my stare. "Were you serious about going out for dinner?"

"Yeah," I say. "I could really go for one of Micky's burgers."

"Sure, I'll just fly back to Denver and get right on that," he teases.

"There's no need to be a smartass," I sulk as my stomach starts to grumble, clearly enamored by the thought of the oily goodness of one of Micky's burgers. God, I haven't had one in so long.

"Yeah, there is," Tank deadpans. "Now, as much as I hate to say this, go get dressed. I can't take you out naked. Others will stare, and I don't like people seeing what's mine."

"You sure seemed to like it those few times in college," I remind him.

"That was different," he grunts as he starts scooting me forward so I can get up and move. "I did that for you. And besides, you weren't my wife then, and you sure as fuck weren't carrying my child."

I get to my feet and turn to face him, a wide smirk stretching across my lips, remembering those few crazy experiences in college. We were sex-crazed and wild back then. Don't get me wrong, we're still both of those things, but now we've grown up. "It was fun though."

Tank rolls his eyes and a grin slowly makes its way across his face. No matter how much he denies it, he liked it just as much as I did. "Go," he demands.

I turn and make my way down the hallway, giving my hips an extra sway. I look back over my shoulder to see him watching me walk away, his eyes darkening with hunger. "I'm ready for round two, if you are," I tell him with a wink.

"Get dressed, Sophie," he tells me, a clear warning in his tone. It would only take the slightest push to get him to cave to my will and take me on the kitchen floor. But I also know that when he heard my stomach rumbling, his only priority was to feed me.

"Love you," I call out, giving in and being a good girl. I mean, there's only so far I can push this caveman before he snaps. And goddamn, when this man snaps, it's one of the most exhilarating things I've ever seen. An angry Tank is sexy as fuck, and when he needs to work it out of his system, good Lord, I see stars.

"Damn straight you do," Tank calls back to me, his voice softening, pleased to find me behaving.

I emerge ten minutes later, dressed and ready for a great night out with my man. "Where are you taking me?"

Tanks brows furrow and he looks at me like I've just asked to peg him with a cactus. "To the burger joint down the road," he says slowly, suddenly unsure of himself.

"What?" I groan with a heavy sigh. "I don't want to go there."

"What do you mean you *don't wanna go there?*" he questions. "You just said that you wanted a burger."

"No, I said I wanted one of *Micky's* burgers. You can't just replace one of Micky's burgers with some cheap shit from down the road. It's not the same."

Tank's face falls and he gives me a hard stare. "Are you shitting me?"

"No," I say, mustering up as much attitude as I possibly can. "I'm not shitting you. I'm serious."

He groans and strides toward me, grabbing my hips and pulling me into him, waiting until I meet his eyes. "Then what do you want?"

I cringe, knowing exactly how he is going to react. "I . . . uhh . . . don't know," I tell him. "You decide."

"For fuck's sake," he groans, looking at me like I've grown another head. "Get that fine ass of yours in my truck. We'll figure it out on the way."

With a grin, I grab my bag off the counter and follow him to the door, stopping as I pass by him. I push up onto my tippy-toes and give him a soft kiss. "You're going to be a great daddy," I tell him before sashaying off toward his truck, as happy as a pig rolling in his own shit.

CHAPTER 2

TANK

"Holy shit," I mutter to Sophie as we let ourselves into Dani and Miller's home. The place is a mess. Baby clothes and toys are all over the place, and there are piles of laundry covering the couch. The trash can is overflowing with takeout containers, and the kitchen sink is filled with baby bottles and other objects I can't identify. It's as if the baby patrol came and ransacked their house.

"Yo?" I call out. "Are you fuckers here?"

"Yes, yes, yes," Dani yells, rushing around the corner of the kitchen. "We're here."

Miller follows behind her, his eyes glued to a baby monitor clutched in his hands, looking nervous as shit. "Please don't go," he begs Dani.

"What if something happens? What if . . . what if she cries or needs something . . . or . . . I don't fucking know. What if she doesn't want me?"

"Miller," Dani says, stopping in her tracks and turning around to face him. "You'll be fine. She'll sleep for the next hour, and I've stuck her schedule to the fridge. All you have to do is follow it and everything will be okay."

She gives him a forced smile as if not believing a word she just said before turning back to continue on her way. "And if she cries?" Miller questions, following behind his wife as she continues ducking around the house, collecting her things.

"It depends," Dani says. "If she cries after she's had a bottle, then she probably has a sore tummy and needs a burp. You know how to do that. But just remember to put a towel over your shoulder because she's been projectile vomiting a bit lately."

His eyes widen in horror before nodding, as if accepting the inevitable. "Okay, but what if it's not a burp?"

"Then she probably needs to take a shit," Dani says, flatly. "Rub her tummy and keep her active. It'll work its way out."

"Right," he says with a cringe. "And if she does shit?"

Dani groans, getting frustrated with him. "Then change her diaper, Miller. You'll be fine. You've done all this before. You're a great dad, and you know what you're doing."

He lets out a sigh, walking over to the dining table and placing the baby monitor down. I glance at the screen, seeing little Mia fast asleep in her bassinet. Some weird plastic thing above her head is spinning and making music, and I'm completely dumbfounded by it. That thing is fucking awesome. I'll have to get Soph to pick one up for our little guy, but I'll make sure it won't play this girly shit. It'll play commentary from the ice hockey championships. Something for the kid to aspire to.

"What the hell happened to this place?" Sophie asks, grabbing the scattered laundry and putting it back into the basket as Dani gathers the rest of her things and jams them into her bag.

"We lost Mia's pacifier last night," she explains. "Hell froze over and took up residence in our home. It was fantastic."

Sophie's eyes widen, slightly horrified for what our future will hold. "Wow, you make me look forward to having this baby so much," she jokes as she rubs that perfect little bump.

"No, I'm sorry," Dani says, still slightly frazzled. "I didn't mean to freak you out. I swear, the good outweighs the bad, but we're still adjusting. We'll get the hang of it. Being a mommy truly is amazing. It's exhausting and the house generally looks like a bomb went off, but it's amazing. You're gonna love it, and when you have your sweet little boy in your arms, you'll realize that every little bit of it is all worth it."

Sophie gives her a warm smile as Dani steps into her and looks down at her belly in awe, making me wonder if she's already considering baby number two. She lets out a calming breath before meeting Sophie's stare again. "Are you ready to go?"

"I'm ready whenever you are," Sophie tells her.

Miller comes up and threads his arms around Dani's waist before pulling her right into him. "Try and enjoy yourself," he murmurs against her neck. "You deserve this."

"I'll try, but your endless worrying all morning has messed with my vibes," she says, turning in his arms and pressing a kiss to his lips. "Remember, the schedule is on the fridge, and if all else fails, call me and I'll come home."

"Okay," he says, though we all know that's a lie. He'll never call her to come home, not unless there was an emergency. He's right, Dani deserves a day off from being a mom. Even if all they plan on doing is driving down the road and sleeping in the car.

"You'll be fine. You have Tank here and he's great with babies," she says. I have absolutely no idea where the hell she got that information from, but I try not to blanch so she doesn't freak out.

"Babe," Miller says. "He used Jaxon's kid as a human football a few weeks ago. Cassie nearly died."

Dani's eyes widen in alarm, and I see her look back at the baby monitor with concern, wondering if she really should be leaving her precious daughter with two inexperienced idiots like us. Her eyes flick back to me and narrow into tight, venomous slits. "Use my baby as a football, and I'll use your throat for chopping practice," she warns me.

"Yes, ma'am," I say, unable to help the wide grin stretching across my face. "No human footballs."

Dani lets out a huff and gives Miller another kiss, which turns into a spontaneous make-out session, reminding me that not a damn thing has changed since college. I turn to Soph and let out a heavy breath, a smirk across my lips, knowing we're usually just as bad. "You better go before he convinces her to stay."

"My thoughts exactly," Sophie murmurs as she stretches up on her tippy-toes and kisses me goodbye, my hands automatically falling to her small bump. After stepping away, Sophie reaches out and grips Dani's hand, pulling her away from her husband before hauling her ass out the door.

The second the door closes behind them, Miller and I glance at each other blankly, the silence louder than a hurricane tearing through a city. What the fuck possessed us to agree to this? When I first walked in, I felt pretty good about this, but now . . . I don't know what's going on, but I swear, Miller's anxiety is starting to leach into me.

"So, uhh . . . what the fuck are we supposed to do?"

He just gives me a blank stare, way out of his comfort zone. It takes him a second to snap out of it before taking a breath and deciding he's got this covered. "Umm, I guess since Mia's asleep, we don't really need to do anything right now. Though, I should probably clean this shit up. I don't want Dani having to do it when she gets home."

Miller gets started on tidying up the living room while I head into the kitchen and wash up Mia's bottles. I notice the schedule Dani stuck to the fridge and I double-check the time. I see that Mia's due for her milk in an hour and a half, so commit that to memory.

I come out of the kitchen twenty minutes later with a couple of beers to find Miller sorting through the clean laundry on the couch. When I drop down across from him, I notice he's watching a rerun of last season's championship hockey game. Even though neither of us knows any of the kids playing for the Denver Dragons anymore, we still feel a sense of pride watching them defend their title.

It's been five years since we skated for the Dragons, and I have to say, I'm damn proud of every single player that has played for them since. Five years in a row, the Denver Dragons have remained undefeated and won every damn championship.

Like I said, I'm fucking proud of those boys.

We're halfway through the game when the cameraman zooms in on the coaches and we see Coach Harris, still red in the face just like he used to be during all of our games. "Fuck, yeah," Miller chuckles, holding his beer up to the screen as if in cheers, but that's not what's caught my attention.

"Rewind that," I say, leaning forward on the couch, as if being just that little bit closer to the screen is going to help me confirm what I thought I saw.

Miller does as asked and I watch intently, telling him when to stop. As I do, he sees exactly what I was looking at. "Is that Shorty next to Coach Harris?" I ask.

"Sure fucking looks like him," Miller grunts. "I only saw him a few weeks ago. I wonder why he didn't say anything."

"Who knows? Maybe he's just filling in or something," I shrug as we hear Mia start to stir.

Miller goes to get up, but I put a hand up, wanting to get her myself. I sneak down the hallway and into her room before making my way over to her bassinet and peering in. She's so fucking tiny, I can hardly wrap my head around it. I go to reach for her when I pause, noticing the way she yawns and drops her face to the side, her eyes still so heavy from sleep.

Dropping my hand to the side of her bassinet, I cautiously give it a little rock and watch in amazement as she settles back into a peaceful sleep. My brows shoot up, my ego practically doubling in size.

I've fucking got this. I can do this baby shit. It's easy.

Heading back out to the living room with my chest puffed out, feeling like the fucking man, I find Miller gaping at me as though he's seeing a whole new person. "How the fuck did you do that?" he asks in awe. "Every time I try, she wakes up screaming."

"I don't know, man. I've just got the touch," I tell him. "Besides, she's a girl. It's in her nature to give her daddy hell."

"Fuck off," he mutters. "That shit ain't supposed to happen until she's a teenager."

I can't help but grin. In all the years I've known Miller Cain, he has always been a cocky, egotistical bastard. But now for the first time in his life, the fucker has no clue, and that knowledge alone makes me the happiest bastard that ever lived.

Mia wakes up shortly after, and I smirk as I watch Miller's face fall. It's clear that he's desperately in love with this little girl, but watching him work out how to parent is fucking hilarious. Though I have no doubt that in a few months, the roles will be reversed and it'll be him with a cocky smirk, watching me make every mistake under the sun.

"Fuck," Miller grunts as he goes to get Mia out of the bassinet. As he walks back into the living room, he holds her up and cuddles her into his chest, trying to soothe her cries.

Double-checking the time, I realize she's woken up right on time to stick to her mother's carefully constructed schedule. "Dani's schedule says she's ready for a bottle," I remind him as he tries to rock and sooth the baby.

His eyes widen, realizing she's hungry, and like clockwork, she turns into a screaming banshee. Not wanting her to wait for her food a second longer than necessary, Miller passes her to me before running into the kitchen and preparing her bottle.

I look down at the screaming baby in my arms and swallow hard. Well, shit.

Not knowing what to do, I stand and start walking circles around the coffee table, gently bouncing her while patting her back. "Come on, kid. It's coming," I say, practically begging her to stop, my boosted ego quickly starting to deflate. Maybe this shit is harder than I thought.

Miller returns a moment later and takes Mia out of my hands before dropping down on the couch. He settles her into his arms and quickly slips the bottle into her waiting mouth, instantly calming her. I watch with wide eyes at just how quickly she knocks that bottle back.

"Fuck, man. I don't know how Dani does this," Miller says as he watches his little girl down her bottle like a pro. "I'm always fucking training and she's left here to work all this out."

"Yeah, I get it," I tell him. "It'll be exactly the same for me and Soph when our little man arrives. You just gotta figure out what works for your family and be there to do your part," I say with a shrug. "I don't know, I guess my kid isn't here yet so I can't exactly offer any advice. But the way I see it, you should think of it like a game plan."

"Huh?" he grunts, clearly confused.

"You know, you have a game plan on the ice. Just apply that same principle to Mia. Think of her schedule as a challenge. You get through the whole thing with no fuck ups, you win. She gets the best of you, she wins. Then you do it all over the next day and make sure you do it better."

"Hmm," he muses to himself, clearly thinking it over before he starts to nod. "I like it."

Mia polishes off her bottle, and he raises her up to face him, Lion King style. "Hear that, Mia? From now on, I'm making your schedule my bitch."

I roll my eyes, unable to resist grinning at the idiot. I watch as he stands and places her up on his shoulder. His hand gently rubs at her back and precisely two seconds later, she comes out with the loudest burp followed by a projectile vomit that drops straight down his back, splattering against the couch and floor with a wet slap.

"Fuck," Miller grunts as he stands before me, dripping in vomit with a very satisfied Mia in his arms.

I crack into booming laughter as he hands her over to me and tries to peel his shirt off without slathering it over his face. "Dude, I think she won this round," I say, smiling down at Mia as her father drops to his knees, using his soiled shirt to mop up the milky puddles on the couch and floor.

That will be me in a few months.

"No shit," Miller mutters under his breath.

Mia reaches up and places her tiny hand on my face, and I can't help but smile at the little she-devil, realizing just how ready I am for my son to come along.

Finding a playmat on the floor, I lay her down before adding a few toys to stimulate her. I watch as Miller finds some proper cleaning tools and gets to work on the mess. "How's Sophie doing with everything?" Miller asks, shoving the couch back to make sure nothing has spilled underneath.

"So far, so good," I tell him. "I just wish she'd slow down on work."

Miller scoffs, knowing the likelihood of that just as well as I do. Hell, Sophie thinks she's Superwoman, and most of the time, she is. But right now, she's pregnant and should be taking time to enjoy this experience rather than working herself to exhaustion. "That's never going to happen."

"Tell me about it," I murmur as I lay a new toy down next to Mia, deciding more is definitely better despite the fact that she can't grip onto them yet. They're still pretty for her to look at. "She caught herself a murderer yesterday, a thief last week, and uncovered a prostitution ring the week before that."

"Shit. At least no one can say she's not good at her job," Miller supplies helpfully.

"Yeah, I just wish it wasn't so dangero—"

My sentence is cut off when Mia lets out a groan, moments before an almighty rumbling comes shooting out of her tiny ass. My eyes widen and I scramble away from the baby, the smell all but whacking me in the face.

Oh, fuck no.

My lips pull up in disgust as Miller's face turns ghostly white. "Oh, please no," Miller begs as he gets up and makes his way over to a very happy Mia. "You want to take the lead on this one?" he asks me as he looks down at his daughter in fear.

"Nah, man," I smirk, enjoying this way too much. "She's throwing down a challenge. She won the last round and now she's checking if it was a fluke or if you meant business. It's your time to shine, man."

Miller shakes his head, clenching his jaw as he bends down and scoops her up by her underarms, refusing to hold her under her ass after an explosion like that.

As he walks past me, the smell wafts with him and I choke back a gag.

He takes her down the hallway and into her nursery again, and noticing the smell hasn't faded away like it should have, I look down at the playmat and all my worst fears stare me in the face. Baby shit is spread far and wide over the playmat, and my heart races as I glance at the door, wondering just how far I could run before Miller hunts me down.

Though if there's baby shit smeared everywhere here, that could only mean . . .

A grin tears across my face. I've got to see this.

Getting up off the floor, I scoop up the playmat by the edges and drop it in the laundry before making my way toward the nursery. Miller gags trying to wrestle his daughter out of her onesie, while also trying not to smear the shit further up her back, and I prop my shoulder against the door, more than enjoying this.

Managing to get the onesie off without making an even bigger mess of things, he drops the soiled garment into what I can only assume is a laundry basket before turning back to Mia. He takes hold of her before immediately pulling away, shit covering his fingers. "Oh, no," he breathes as his daughter smiles up at him as innocent as ever.

Mia giggles, and it's almost as if she's done it on purpose, like a big fuck-you for trying to conquer her schedule. Wanting to get it over and done with, he tackles it head on, just as he does on the ice, taking charge and making the challenge his bitch. Within seconds, the naked baby is held out as he races to the bathroom, demanding I hurry up and run her a bath.

After getting her bath ready and checking the temperature, Miller gently lowers her into the water, supporting her head the whole time. He gives her a quick wash, rinses through her barely existent hair, then lets her have a splash before wrapping her up in a towel, all while I'm left wondering how the hell we got ourselves into this situation?

Miller passes her off to me to dress while he cleans up the rest of the poo explosion. I take her back to her nursery and lay her on her changing table, trying to figure out where to go from here.

Keeping a hand resting on her stomach so she doesn't roll, I pull a new diaper out of the drawer beneath the table and study it for a moment. That's when my *can-do* attitude burns to ashes around me. Shit. Do the tabs fasten in the front or the back? I look at it from every angle before checking the drawer to see if there's some kind of instruction manual. Having those scratchy tabs in the front could be uncomfortable, right? I settle with hooking them in the back and try to figure out how to get the damn thing to stay on. Satisfied with my work, I go about getting her dressed into her little hockey jersey. The same one I know Dani has stashed in her closet.

"Dude," Miller laughs as he comes into the nursery and sees my progress. "You got her diaper on backwards."

"Fuck," I groan before starting the whole process over again.

Ten minutes later, I've successfully gotten her changed, and I take her back out to the living room. After making her up a new play area, I put her down as Miller comes out of the kitchen with two more beers. We each crash down onto the couch in relief and take pleasure in our drinks, never feeling so deserving of one in my life. Shit, I've played multiple championship games and nothing was harder than what we just endured.

I'm so glad that's over. Mia couldn't possibly throw any more surprises our way.

ESPN goes straight back on as Mia giggles to herself while she plays with a toy elephant. I look over at her, as happy as can be, and I know without a doubt that Sophie and I are doing the right thing. Being a parent is going to be the most rewarding thing we'll ever do.

CHAPTER 3

SOPHIE

Dani and I walk out of our couples massage and I let out a heavy sigh, never having been so relaxed in my life. It was so damn good, and only serves to remind me that I've waited far too long to do this. I swear, nothing will ever compare to how good Tank makes me feel, but that massage came in a close second.

Dani groans as we make our way up the hallway and into the bathroom, our matching robes pulled tight at our waists. "What's wrong?" I ask, as we reach our lockers and I start pulling off my complimentary robe to get dressed.

"I fell asleep," she whines, her bottom lip pouting out. "All I wanted was to relax and enjoy my massage, but then I had to go and fall asleep. It's like I've missed the whole thing. Like, why wouldn't she wake a bitch up?"

I can't help but grin at the idiot. "Come on, it's not that bad," I tell her.

"Are you kidding?" she grunts as she strips out of her robe. "I pushed a watermelon out of my lady taco three months ago, and that watermelon has been sucking on my tits ever since. I hardly know what sleep is, and my stomach looks like it's suffered through a hurricane," she says. "Is it too much to ask that I actually enjoy my massage rather than be unconscious for the whole thing?"

"Okay, Momma," I say. "Calm down. We're getting our nails done next. You've had your power nap, so you can relax while some lady fusses over you without the fear of falling asleep. What do you say to a pedicure as well? And if that doesn't do the trick, I'll bring you back next week for another massage."

Dani pouts, but the idea of getting pampered cheers her up. "I mean, my nails really have been neglected these past few weeks," she says with a little whine as she grabs her bra and starts to get dressed. She drops her robe, completely naked in the big bathroom without a hint of shame, and goddamn, she looks great after pushing out that watermelon.

She reaches behind herself to clasp her bra, and in any other scenario, I would have looked away to give her just a fraction of privacy. But when she shoves pads inside her bra, all I can do is gape. What the hell is she doing? They're definitely not chicken fillets. I've seen her tits before, and it's not as though she needs the extra padding.

Her boobs are huge right now.

Unable to help myself, I let my intrusive thoughts fly free. "What the fuck are you stuffing your bra with?" I ask as I stare at her.

A massive grin cracks across her face, and suddenly her untimely afternoon nap is all but forgotten. "They're breast pads for when you're breastfeeding or pumping," she explains.

"What?" I ask, dumbfounded, realizing just how much of this baby momma stuff I've still got to learn. "You mean, like, menstrual pads for your tits?"

Dani laughs. "Kind of. Watch this."

She reaches behind herself and unclasps her bra, letting the straps fall down her arms, the pads going right along with it. Then I watch in shock as milk starts leaking from her swollen tits. "Oh, my God," I gasp, holding onto my own, fearful for their future. "Is that shit going to happen to me?"

"Probably," she laughs. "If I give it a squeeze, I could squirt you," she adds, facing away, unable to resist giving me a demonstration. I watch in horror as a perfect arc of milk squirts from her left tit and splashes against the bench. "Miller hates it when I do it."

"Yeah, no shit," I sputter. "Does that hurt?"

"Eh," she shrugs. "It's not exactly comfortable, but you get used to it. Some women really hate it, while others think it's great. I'm chilling somewhere in the middle. It certainly has its benefits. You know, like when you need to put your husband back in his place. Full disclaimer, this shit can get sticky. Like if it gets on you and you don't wipe it away, you'll feel it there until you wash it off properly. Also, sometimes during Mia's feeds, she'll just kinda pull away for a break, and it'll just leak all over her face."

My mouth drops open, feeling like I need a notepad and pen just to write down all these things I've never even thought about before. "Don't get me wrong, I'd love to sit here and talk about your leaky tits all day, but if we don't hurry up and get dressed, we're going to miss our manicures."

Dani shrugs and gets back to clasping her bra again. "You're the one who asked," she says with a grin before sliding her clothes back on.

Pulling my phone out to check the time, I find a text from Tank and open it to find a photo of Miller changing Mia's diaper, shit literally up the walls. A barking laugh tears from the back of my throat and I hand Dani the phone, knowing she lives to see her husband like this.

"Oh, shit," Dani laughs, tears springing to her eyes. "Miller is never going to let me leave again."

"Yeah, he will," I say. "He's way too in love with you to hold it against you."

"He is, isn't he?" she says with a sweet smile, getting that same dreamy look on her face that appears every time she thinks about how much she loves her man.

"Ugh, don't start this shit," I groan as I take the phone back and actually checking the time, my eyes bugging out of my head. "Oh, shit. Our appointment at the nail salon starts in like . . . three minutes."

Dani gasps as we collect our belongings and make our way over to the nail salon, making sure to thank our masseurs on the way.

We make it to our appointment right on time, and they are more than happy to squeeze us in for pedicures as well. The lady sends us off to choose a nail polish color, and I pick out a deep red as Dani chooses a dirty brown color that looks suspiciously like the shit I saw smeared across the nursery room walls. I try to hold in a cringe at her choice as we take our seats to be pampered, but let's face it. I don't have enough self-control for that shit.

The ladies taking care of our manicures are speaking in another language, and I can't help but feel as though they're talking about us. I mean, do I have something on my face? Did I put my dress on wrong? Are Dani's tits leaking through her breast pads? Seriously, what's up?

I try my best to tune them out, and when I finally do, my little guy starts kicking me in the ribs, reminding me he's there and ready for a little attention. I place my free hand on my stomach and feel as he kicks me while I relax further into the chair, realizing just how badly I needed this.

This pregnancy has been exhausting. I've just sailed through the five-month mark and have only just stopped throwing up. Though, I haven't had much time to be thankful for the reprieve since the heartburn began. My feet ache by the end of each day, and I spend the majority of my time uncomfortable, especially when I'm trying to sleep. I have to tuck a pillow between my legs to ease the pain in my back, but apparently there's a special pillow made for this shit that I've been searching for everywhere.

I have no idea how I'm going to cope over the next few months, but it will be worth it when I hold my beautiful little boy in my arms.

Hearing a light snore beside me, I glance over and grin as I take in the sight of my best friend, fast asleep, barely able to hold her head up as her manicurist goes about her business. I consider waking her, knowing she'll be pissed she missed yet another chance of being pampered, but despite how she feels about it, she needs her sleep more.

Forty minutes later, I wake Dani and she glares at me for allowing it to happen again.

After piling back into Dani's car, we head out for something to eat and I listen to her constant ranting about allowing her to sleep through her nail appointment, when out of nowhere she slams on the brake in the middle of the busy street, almost sending me crashing into the dash.

I barely manage to catch myself, gaping at her with wide eyes when overwhelming sobs tear from deep in her chest, tears rushing down her face. I gape at her for a moment, wondering what the fuck just went down in the last few seconds that I clearly missed. "What the hell?" I gasp as I stare at her like she's gone insane, my gaze flicking over her body, making sure she's physically alright.

When the broken sobs don't stop, I unbuckle my seatbelt and lean across, pulling her into my arms, letting her cry it out on my shoulder as we ignore the pissed off drivers making their way around us, horns blaring.

"I . . . I . . . I miss Mia," she cries.

Ahhhh, and it all makes sense. She's an overtired, emotional wreck, still trying to figure out this whole parenting thing. But hell, she's handling it like a pro, much better than I'll be doing it in a few months.

"You've only been away from her for a few hours," I remind her, but apparently that's the wrong thing to say.

"Four hours is a lot when I've never left her before," she tells me. "I tried to be brave for Miller so he'd be confident when I left, but the second I stepped out the door, I just wanted to go back. And I know that's a shitty thing to say to you because I really have had a good time with you, but I miss her so much. And my tits hurt. I need to pump, and I just . . . I just . . ."

"It's okay," I say, desperately trying to calm her down. "Mia is doing fine. The boys would have stuck to her schedule and she did a great big shit. They would have called if there was any trouble."

"You don't really believe that do you?" she scoffs. "Miller would have been all like, *I can handle it, don't call Dani. She needs her girls' day.*"

I cringe. He definitely would have said that. "Yeah. You're probably right, but don't stress. We can skip having lunch out. We'll head home and have lunch with the boys instead."

"Are you sure?" she asks, pulling back and looking up at me with blazing blue eyes, red-rimmed from her tears.

"Yeah, babe," I smile. "Besides, after that massage, I could really use a little attention from Tank."

"Ugh," Dani groans. "That was supposed to relax you, not get you hot."

I shrug my shoulders. "What can I say? She had her hands all over me."

"Oh my God, Sophie," she sighs, shaking her head.

Realizing she's in no position to drive, we quickly change positions by climbing over the center console, reminding me of all the times I did this as a teenager. Though the situation was extremely different, and I didn't have this baby bump in the way back then. After we're both settled in our seats, I hit the gas and get back on our way.

We get another few minutes down the road when Dani's tears finally stop and she glances at me, ready to say something, when an excruciating pain shoots through my stomach. "Ahh, fuck," I cry as my hand wraps around my bump, tears instantly springing from my eyes.

I do my best to swerve off the road without hitting anyone and come to a screeching stop, Dani's hand clutching the *holy shit* bar with wide eyes. "What's wrong?" she rushes out, her gaze sailing over me.

I can't answer. All I can do is remember to breathe.

Clenching my eyes, I recline the chair all the way back, desperately needing to stretch out as the pain only gets worse. I hiss through my clenched jaw, barely holding on. "Fuck, Sophie. What's wrong?" she repeats. "Is it the baby? Are you having contractions?"

"I . . . I don't know, I don't think so," I cry as I try to get back to focusing on breathing, my hands roaming over my stomach, willing the pain to go away. "It hurts. Something's wrong."

"Can you move? I'll drive us home. Or do you want me to call an ambulance?" she questions. "I can get Tank to meet us at the hospital."

I focus on taking quick, short breaths, and the pain starts to fade a little. "I . . . I don't know. I think it's getting better," I tell her.

Her lips press into a hard line, not wanting to take any chances. "Yeah, I'm coming around," she says before pushing her door open and jumping out onto the road. She quickly hurries around the car, and if I hadn't pulled over, I'd be bitching her ass out for being so stupid.

Dani meets me at my side and helps me out, before walking with me around to the other side. She helps me climb back up into the car and reclines the seat so I can be comfortable. Within seconds, she's back in the driver's seat, both of us a complete mess. "Home or hospital?" she questions, letting me make the final call.

"Home," I tell her, the pain starting to get much better, definitely not hospital material. But hell, the second I can, I'll be knocking down my obstetrician's door and asking what the fuck just went down.

Dani pulls out into the traffic, concentrating on getting us home, but her eyes never once stop flicking back to me. "Are you okay now?" she asks as she quietly turns the radio back on, both of us needing that background noise to help relax us.

"I think so," I tell her, rubbing the spot on my stomach that had me in excruciating pain. "I don't know what the hell that was, but if that was a contraction, there's no way I'll be doing this without the drugs."

"I don't think it was a contraction," she muses, her face scrunching, deep in thought. "I mean, definitely check with your doctor. Every woman's contractions aren't going to feel exactly the same. But my guess is that it was probably muscle cramping or round ligament pain. It happened to me quite a bit, but I apparently have a higher pain threshold."

A grin splits across her face, never missing a chance to tease me and I roll my eyes. "Whatever," I scoff. "I was there when you were giving birth, remember? And that was not the picture of a woman who has a high pain threshold."

"Give me a break," she laughs as she pulls up at the gate of her home and punches in the code. "I was pushing a watermelon out of my vag. That's a little different from having a little cramp."

"Shit, girl. I'm gonna smack you if you refer to that as a little cramp again," I tell her, when a male's voice coming through the radio pulls my attention away.

"Breaking news," the guy says, prompting me to lean forward to turn up the volume. "Marco Cincinnati, founder and CEO of MC Construction, one of the big five developmental leaders of LA, has been found dead. The body was discovered at 9:37 this morning in what was believed to be a brothel. Officials say his cause of death was drug and alcohol related."

My eyes bug out, my spidey-senses tingling. Something inside me screams there is so much more to this story as I reach forward and turn the volume up a little more.

"Holy shit," Dani grunts as she brings the car to a stop at the top of her driveway.

"Shhhh," I demand, waving my hand at her, needing to hear what else is being said.

A response comes from the other news reader. "Wow, John. Can you believe it?" she says, a strange suspicion in her tone. "This comes a week after the death of Andrew Taylor, the CEO of Taylor Developments, who died of a heart attack. And of course, Phillip McDonald, the CEO of McDonald Construction, who passed from natural causes in his sleep just a week before that."

"Right," John replies. "Sounds like someone's been sticking needles in voodoo dolls. This screams foul play to me. I'd hate to be the CEO of Baxter Corporation or First Choice Construction. Looks like they might be up next."

Too freaking right. What's the bet that one of these CEOs had something to do with it? I mean, I could only imagine the type of money that would be coming their way if all the competitors are out of the way.

"Indeed," the woman replies. "It will be interesting to see how these companies recover from these tragic losses."

The news bulletin cuts over to an ad, and I turn the radio down before getting out. "You've got that look again," Dani murmurs with disapproval as she reaches into the backseat and grabs her handbag.

"What look?" I ask, knowing exactly what she's talking about.

"You're not seriously going to investigate this, are you?" she asks.

"Of course I am. Did you not hear how suspicious that was? Three of the five leading CEOs in the construction world are dead within three weeks of each other. It's practically begging for an investigation. There's no way I'm not looking into this story. If I'm right, which I usually am, this could be huge."

"Soph," she sighs. "It was an overdose in a brothel. The other guy had a heart attack, and the one before that died in his sleep, probably right next to his wife. There's nothing to look into, they're all just terrible tragedies. It's just a coincidence that it all happened in such a short time frame."

I arch a brow. "You know I don't believe in coincidences."

"Sophie," she grunts, the disapproval thick in her tone. "You're five months pregnant. You really shouldn't be doing this. If you're right, then the police should be handling it. You should be concentrating on growing that baby."

I roll my eyes. God, she sounds like she's been letting Tank get in her ear. "Come on, Dani. You know I can't just sit around and do nothing. If there's a story here, I'm going to find it. I'll be careful," I promise her.

She lets out a huff, knowing that once I have my mind set, there's no going back. "Tank's going to be pissed."

"Please," I scoff. "I can handle Tank."

Dani shakes her head before pushing through the front door to find the boys fast asleep on the floor next to a snoring Mia, and a grin stretches across both of our faces. "Looks like she wore them out," Dani laughs, her eyes sparkling with undeniable love and happiness.

"It sure as hell does."

CHAPTER 4

TANK

My blades cut through the ice as I push out into the middle of the rink. I know the season hasn't started yet, but I'm in the top position for becoming captain, and not a damn thing is going to stop me from earning it. So, here I am, taking every chance I can get to improve myself. To push myself to my absolute limits.

I will be captain of the LA Storm. No. Matter. What.

I'm about to have a son who's going to look up to his daddy, and when he does, I want to see the pride shining through those little eyes. Eyes that I hope will look just like Sophie's. I want him to learn that anything is possible, that if you work hard for something and put in the hours, his dreams will come true. Hell, I want him to be so proud of his daddy that he'll brag to all his little friends that his daddy is better than theirs, and if that's taking it too far, I don't give a shit.

It's amazing what that thought does to me. Just knowing I have a beautiful little boy growing inside my wife's stomach fills me with something I've never felt before. Honestly, I have absolutely no fucking idea what this feeling is.

Pride? Love? Excitement? Maybe it's a mix of it all, but whatever the hell it is, it spurs me on to be the best possible version of myself.

It was first thing in the morning when I snuck out of bed earlier than usual. Usually, I have no problem getting up and out in the morning, except today. Ever since Sophie got home from the spa with Dani, she's been off . . . Well, maybe off is the wrong word. She has been distant . . . distracted.

To anyone who doesn't know her, they would assume she's hiding something. Whereas I know she only gets like this when she is deep in thought and planning a strategy to get the next big story, to put her name on the map, right up there with the best investigative journalists before her.

Don't get me wrong, I love that she loves her job. I love that she has the drive to push herself to be the best. It's fun and exciting for her, and when she gets to help put some sick bastards behind bars, right where they belong, she's giving closure to those who need it. But she's five months pregnant, and she needs to slow down. A new project is not what she needs right now.

This can't be healthy for the baby, right?

I don't know. Maybe it's just me being overprotective. She likes to remind me of that all the time. Maybe I should just let her do her thing. Then again, if she got hurt, I would never forgive myself.

Damn it.

Someone pushing out onto the ice has my attention finally snapping away from the horrors of my own mind, and I'm thankful that now I'll actually be able to concentrate.

Coach Larsden skates up to me with a slight lift of his chin. "How's it going, Tank?" he asks, coming to a standstill beside me.

"Pretty good," I say to the guy, who's been my coach for the past five seasons, going on for what should be one hell of an amazing sixth. "It's a bit early for you."

"Yeah, I wanted to get an early start," he grunts. "The season is starting soon, and I have a shitload of work to get through. Not to mention the paperwork you assholes bring along with it."

A grin pulls at my lips, glad it's him and not me. "Sounds riveting."

Coach rolls his eyes as he pulls a puck from his pocket and drops it at his skates. "How's your training going? I've noticed you've been logging a lot of hours in the gym."

"I have," I say. "I'm feeling good. Ready for the season."

"I know you are," he says with pride, a rare compliment from a guy who's often harder than the ice he skates on. "That's why you're at the top of my list for being captain this season."

I nod, trying not to let my ego soak that in. Man, it feels so damn good to hear those words, no matter how much I've heard it over the past few months. It's been rumored up until now, but that confirmation is all I needed to know I'm heading in the right direction. "Thanks,

Coach," I say with a curt nod. "Appreciate it."

He shrugs off my thanks, just as I knew he would. He isn't one for accepting thanks, nor giving it. He's a believer in getting what you deserve. If you've put the work in, then why shouldn't you be rewarded? Either way, I'm not going to accept this position without letting him know how damn thankful I am. But one thing's for sure, I won't be letting him down, and I sure as fuck won't be letting my team down.

"How's Sophie?" he asks as he pulls the goals into position.

"Great," I smile as I head over and grab a few more pucks out of the bucket by the gate and drop them to the ice. "She's starting to get uncomfortable, but she's too fucking stubborn to admit it."

He lets out a sympathetic laugh, knowing all too well what I'm going through after his wife recently gave birth to their fourth baby girl. "Just wait a few more months. You won't stop hearing about it."

I grin at his comment. Most guys can't stand it when their women bitch and complain about shit, but I love it. It gives me a chance to fix it, which makes her see me as her hero, and that always comes with benefits. Besides, if she's still complaining to me, that means she still cares. A woman who doesn't bitch to her man is a woman who no longer gives a shit. "I can't wait," I smirk.

Coach Larsden shakes his head and leaves me to concentrate on my training. I get to work, and one by one, the other guys show up and join me on the ice. Since the season hasn't started, the boys don't have to be logging as many hours, but I'm glad they're here. It always pays to push ourselves, to better the team.

This season we're defending our title and I couldn't love a game more. This shit is different from high school or college hockey. The games get harder and faster and the skill I've seen out on the ice is incredible. No matter how good I think I am, there's always going to be someone better, someone to motivate me to keep going. But this season, I'm at my best. It doesn't get better than this.

Miller cuts past me and being the smartass he is, steals the puck right out from under my skates. He smirks as he flies by, calling me a "Pussy-whipped bitch," as he goes, but the fucker isn't going to live it down.

I take off like a bull after him, raging down the ice like lightning. He glances over his shoulder to laugh and smirk like a fucking idiot, thinking he's got the best of me, and I have to grin as his eyes widen in shock. He didn't expect me to come after him, but now that I've started . . . there's no way in hell I'm stopping.

"Ahh, fuck." Miller pushes forward, and I cut across the ice, recognizing his tells. After all, I've been skating with the guy for over eight years. Back in college, we were known as the Dream Team. Hell, some people still call us that. Miller was the big playboy on campus, the king of the fucking ice, but right now, he's a sleep-deprived new father who just messed with the wrong fucking guy. He's on my ice now.

He flies around the back of the net, and I distantly notice a few of the guys move away, knowing if they get between us, their asses are going to get laid out. I cut across the front of the net and end up right in front of him.

Miller attempts some of his fancy-ass footwork, but I come at him with the kind of brute force he simply can't match. They don't call me Tank for no reason. As he gets closer, I see the look in his eyes. He thinks he's got this in the bag. He thinks he's got me.

My gaze levels on the puck, and for just a second, I let him think he's got me, let him put his guard down. In a split-second movement, my stick cuts out in front of him and scoops up the puck like fucking magic. He continues past me, enjoying his win far too much to notice he no longer possesses the puck. A mistake made by someone whose head clearly isn't in the game yet. I can't even blame him. If I spent my weekend scrubbing baby shit off my walls, my head wouldn't be in the game either.

I shoot around and fly up the other side of the rink, and after realizing he's got to step it up, Miller takes off. I shoot the puck forward and watch as it flies through the air in a beautiful arc, slamming into the back of the net.

"Fuck, dude," Miller pants, coming to a stop beside me. "You've picked up speed."

"Nah, you lost it when you left your balls back there," I laugh, pointing out the patch of ice where I took the puck from him, which is when I notice some of the younger guys applauding my efforts. Besting the great Miller Cain isn't an easy feat. It's one they could only dream about. There's only a handful that could achieve it.

"Fuck off," Miller grins. "Give me a few weeks, then I want a rematch."

"You're on," I smirk. "But you better be ready before the season starts."

"You know I will be," he states before taking off with another puck and running some drills with the guys. He pushes them to their limits, the same way he's always done, ever since college.

I continue for another few hours before getting off the ice and heading into the locker room. I have a quick shower and get myself dressed before pulling out my phone to call Sophie, only to find a new text. I groan, seeing the name across my screen.

Crazy Jill - Tank, I love you. I can't wait to be together.

Fuck me. This chick is relentless. She's been texting and calling for the past four years. It's getting ridiculous. Sophie and I even make bets on how long she'll wait between texts.

In the beginning, I would reply and tell her to stop, but that only spurred her on. Every time I block her number, she gets a new one. I've changed my number many times, but she always manages to find it. So now, I just let it go. She messages, and I ignore it. She calls, and I decline it. Everything's been harmless so far, just an enthusiastic horn-dog fan who dreams of screwing her celebrity crush. Just another perk of the job.

Sophie will get a kick out of it though. She always wins these bets, and today isn't any different. Loser cooks, but there's one certain stipulation. He or she must be naked, and I'm not gonna lie, the thought of accidentally closing the oven on my cock lives rent free in my head and scares the shit out of me. Obviously I'm up tonight, but I don't really mind it. All it means is Soph's going to walk by a million times to grope me until I make her scream on the kitchen counter.

A smile comes to my face as I make my way out of the ice rink. I press on Sophie's contact details and hold the phone up as I walk out to my truck, listening as it rings out. I get her voicemail and leave a quick message. "Babe, Crazy Jill messaged, so it's on tonight. You better be ready. Call me back when you can."

I hang up before trying her office number.

"Daily Star, this is Jen," the receptionist greets.

"Jen. Hey, it's Tank. Is Sophie around?"

"No, sorry," she says with a slight cringe in her voice, telling me exactly what I need to know. "She hasn't been in all morning."

"Damn it," I grunt. "What story is she chasing?"

"Ahh . . . let me have a look," she says as I hear the familiar sound of her fingernails tapping away on the keyboard. "It says she's working on that story about that guy who wanted to clear his name."

"Nah, she wrapped that last week. The guy was guilty of that and more."

"Shit, seriously?" she breathes, her tone hitching high. "I could have sworn he was innocent." For fuck's sake. Is this chick serious? How could she not know that the story was done by now? Sophie sent it in days ago. It's probably in the middle of being printed for their latest issue. "Look," she continues. "This is Sophie we're talking about. If her last story is wrapped and she isn't here, she's probably following a new lead."

"That's what I was afraid of," I tell her before hanging up and unlocking my truck. I jump in and get busy writing Sophie a text.

Tank - Babe, where are you? I hope you're being safe. Don't get yourself into any trouble.

I hit send and take off to grab lunch, and I'm back at the ice rink an hour later. "Dude," Cameron, one of the guys on my team, says with a pitiful scoff. "Where'd you fuck off to? We've all been here sweating our asses off and you're off taking a fucking break."

"The fuck?" I grunt, fixing to put this motherfucker in his place. "I was here four hours before the rest of you, and as I recall, you were the last through the fucking door."

"Chill out, bro," he grunts, having the decency to look ashamed of himself, but then goes and puts his foot in it. "I was just fucking with you. No need to take it so hard."

Not wasting my time on him, I walk straight past and dump my shit in the locker room before grabbing my water bottle and making my way up to the rink gym. After walking through the door, I come to a stop, finding Miller across the room. A grin pulls across my lips. Apparently, this morning's smackdown has pulled his motivation right back to where it needs to be.

Miller was in the same position at the end of last season, both of us neck and neck to claim captainship for this coming season. But since Mia came along, he's more than happy to take a backseat on this one. Even if he didn't, I still would have fought for it because I've done my time. I fucking deserve it.

I know it's always been a dream of his to be captain in the professional league, but I guess things change when you have kids.

Now he's just happy to be along for the ride. Don't get me wrong, he still works his ass off for his team and is one of the best players in the league, but being captain is no longer on his radar.

But me, I want this. I'll stop at nothing until I've succeeded. That doesn't just mean I only want the title. I want to earn the position and be the best damn captain the LA Storm has ever seen. I want my team to look at me and know I was the right decision, and trust me to get them right through to the championship.

I'm going to lead this team to victory, even if it's the last thing I do.

CHAPTER 5

SOPHIE

Well, don't I just feel like a big, old, saggy cunt?

Tank knows me well enough to know that I'm following a new lead, despite me not saying a word, but it feels wrong that I didn't come right out and say it.

I guess I was trying to avoid the inevitable fight that would have come with it. Maybe fight is the wrong word. He would have gone on and on about how I should be relaxing and how my job is too dangerous, blah, blah, blah. But then I would have jumped his bones and rocked his world until he forgot what we were talking about. Though jumping his bones is a little harder now that this bump is in the way, but that just means we have to be a little more . . . creative.

Dani always complained that sex during pregnancy was

uncomfortable and that Miller hated the idea of invading his unborn child's space—as if he was going to poke his baby in the eye or some shit like that. Tank and I certainly don't have those reservations. No matter what the occasion, sex is fun . . . Actually, it's a hell of a lot more than fun. It's explosive, especially with a machine like Tank. Mind blowing doesn't even seem to cover it.

I got up at the crack of dawn this morning to find Tank already gone, probably already a few hours into his training. Even though the season hasn't started yet, his training sessions have been getting longer and harder, pushing himself to his limits. I have no doubt that his dedication will earn him captain this season, and I'm already so damn proud of him. I can't wait to see him in action again. Watching him dominate the ice is one of the sexiest things known to man. God, it makes me so proud . . . and hot.

After planning out my day and putting my breakfast dishes into the dishwasher, I shower and get ready for work, making sure I look professional, yet innocent.

I go over the notes I made last night about the case of the dead CEOs and get myself out the door. Twenty minutes later, after checking in with Jen, I pull up at the office of First Choice Construction, and I'm back out the door within the hour. There's no way that old guy did it. That old asshole could barely lift his hand to scratch his own ass, and as bad as it sounds, I wouldn't be surprised if he were to croak over the next few weeks anyway. Besides, I didn't feel it in my gut. This guy might be guilty of something, but he's not guilty of this.

Getting back in my car, I make my way across the city to Baxter

Corporation. I double-check my notes and take a quick look at the photo attached to his name, Christian Baxter. The guy is in his mid-thirties and looks like an absolute sleazeball. He built his company off the money given to him by his mommy and daddy, and from the news articles I could find, he's a real loser.

After touching up my lipstick in the rearview mirror, I get out of my car and glance up at the massive skyscraper before me. Not wanting to be here any longer than necessary, I head inside and over to the reception desk. "Hi, I'm Sophie from Daily Star. I'm here for my scheduled appointment with Mr. Baxter," I lie.

The receptionist inspects her schedule and gets a nervous look on her face, her brows furrowing with unease. "I'm sorry. Sophie, is it? I don't have you down for an appointment."

"Oh? I spoke with Mr. Baxter himself last Thursday. He specifically scheduled an appointment with me for 11 a.m. Shall I give him a call?" I ask, pulling out my phone and making a show of searching through it.

Her eyes widen with fear and it makes me wonder what kind of boss Baxter is to have his staff running scared of a hypothetical schedule mix up. "Oh, no, no. That won't be necessary," the girl says, looking deathly pale. "Go on up. He's on level 38."

Works like a charm.

I give her a polite smile and turn on my heel before a wicked grin spreads across my face. I'm too fucking good at this.

After pressing the elevator call button, I wait, watching the numbers on the little screen as the elevator flies up and down the many levels. Once I step into the glass box and press number 38, the doors inch shut, and I watch the view as the elevator takes off through the beautiful skyscraper. I have to admit, when it comes to developing high-rise buildings, Baxter Corporation clearly knows what they're doing.

Reaching level 38, I step out of the elevator and find a heavy glass door with *Christian Baxter, CEO* written across the front.

Pushing through, I come face to face with yet another receptionist, or maybe it's his personal assistant. Who knows? But the one thing I do notice about her is that she looks a lot like me, and within seconds, my mind is racing with the endless possibilities of how I can use this to my advantage.

I step up to the young girl who looks at me with a bright, welcoming smile. "Hi," she starts. "You must be Sophie. Welcome to Baxter Corporation. My name is Aimee."

"Thank you, Aimee," I say, pleasantly surprised that the front desk actually communicated with upstairs.

"Forgive me for asking, but can you remind me of the nature of your appointment?"

"Of course," I smile. "As I mentioned to your receptionist downstairs, I'm from Daily Star Magazine, and I have an interview with Mr. Baxter."

"Oh," she says, with her eyes widening in surprise. "What's the interview in relation to?"

"Mr. Baxter has been nominated for this year's Sexiest Bachelor award," I say with an immature giggle, acting like a dumb high-school bimbo excited about his nomination. "I just need a few comments from him, and I'll be on my way."

"Right," she says as her eyebrows crease together in confusion. "Wasn't he awarded that last month?"

"No," I say with a slight shake of my head, trying to appear as professional as possible while also pulling out the dreamy *Oh my God, your boss is so cool* vibe. "That was the Money Makers Under Forty award. Now all the ladies are going to know he's not only a bachelor, but he's raking it in too," I grin with a playful wink.

Aimee's face flushes, and she finally agrees to take me in. She leads me down a long hallway before taking me through a maze of glass-windowed offices, and I make sure to commit her every move to memory. At the end of the hall, she swipes her key card, and I'm ushered straight into Christian Baxter's office.

His office is huge, and I spot Christian instantly, talking on his phone as he stands at the massive room-length window. I know he heard my entrance by the sound of my heels clicking on his polished marble floor, though being the pompous ass that he is, he ignores me and forces me to wait until he's good and ready.

Making myself at home, I head over to his bar, grab a glass tumbler, and fill it with ice water. I gingerly take my time shuffling toward the massive couch to get comfortable, wanting to see what vibes he gives off when frustrated or just slightly inconvenienced. As he ignores me, I pull out my notepad of ridiculous questions and my pen, making sure to click it a few times before absentmindedly tapping my fingernails on the side of the glass tumbler.

I do my best to take in his office, working out where he would keep personal files and any kind of information on his competitors. Let's face it, this guy hasn't said a word to me yet, and I can already tell he plays dirty. Whether or not he did what I think he might have done, there will be some sort of story within these walls. The fun is digging it out.

Five minutes later, Christian finally ends his call and turns to me with an annoyed scowl. The moment he takes me in, his gaze narrows and a sleazy grin takes over his face, making my skin crawl.

He takes a few steps toward me and I rise up off the couch, not wanting to put myself in a vulnerable position. Placing himself before me, Christian holds a hand out, and I do the same. The moment he takes in my wedding rings and protruding baby bump, his face pulls up in disgust and disinterest.

Score one for me . . . I think.

"I'm Christian Baxter. How can I help you?" he asks, dropping my hand, trying to sound the least bit professional.

I give him a polite smile. "Sophie Meyers," I inform. "I'm here with Daily Star Magazine, covering your *Sexiest Bachelor of the Year* nomination."

"Huh?" he grunts. "Did I not do this interview a few weeks ago?"

"No," I say with a flirty smile. "That was a separate nomination. Apparently, you're quite a popular guy."

He gives me a cocky grin as he takes a seat opposite the one I just vacated, making sure to check his watch. "I have a few minutes, so by all means," he says, sweeping his arm out and inviting me to take a seat.

I make myself comfortable, but before I can launch into my questions, he holds a hand up. "Hold on," he says with creased eyebrows. "I've heard of you. Aren't you that investigative journalist who has been putting assholes behind bars?"

"Guilty," I say with a proud smile that has his interest returning. Apparently, this guy is willing to look past the baby bump and wedding band after all.

"Right, so why are you doing an interview like this?" he asks skeptically.

I let out a frustrated scoff and put my acting skills into gear. I rub my baby bump, bringing his attention to it once again. "Apparently, my boss doesn't approve of my risky projects while I've got this little guy growing inside me. Though I'm sure he's just concerned about the premium of his insurance if something were to happen. So until further notice, I'm stuck doing these fluff pieces, even though my usual projects are what bring in the most money for the magazine," I explain. "That and my husband would have a heart attack if I was doing what I really wanted to do."

"Bad luck for you, huh? Though I must agree with your boss. From a business perspective, he was right to bench you."

"I know," I agree with a heavy sigh. "Anyway, I should get started. You're clearly a very busy man, and I don't want to take up too much of your time."

He nods his head, and I launch into my questions about his sexy, good looks and bachelor status, making sure to hit all the fitness and diet questions. After doing my best pretending as though I'm actually interested in his clinical, rehearsed replies, I wrap it up when I go ahead and take a risk. "Thank you, Christian. That concludes my questions for the article, but may I be so bold to ask for a statement?"

His gaze narrows and my gut screams to go for it. "A statement for what?" he asks.

"A colleague of mine is doing a piece on the recent passing of Marco Cincinnati. I'm sure you must have known him quite well."

"Recent passing?" he asks with concern, his brows furrowed.

Hmm . . . curious.

Either he truly has no idea, or the guy is pulling out his own impressive acting skills. But how could someone in his position not know about Marco's passing? It was major news that rocked the construction world.

"Yes, sir. His body was discovered on Saturday morning," I inform him like the good little girl I am.

Christian hangs his head. "That's truly devastating. I have known Marco for quite some time."

"I'm so very sorry, I wasn't aware you knew each other personally," I tell him. "I would have broken the news in a more sensitive way."

He nods his head. "How did he pass?" he asks.

Bingo. Just the question I was hoping for.

I watch Christian closely as I go about my description. "His body was discovered in a brothel. He was highly intoxicated, and there was evidence of drug use. Though I believe they are still waiting for the toxicology results to determine if he was using."

He nods his head, and I watch as his features remain schooled.

No shock, no surprise, no dilation of his pupils. This is not news to him, and that tells me that there is indeed more to this story. "That's a shame," he says, shaking his head with disapproval. "I hadn't realized he was one for wild partying. If I'd known he was in trouble, I could have reached out and gotten him the help he so clearly needed."

Liar. There are plenty of news articles that show the two of them out having wild, drunken nights together. All of which include alcohol, drugs, hookers, and DUI charges.

"Of course," I say, giving him a tight smile. "Again, I apologize for being the one to have to break the news. I'm sure you must need a moment to yourself to grieve. So, I'll get out of your hair and I'll be sure to email your office when the article is ready for approval."

"Wonderful," Christian says, getting to his feet. He holds his hand out once again, and I reluctantly take it. "It was lovely meeting you, Sophie."

"Likewise," I nod. "Thank you for your time this morning."

With that, I beeline for the door, knowing that without a doubt I will somehow find my way back into that office. I head back out to the reception area and find Aimee at her desk. "All done?" she asks with a clinical smile.

"I am," I say. "Thank you for finding the time. The article is going to be great."

"Oh, fantastic," Aimee beams as I spy her key card left carelessly on her desk. The idea is in action before it has even fully formed.

"Oh," I gasp as I double over and clutch onto my stomach in pain.

Her eyes widen in fear. "Is everything okay?" Aimee shrieks as she comes rushing around the side of her desk and does what little she can to help me.

"It will be," I pant, pretending to concentrate solely on my breathing. "I've been getting a lot of cramping," I explain. "Could I trouble you for some water?"

"Of course," she says before hurrying around the office, desperate to help the needy pregnant woman.

The moment she turns her back, I make my move and swipe the key card off her desk before sliding it into my purse. I make myself comfortable on the couch opposite her desk and put on a show of rubbing my stomach as I wait for her to return.

Aimee comes back moments later with a glass tumbler filled with frosty water. "Thank you so much," I say, graciously, as I take the glass from her and sip the chilled water.

"No problem at all," she says, gently placing a hand on my shoulder. "Are you feeling better?"

"Yes, much. Thank you," I say. "It happens at the worst times."

"I can only imagine."

I give her a friendly smile before getting back to my feet. "May I ask where the nearest bathroom is? This baby likes to use my bladder as a squeeze toy."

She gives me a fond, knowing smile and points out a doorway just off the reception area. I thank her once again and get on my way, ready to put this plan into action.

Walking into the bathroom, I go up and down the aisle twice before declaring the coast officially clear. Glancing around, I try to figure out the best way to do this. I glance up at the ceiling and spot a smoke detector directly above the sink.

Excellent.

With a grin, I search through my bag and find my trusty lighter. I remember when I first bought it, Dani had insisted that I'd never use it seeing as though I don't smoke. But I was really into having those flaming shots at the time, so I've never once regretted buying this bad boy. Especially now.

Placing my handbag down on the counter, I do my best to hoist myself up. I latch onto the mirror carefully, not wanting to fall, as I grab some paper towels off the counter and hold them to the lighter. The flames catch instantly, and I quickly look back at the door, knowing now would be a really bad time for someone to come in.

Holding the paper towel up to the smoke detector, I let it do its thing.

I listen out, and just as I hoped, I hear the magical sound of the fire alarm starting up. I drop the flaming paper towels into the sink and reach down to turn on the tap. The second the fire is out, I scramble off the counter, being as careful as possible before rushing into a stall and hiding.

The people outside the bathroom groan and fuss as they jump straight into their evacuation procedure, and I can't help but grin to myself at my quick thinking. I mean, this is a pretty epic plan. Though, it's definitely one I won't be able to share with Tank. If he knew . . . shit. I don't even want to think about it.

I hear Christian Baxter's voice outside the bathroom. "This is the fourth fucking time this month," he snaps. "Organize for someone to replace the system."

"Yes, sir," Aimee hastily responds.

"Grab your things," he demands, acting like the jerk I knew he would be out of the public eye. "You'll have to reschedule my video conference for a lunch appointment. Who knows how long this bullshit will take."

"Yes, sir," she stutters out again, making me feel bad for the poor girl. She's doing everything for him, he could at least pretend to be a nice guy. I know if it were me working for him, I would have told him to shove it up his ass ages ago then done everything in my power to inconvenience him in the most frustrating way during my strut out the door.

The noise coming from outside the bathroom starts to dwindle, but I wait a few extra minutes just in case. I pull my phone out of my bag and find a new voice message and an unread text. I read the text first and feel bad when I notice it was Tank checking in on me and I didn't respond. Then I listen to the voicemail.

"Babe, Crazy Jill messaged, so it's on tonight. You better be ready. Call me back when you can."

I close my eyes as I listen to his voice. Even after all this time, the guy still makes me feel like a horny teenager. I grin at his message. That Crazy Jill is so annoying. In fact, all the women who are pining for my husband are annoying, but she's like an extra special dose of fucked up. The woman is clearly taking the wrong meds. Get the picture already! He's happily married with a baby on the way. He isn't interested.

But then, the little bets we have make for some very interesting nights together. And it looks like tonight will be no different. I quickly type out a response.

Sophie - Hey big guy. I'm already thinking about all the ways you could take me over the kitchen counter. Actually, I'm not sure I'll make it to the kitchen counter. I'm just finishing up work, I'll be home within the hour. Love you.

Tank - I can't fucking wait. I'm in the gym, I won't be long.

With a grin, I tuck my phone into my pocket and quietly tiptoe to the bathroom door. I stick my head out and look up and down the hallway.

The coast is clear.

A burst of adrenaline rocks through my veins as I slip out of the bathroom, putting my hair up the same way Aimee had hers, and I steal her jacket off the back of her chair. I pull it on and walk through the office with my head down, making myself look as much like Aimee as possible, just in case there are any cameras or if some office rebels decided to stay behind during the evacuation.

Pulling the key card from my purse, I swipe myself into Christian's office, feeling like a goddamn mastermind. I rush around the office with my head down, making sure to go as quickly as possible since I have no idea how long this evacuation should take. I find the filing cabinet I spotted earlier and get to work. Unfortunately, it's all your typical construction shit with lists upon lists of clients.

I move to his desk and notice his bottom drawer is locked. Bingo.

Searching the office for a key, I head over to his bookshelf and find a photo frame of him with two older people, likely to be his parents. I lift up the frame and grin as I find a shiny silver key.

Too easy. What a rookie error.

Hurrying over to the desk, I hastily slide the key into the lock and give a quick turn, grinning as the key swiftly unlocks the drawer. I open it up and sure enough, there are four other files, all with the names of the four other leading construction companies.

I stare at it in shock for a moment. I can't believe this shit is actually here. Personally, if I was going to be a slimy bastard like Christian Baxter, I would have kept this shit at home, locked far, far away from prying eyes. But when you get cocky, you make mistakes.

I flick through the files, taking quick snapshots of each slip of paper on my phone before placing each file back in the drawer in the exact same position. I look over Christian's desk once again as the alarm comes to a stop and I realize it's time to bail.

I return the key to the shelf, placing it under the frame before making my way out of his office and feeling my pocket to make sure I have my phone. After all, the second I'm home in front of my laptop, I'm going to be uploading the photos and studying each one very carefully.

After making my way back down the hallway, I slip off Aimee's jacket, and place her key card on her desk. I shake out my hair and narrowly escape being caught by the Fire Chief as I slip into the fire escape stairwell and make my way down the thirty-eight flights of stairs.

My legs ache by the time I reach the bottom, and I do my best to blend in with the rest of the anxious crowd, desperately keeping my eyes open for Christian or Aimee. The last thing I need now is to be seen or recognized.

I manage to slip across the road and finally come to the safety of my car before jumping in and speeding away. A sharp laugh pulls from within as I fly through the city, unable to believe I just pulled that shit off.

CHAPTER 6

TANK

It's just after four in the afternoon when I stride through my front door, more than ready for tonight's naked cooking. As usual, I drop my hockey bag just inside the door and kick off my shoes. I can't wait to go find my girl.

Seeing something in my peripheral vision, my gaze snaps up, and I stop dead in my tracks as my wife stands before me in nothing but a black harness, thick straps covering her body and leading down to a pair of thigh-high stockings, all connected to suspenders. But fuck, it's the heels that get me. Always the fucking heels.

Sophie gazes at me with a hungry stare, and I slowly walk toward her, my cock springing to life, watching as her eyes flame with need.

Hell fucking yes.

Starting with her long blonde hair, my eyes trail down her lean body, coming to a stop on her full tits, which sit perfectly plumped underneath one of the straps. My eyes continue down past that incredible bump to the tiniest black thong, and the sight alone has me wanting to tear it from her body with my teeth.

I hit the fucking jackpot with Sophie. The day I saw her in the gym doing her squats is still, to this day, the best day of my life. Well, right after our wedding day, and the day I found out she was carrying my son. After six years together, life with her has gotten better every fucking day.

I stalk her as she licks her lips in anticipation, my hand coming to my belt as my eyes lock onto hers with undeniable hunger. My belt whips out and drops to the ground with a heavy thud before I pop the button of my jeans, already rock hard for her.

"What's this for?" I murmur as I finally reach her.

Sophie's hands slide under my shirt before pressing flat against my chest, feeling the hard ridges of muscles beneath her fingers. My hands come down on her soft body, roaming up and down as I take in the feel of the barely-there leather on her skin. "I couldn't wait for dinner," she purrs, lifting my shirt.

Fuck, she's perfect. The way she needs me like this, I will never tire of her.

I help her to lift my shirt the rest of the way as I watch her eyes greedily take me in. I step into her personal space and press my lips to her neck. "Mmmm," she moans. "It never gets old."

Too fucking right.

Sophie's petite hand slips into my open pants, freeing my cock as she wraps her tight fist around me. I let out a groan as she works me up and down.

"Fuck, Soph," I hiss through a clenched jaw. This is just what I needed.

I'd been with many women before I met Sophie, and not one of them could affect me the way Sophie does. She's like a damn firecracker, always ready to go off, but only ever for me.

My hands roam over her perfect body, more than ready to dive down between those delicious thighs, when she gives me a seductive stare, rolling her tongue over her bottom lip, then drops to her knees before me.

My whole body shudders, and the anticipation of her mouth closing over my cock brings me to fucking life. Did I mention my woman is perfect?

Sophie looks up at me with those big blue eyes before making a show of licking her lips and spreading her knees as wide as possible. Then, keeping her stare locked on mine, she leans forward and takes me in her mouth.

Sophie takes me deep, her fists locked tightly around the base of my cock as her head bobs up and down. She takes me right to the back of her throat, past her gag reflex, and as she pulls back, her tongue rolls over my tip, making me groan. I knot my hands into the back of her hair, and she doesn't take her eyes off me. Despite the way she works me, it's those eyes that hold all the power and keep me captive, prisoner to her every will and desire.

My cock twitches from the motion of her tongue, and as I feel myself getting closer to spilling into her mouth, I pull back a little, not even close to being finished with her yet. I reach down, grabbing her under her arms and hoisting her to her feet before turning her around and bending her at the waist. Her hands catch on the wall to hold her steady as that perfect ass looks up at me. I can't help but give it a good spanking, grinning as she lets out a gasp and pushes her ass back into me, begging for more.

I fist my cock as my other hand finds her center. Even through her thong, I can feel she's soaking wet for me, and I move the flimsy fabric out of my way before plunging my fingers deep inside her. She cries out for more, and I give her what she needs, curving my fingers and massaging deep inside her sweet cunt.

"Fuck, Tank. I need you inside me," Sophie pants as she presses her ass into me, causing my fingers to deepen within her. Using my thumb, I press it to her ass and grin as she groans with need.

"You're gonna take me like a good little whore," I tell her, bringing my hand back down to spank her again.

Her whole body shudders, and I feel her pussy clench around my fingers. "Oh God, yes," she groans. "Now, Tank."

Yeah, fucking firecracker. I don't need to be told twice.

Stepping in close behind her, I guide myself to her entrance, and with one swift thrust, I bury my cock inside, feeling her stretch around me.

Sophie lets out a low moan and my fingers tighten on her hips as she presses back against me, taking it all. Fucking perfection.

I start to move, giving her exactly what she needs while being careful not to be too rough with her. My hand winds around to her clit and begins rubbing tight little circles. She screams out as I fuck her, each of us in a world of pure ecstasy.

"I'm going to come," she warns.

"You're going to do more than come," I tell her. "You'll wait until you explode."

"Fuck," she cries. I can just imagine her clenching her eyes, concentrating on holding out. "I can't, Tank," she pants, letting out a low, throaty groan. I feel her come as she clenches down around me, her walls convulsing as I continue to fuck her raw. Her hands ball into fists against the wall as I watch her come undone. Reveling in her high, I come with her, shooting hot bursts of cum deep inside her sweet cunt.

After catching her breath, Sophie straightens so her back is pressed firmly against my chest. My hands wind around her body, one latching onto her full tit while the other circles our son. "I love you so fucking much," I murmur against her neck, my lips moving against her sensitive skin and prompting her to tilt her head away, silently asking for more.

"Mmm," she groans, her hand lifting to mine over her tit, those perfectly manicured fingers slipping between mine. "I love you, too."

"You want to explain what that surprise was about?" I ask. Sophie's body goes rigid in my arms, and I let out a sigh before turning her around and lifting her. She wraps her legs around my waist, and I walk us into the bathroom to help clean her up.

"I had a really good day," she tells me before cringing. "But, it's my kind of good day, not yours."

My face falls and my stare locks on her, realizing that the surprise at the door wasn't a surprise at all. It was her guilty conscience working overtime, but I'm not complaining. She can greet me at the door like that any time she pleases. "You have three fucking seconds to tell me what you did."

Not two minutes later, I'm gaping at my wife in horror. "You're telling me you started a fire in order to set off the fire alarm, broke into a possible murderer's office, impersonated someone, and stole legal documentation?" I question.

A wide grin stretches across her face, her fingers remaining on my body, knowing how her touch has a way of keeping me calm. "Yep," she says proudly.

"Should you really be doing all this?" I ask, bringing up the old argument. "You could have hurt yourself. You really need to slow down. You're five months pregnant, for God's sake. What if you had been caught in there?"

"Then instead of getting a sexy surprise at the door, you would have gotten a different kind of surprise," she says with a guilty smirk. "But getting back on track, I'm kind of hoping there's something in the documents I found. So, you'll be happy to know that I'll be at the office for the rest of the week. I might even work from my home office. We'll see how I feel."

"Good," I smile in relief. The last thing we need is for her to exhaust herself. I know she likes to think she's Superwoman, and yes, most of the time she is. But right now, she has a growing baby to look out for.

"I finally got to use my lighter again" she grins, changing the topic.

"What?" I grunt, raising a brow as she hops off the bathroom counter. "I thought that was only to be used for shots?"

She smirks up at me with laughter in her eyes. "It was important. I had to use it."

"Yeah," I scoff. "It was important when I needed to use it too."

"Babe," she says, trying to keep a straight face. "I was not going to let you use my lighter so you and Miller could set your farts on fire."

"It was important," I repeat.

Soph rolls her eyes, and we make our way out of the bathroom where I find my shirt discarded in the middle of the hallway. Bending to pick it up, I hear Sophie clear her throat behind me. I turn on her, letting out a heavy sigh, knowing what's coming next. "Yes?" I ask slowly.

"You lost a bet, big guy," she reminds me, looking all too proud of herself. "You should be stripping off, not putting more clothes on."

"Seriously, babe?"

"Yep," she grins. "You made me follow through when I lost the bet. Now it's your turn."

With a sigh, I throw my shirt at her and watch as she gingerly pulls it over her head, covering up that sexy lingerie before I lose my jeans, which somehow managed to stay up during the whole screwing in the doorway thing. I stand before her in my birthday suit. "Better?" I ask.

"Much," she grins, clearly very proud of herself.

With a sigh, I go about the kitchen, preparing everything I need for dinner. It's still a bit early, but I might as well get on with it.

I'm just finishing up when the intercom for the front gate buzzes, letting me know someone is here. Sophie gets up and checks the camera. "Oh, it's a delivery," she announces excitedly as she buzzes the driver through.

I double-check that my shirt is properly covering all her bits before she makes her way to the door, but I should know better by now. My shirt practically falls beneath her knees. I hear her opening the door and she thanks the driver before the door is closed once again.

I go about my business in the kitchen when I hear her entering the living room. "Babe, my stroller came," she announces with a clear smile in her voice.

"Awesome," I murmur, bending down to get the dinner out of the oven.

"Uhh," comes an unfamiliar voice. "Where do you want this?"

What. The. Fuck?

Abandoning dinner, I whip around wearing nothing but a pair of oven mitts and find the delivery guy standing right in the center of my living room with a beaming Sophie right beside him. I quickly realize my cock and balls are out and that I just mooned the guy getting dinner out of the over, so I hastily cover myself with the mitts.

My eyes narrow on Sophie, but all she can do is smirk, letting me know that she invited the guy in on purpose. Hell, she probably gave him the big puppy-dog eyes and pointed out her pregnant belly, and the asshole would have fallen at her feet. Damn little hussy is going to pay for that one. "Just pop it down here," Sophie says pointing toward the floor of the living room.

The delivery guy does just that, and Sophie can barely wait until he steps away before she starts ripping into the box. The delivery guy shuffles toward me with his tablet held out. "I need you to sign for it, here," he says as he finally looks up at me. His eyes go wide and I recognize the look immediately—he's a fan.

"Holy shit," he gasps. "You're Tank Meyers."

"Yep, that's me," I say as I take the tablet from his hand and awkwardly try to sign for the stroller while still covering my junk.

"Wow. Fuck. I'm one of your biggest fans, dude," he says. "Can I get an autograph?"

"Uh, well, I'm sort of in the middle of the first one you wanted," I grunt. I wonder what planet one must be living on to even think now might be an appropriate time to ask for favors. I mean, shit. I'm in my fucking kitchen, covering my cock with my wife's *Hello Kitty* oven mitts. This is not the time for autographs.

"Right, yeah," he says, dropping the autograph thing. "I went to all the games last year. I think you'll make it as captain this season," he tells me.

"Thanks for the vote of confidence," I say as he moves around the kitchen, unable to stand still in his excitement. Annoyingly, his movements mean I have to keep adjusting the oven mitt so the poor kid doesn't get another eyeful of my dick.

"Yeah, no problem," he says. "I actually applied for a position on the team a few weeks ago."

"Really?" I ask, my brows dipping low, not aware that we had any openings.

"Yeah, I really want to be a hockey player. I don't skate yet, but I figured they'd teach me once I got the position," he says. "You know, that's what the coach is for, right? I sent in my resume. Maybe you could put in a good word for me?"

He's shitting me, right? Does he really think professional athletes just send in their resumes one day and cross their fingers, hoping they get a callback? Was he going to hire a pair of skates from skate rental, or maybe he was thinking of asking to borrow a pair off one of the boys?

I look at Sophie, who's standing with a stroller wheel in her hand, trying her hardest not to burst out laughing. "Is he for real?" she mouths with a wicked grin.

I give her a slight shrug and turn my attention back to the stranger in my kitchen. "Sorry, buddy. That's not quite how the recruitment process works," I tell him, hating to shoot down his dreams.

"What do you mean?" he asks, suddenly stopping.

"The guys on the team have all been skating since they were kids. Training day in and day out. All were drafted from their college hockey teams," I inform him. I can't believe I'm actually having this conversation in my kitchen right now. I figured this was general knowledge, but even if it wasn't, at some point common sense has to enter the chat.

"Fuck," he grunts, looking as though I've just taken a massive dump over his whole career plan. "What am I going to do now? I practically told my girlfriend I was already on the team."

"Tough break, man," I say with a tight smile, really not interested in the exaggerated lies he tells his girlfriend. "Anyway, now's not really a great time," I tell him as I hand the little tablet back to him.

He takes it from me and slides it into his pocket before giving me a sad smile. "Right. Well, it was great to meet you," he says before turning his back and making his way to the door.

Sophie follows to make sure he actually leaves, rather than taking a crapload of our shit to sell on eBay like the last obsessive fan who wandered into our house did. She sends him on his way before returning to me with a massive grin. "Can you believe that?" she asks, as she bursts into laughter.

"I know," I grunt. "I kind of felt bad bursting his bubble like that."

"You did the right thing," she says, walking up to me and wrapping her arms around my body before letting her hands wander down to my ass.

"Speaking of doing the right thing," I say, narrowing my gaze on the little she-devil. "You brought him in here on purpose."

"I don't know what you're talking about," she grins.

"You're going to pay for that."

"Really?" she asks as her nails dig into the flesh of my ass. "How so?"

"You'll find out," I tell her with a grin, imagining the position I'll be putting her in later. "But first you need to feed my son."

"Fine," she says, reaching up onto her tippy-toes and planting the sweetest kiss on my lips. "Can you help me put the stroller together after that?"

"Sure thing."

Together we go about the kitchen, dishing up dinner and flopping down onto the couch to eat. I decide to get started on the stroller while Sophie takes her sweet ass time with dinner. Apparently, now that the baby is taking up so much room, she has to eat slowly to avoid throwing it all back up again. Just to make my point, she belches so loud, the fucking neighbors can hear.

My wife is so fucking charming.

Twenty minutes later, I finish with the stroller just as Sophie finishes her dinner. I collect her plate off the side of the couch and make my way into the kitchen before rinsing off the dishes and placing them in the dishwasher, all while Sophie clings to my back.

I turn in her arms and lift her so I can easily kiss her, and she wraps her legs around my waist as I place her down on the kitchen counter. "Thanks for dinner," she murmurs against my lips.

"My pleasure."

Sophie pulls back just enough so that we can have a decent conversation without our lips mushing together. "Should we go to bed?" she asks with hooded eyes, clearly having her own agenda for the night.

"Nope," I say with a shake of my head as my fingers grasp the bottom of my shirt and start pulling it over her head. She raises her arms and allows the shirt to come off before dropping it in a heap at my feet. "You owe me," I remind her.

"And what is it that you so desperately desire?" she asks, her eyes sparkling with hunger.

I step back from her and take her in, still in the harness, minus the heels, and looking as stunning as ever. I continue backing away from her until I'm leaning against the opposite counter. "Spread 'em," I tell her.

She does what she's told, extremely slowly, and I feel the blood rushing to my dick as I watch her move. She shuffles back onto the center of the counter to give herself some room as she spreads her legs as wide as possible. She places her feet up on the counter, making sure she gives me the best possible view.

Fuck me.

I take my dick in my hand and watch as her eyes zero in on the movement, flaming with desire. "What now?" she purrs in that velvety voice.

"Harness. Off." I order.

Once again, she happily obliges, though naturally, she does it as slowly as she possibly can, making it pure, sensual torture. Then finally, those perfect tits look back at me, desperate to be touched. Sophie sucks her bottom lip between her teeth, nearly driving me to the edge. "Touch yourself, baby," I tell her. "I want to watch."

A devilish grin crosses her face as her hand comes up and cups her breast, squeezing it and rubbing her nipple between her fingers, the same way I would have done had it been my hands on her body. Those hungry, blue eyes remain locked on mine, but I'm far too busy watching her body.

Leaning back, her hand starts traveling down her body, and I watch with bated breath as she moves the fabric of her thong out of the way.

She sucks in a gasp before pressing two fingers to her exposed clit and rubbing little circles.

The view has my hand pumping faster and tighter on my cock, desperate for more. Sophie lets out a moan and her eyes close in satisfaction before she lowers her hand just a little further. Her eyes open and she watches me as those same two fingers push into her entrance, coming out glistening before making their way back in.

Fuck, seeing her this turned on has me wanting to cross the kitchen and plunge deep inside her, but then I also want to watch until the end. Her other hand comes up and starts caressing her tits once again as the moaning and grunting become more frequent in our quiet kitchen.

Her hand moves faster, but I know she needs more, more than what she can offer herself right now. "Please," she begs from across the kitchen.

I can't say no to her.

I make my way to her in two quick strides, grabbing her ass before scooting her right to the edge of the counter, perfectly lined up with my dick. She pulls her fingers out and presses them to her clit as I bury myself deep inside her.

"Holy shit," she pants. "This is so much better than what I had planned."

"Bet your sweet ass, it is," I grunt as I slam into her one last time and come hard, just as she detonates around me.

CHAPTER 7

SOPHIE

I make my way into my office bright and early, more than ready to blow this case wide fucking open.

While I wait for my computer to power up, I head into the staff kitchen and reach for the coffee pot. Thinking better of it, I put some water on and grab a tea bag instead. I know I'll need the caffeine today, but this little guy inside me doesn't appreciate it.

Heading back to my office with my tea in hand, I close the door behind me and prepare for a big day. As much as I love my team here, they can get loud, and the last thing I need is distractions. I need to focus. So I place my tea down on my desk and move every last piece of paper that has nothing to do with the CEO case onto the floor.

Next, I make my way over to my corkboard and take down

everything from my previous investigation. I make sure to put it all away in a folder, just in case any of my information is needed in court. After all, one can never be too careful in my line of work.

Ready to get started, I pull my phone out of my bag and attach it to the USB cable connected to my computer, before selecting all the images I wish to transfer over. Seeing as there are so many, I start printing off images of all the people involved and attach them to my corkboard, making sure to put a big red cross over the faces of the deceased because, well, that's what they do in the movies.

Ten minutes later, once I've finished setting myself up, my computer beeps to notify me that the transfer is complete, so I make myself comfortable and get started.

A few hours and a headache later, I finally stumble upon something interesting that could possibly blow this case right out of the water. It seems that a company by the name of CB Construction anonymously bought shares in all of the construction competitor's companies, each with hidden clauses stating that if the CEO should pass, his or her remaining shares would go to CB Construction. After digging into the background and financials of this company, it becomes clear that it's a shell corporation, set up to cover the ass of none other than Christian Baxter.

My brows furrow. I've never been one to have an interest in shares, so I have to do some research on the standard practice, but either way my gut is telling me that this isn't right. No CEO in their right mind would have approved a deal like this, even without knowing if the other party was a direct competitor.

I keep digging into this whole shares thing and realize that with these CEOs dead, Christian is now the anonymous major shareholder of each of these companies and making a shitload of money off it too.

He also has the power to shut down these companies, which would drive all potential clients his way, or he could buy them out. Really, as the major shareholder, he could do whatever the hell he wants with all the competitor's companies now.

And I think I just found a motive.

My brain swirls with information, and I know in my gut that he had something to do with these deaths . . . Well, I guess death is the wrong word. They were murders made to look like deaths from natural causes.

I print off the contracts and pin them to my corkboard, making sure to highlight the evidence. I can't find it in me to sit back down, so I pace my office instead. How the hell am I going to prove that he did this, or at the very least, that he had something to do with it?

A man like Christian Baxter would have every moment of his day carefully scheduled. If I could somehow get my hands on his calendar, I could cross match his schedule to the time of the deaths to see if he has any type of alibi, or if it's even worth digging deeper.

I start wondering how I'm going to get what I need when I remember his PA's planner that sat on her desk. She should have every tiny detail of Christian's whereabouts in that thing. The only question is, how the hell am I going to get my hands on it?

Realizing this means another trip out of the office that Tank isn't going to approve of, I start thinking about how I'm going to make it up to him.

My phone ringing on my desk startles me out of my thoughts, and I grin at the caller ID. Shit, it's as though he knows I'm about to get up to something. I hit answer and hold the phone up to my ear.

"Hey, big guy," I smile.

"Hey, babe. How's your day going?" he asks. "Are you still at the office?"

I roll my eyes, knowing that would have been his first thought. "Yes, I'm still at the office," I tell him. "My day's been huge. I found motive."

"Seriously?" he questions in surprise, making me wonder if he doubted me. "What kind of motive?"

I go through everything I've found today, and even though I know Tank hates when I do this, he also won't stop me from putting someone behind bars. Especially if that's where they need to be.

"That's some pretty damning evidence, but it's not enough to get him convicted. It just proves he's the majority shareholder of their companies," he points out.

"I know," I say with a cringe, hating to disappoint him. "Which is why I need to go back to his office."

"No, babe. Absolutely not. I don't want you going there, especially now you suspect him of actually murdering those guys," he says. "Who knows what could happen if he finds out you're digging. You don't have a good enough reason to be there."

"Actually," I say, cringing again. "I think I might."

"Babe," he warns.

"It's fine," I promise. "I won't even need to see him. I just need to hand something to his PA."

Tank lets out a frustrated sigh before finally giving in. "Are you sure?"

"Promise," I say. "I'll be in and out in no time. I won't even need to escape down the fire stairs." I can picture him rolling his eyes, and when he doesn't say anything, I know I've won this round. "How's your day going?" I ask, hoping to change topics.

"Good," he says, a strange tone in his deep voice.

"Spill it, buster," I demand, unable to stop the massive grin spreading across my face.

I can practically hear the smile in his voice. "Coach Larsden has called a meeting for tomorrow. He has a few announcements."

"And you think this is when you'll be crowned king of the ice?"

"Well, yeah, I'm kind of hoping," he says a little bashfully, knowing damn well that he's going to be captain.

There's no doubt in my mind that he's going to get that position, and I know he feels that too. He just doesn't want to get his hopes up. "You'll be fine," I tell him, knowing just how much he deserves this. "You've got this."

"I know," he replies, softly. "What are you doing?"

"Nothing. I was just thinking about getting lunch before I head out to Baxter Corporation," I tell him.

"Could you hold off for half an hour? I'll swing by and take you out."

I twirl my hair around my finger like a teenage girl, despite knowing he can't see me. "Ooh, are you asking me out?" I tease.

"Shut up," he grunts. "I'll be there soon."

"Okay, love you."

"Love you too," he murmurs before ending the call.

I grin as I put my phone back down on my desk and get busy. With Tank arriving in half an hour, that gives me just enough time to put together a mock article that I can use to weasel my way back up to Aimee's desk.

As usual, I get carried away when I'm writing, so I practically jump right out of my seat when a knock sounds at my office door. I look up to find the world's largest man looming in my doorway, looking as sexy as ever. "Are you ready to go?" he asks with a smirk.

Shit. Where did the last half an hour go?

I hit print on the article and rush around my office, collecting all my crap. "Sure am," I beam as I pick up the paper from the printer.

Tank makes his way inside and quickly looks over my corkboard. "He's a real fucking scumbag," he comments, taking my hand and leading me out the door.

"How was training?" I ask, pressing the button for the parking lot as we step into the elevator.

"Good," he says, pressing me into the wall of the elevator and kissing me deeply. His hands travel down my body and cup me between my legs. "I love it when you dress for the office," he murmurs.

"There's cameras in here," I remind him with a gasp. Honestly, it wouldn't be the first time we've been sprung in this thing.

"Damn it," he grunts, pulling away and leaving me desperate for more.

The elevator opens and he takes me by the hand as he leads me toward his truck. He helps me up into it like a gentleman, kisses my temple while his hand caresses my stomach, and then finally closes the door, leaving me pining for him as he makes his way around to the driver's side.

Fuck, I love this man.

Tank takes me on our lunch date and all too soon, the bill is paid, and we're getting back in his truck. "Are you heading back to the office?" he asks.

"Um . . . I don't really need to. I have everything with me if you wanted to take me to Baxter Corporation. I'll be like, five minutes, and then we can go home."

"You don't need your car?" he questions.

"Nah, I'll work from home tomorrow."

"Okay. I was going to hit the gym, but I can use the one at home."

Oh, shit. Just the thought of him getting all hot and sweaty seems to do the same thing to me. My eyes become hooded as I look over at him, wondering just what kind of workout he has planned. After all, if it's hot and sweaty that he wants, I could certainly help with that. "Can I watch?"

He rolls his eyes, but I see the enjoyment in his satisfied smirk. I know without a doubt that I'll end up bent over his gym equipment at some point this afternoon.

It's a short drive to Baxter Corporation and after Tank pulls up out front, I hop out of his truck with a promise to be back as soon as possible. "If you're not back in five minutes, I'm coming to get you," he warns.

I give him a salute. "Yes, sir," I grin before disappearing into the massive skyscraper.

I head straight for the elevator, ignoring the disgruntled receptionist in the lobby, and hit the up button. Once again, I'm in awe of this incredible building, and find myself wondering just how much something like this would have cost to build. The elevator arrives with a *ding*, and I wait patiently for the doors to open before stepping in.

It takes no time for the elevator to shoot through the sky and chime my arrival at level 38, and as I push through the heavy glass door, I'm faced with a smiling Aimee, ready and waiting to greet anyone who graces her boss' office.

"Sophie, right?" she questions as she raises from her desk.

"Yes, that's right," I smile. "Sorry to just drop in like this. My husband surprised me with lunch in the area, so I thought I'd pop in while I was close."

"Oh, no problem. How can I help you?"

I reach into my bag and pull out the mock article on Christian Baxter's Sexiest Bachelor nomination and hand it over. "I've finished the draft article. I was hoping Mr. Baxter could give it the okay so I can send it to print."

"Oh, sure," she says. "I'll get him to check it over now. Would you care for a seat?" she says, indicating to the one I had faked my baby pains on yesterday.

"Thank you," I say with a polite smile.

The moment she turns her back, I make my move. Just as I thought, the planner sits right on her messy desk, and I quickly slip it into my bag before taking a seat on the couch.

Moments later, Aimee returns and hands me the draft article. "He was pleasantly surprised. You are quite the writer."

I give her a beaming smile. Despite who her boss is, a compliment for my writing never goes astray. "Thank you. I'll send it off to my editor and be sure to send you a copy of the magazine with his article in print."

"Excellent."

With that, I duck out of the office and make my way back out to Tank's truck. "All good?" he asks as I climb in.

A wicked grin cuts across my face, once again reminding myself that I'm the baddest mastermind in town. "All good."

The next day, after sending Tank on his way to his meeting with Coach Larsden, I hole up in my home office with Aimee's planner until I have memorized every last detail of Christian Baxter's whereabouts for the days surrounding the murders.

Honestly, it's more work than I thought it was going to be. It's not like *Kill Marco Cincinnati in a brothel* is written in red capital letters in her planner.

Though, I do find out that at the time of each death, Christian Baxter has no alibi. Well, at least according to this planner he didn't.

I've also worked out that the appointments surrounding the times of the deaths have all had him smack bang in the center of the city, giving him plenty of time to do away with his competition and return to his office or home without anyone noticing his absence.

Damn. If I didn't love writing so much, I could have been a detective. I'd be nailing bastards all over the country and putting their scum-asses in prison.

At precisely eleven in the morning, my stomach starts rumbling, and I look down at my swollen stomach. "Dude, I just ate like an hour ago. You're already hungry?"

I know he can't respond. Well, actually he will in his own way. He'll probably start kicking me in the ribs the moment I eat, letting me know just how much he appreciates the yummy goodness I'm filling my body with.

I always found it strange when women talked to their unborn children as though he or she can hear them from inside, and maybe they can. Either way, they literally look like they've gone bat-shit crazy, and trust me, I let Dani know it every time she did. Now that I'm experiencing pregnancy firsthand, it feels right. Like communicating with my baby is the most natural thing in the world.

I guess that's just one more thing Dani gets to say *I told you so* about.

Getting up, I head into the kitchen to make myself a sandwich, when I begin thinking about Tank's meeting today. I wonder if he's had it already. He would have likely called me right after to tell me the good news if the meeting was over. And no doubt, there will be good news. Otherwise, I'm going to have to go down there and bang some heads together. If Coach Larsden does my husband dirty, there'll be hell to pay.

I place my sandwich delicately on a plate as if I'm about to deliver the bastard to the king and make my way back into my office. I sit down and annihilate it while I stalk all of Baxter's personal social media pages, hoping to find something that could actually tie him to any of this bullshit. After all, the planner was great and shows he doesn't have an alibi, but it still doesn't prove he actually did it.

By the time I push away my empty plate, I let out a long sigh of frustration. I really should have made two of them, maybe three. I consider getting back up when my phone rings.

I grin at the caller ID.

"Hey, bitch. What's up?"

"Don't call me that. You're on speaker and Mia is listening. I don't want her growing up with a potty mouth like yours," Dani says.

"Oh, please," I scoff. "Mia would be lucky to have a mouth like mine. Besides it's a cutthroat world out there, maybe a little cuss word here and there would do her good."

I can practically hear her rolling her eyes. "Whatever," Dani groans. "Can we come over? Mia really needs to get out of the house."

"Yeah, but can you give me a few hours? I'm in the middle of some research. I'm going to crack this one soon. I can feel it."

"Okay, sure. I'll head out and do the groceries first, then come your way."

"Excellent," I say and am about to hang up when a thought occurs to me. "Have you heard from Miller? Have they had their meeting yet?"

"No. It's at one, so they're still training. Don't stress," she says in a soothing tone, knowing just how anxious I've been over this. "He'll get it."

"I know he will," I say as confident as ever, though that doesn't change the fact that I've been nervous for him all day. God, I'd like to be a fly on the wall during that meeting. "I'm just excited."

"I know. We'll see you soon," she laughs.

"Okay, bye."

I end the call and instantly head back into the kitchen. I know Dani will want to have a late lunch when she comes over, but that's still another few hours away. I'm definitely going to need another sandwich if I'm going to survive that long.

CHAPTER 8

SOPHIE

I'm busy searching through all the dead guys' Facebook pages and social media accounts when the buzzer for the front gate sounds through the house, and I glance at the time. My brows furrow. It's only been an hour since I spoke with Dani. Is she really struggling that much with Mia today?

Letting out a sigh, I lean across the desk as best I can, trying to reach the button for the gate, but my bump just won't let me bend the same way I used to. Groaning with frustration, I search my desk and spot a ruler, determined to do this without having to get up.

Stretching out again with the ruler, I easily press the button and feel as though I've accomplished some kind of miracle. I'm such a fucking genius. A brilliant, lazy, fucking genius.

A moment later, there's a knock at the door and I groan to myself. Seriously? Can't she just walk in like she usually does? I ignore her and get back to searching Facebook, knowing she'll eventually just let herself in, when the knock sounds again.

Damn it.

I huff in frustration and get to my swollen feet. She better have her hands full, making it physically impossible to open the door. And by hands full, I definitely mean she better have snacks. At this point in my pregnancy, I only get off my ass if it's extremely important, when food is involved, or if the baby is squishing my bladder and I'm about to wet my pants.

I fling the door open with a little more force than necessary and start digging into Dani before the door has fully opened. "Are you kidding me right now?" I scold as I take in the people on the other side of the door, before quickly cutting myself off.

My eyes widen in shock.

What the hell is he doing here?

A very disgruntled and annoyed Christian Baxter stands at my door with two extremely imposing men. Bodyguards? Hired muscle? I don't know, but they don't look friendly.

Christian immediately steps into my home with his two beef heads following behind and I take a hesitant step away as one of the guys closes the door behind him, then flicks the lock.

I swallow hard, realizing this is not going to be a friendly visit.

"It's very unfortunate that we must meet again like this, Sophie," Christian starts as he looks me over, before welcoming himself deeper into my home.

The shock wears off, and I quickly hurry after him. "Excuse me? What do you think you're doing?" I ask as he gingerly takes a seat on my couch.

"Please," he says, sweeping his arm out toward the opposite seat. "Make yourself comfortable."

"No, thank you," I say, my voice thick with sarcasm. "What are you doing, coming uninvited into my home?" I ask calmly as I cross my arms over my chest and pull my bitch face into position.

He looks up at me as he throws his arm casually over the back of my couch. "You think I wouldn't realize what you were up to?" he asks. "I figured it out the second you told me who you were."

"I haven't a clue what you are talking about. I told you exactly what I was doing by coming to your office. In fact, your article was finished yesterday. It was approved and sent to print, so you have no reason to be here."

Christian lets out an irritated scoff. "You think I'm here because of some bullshit fluff piece? I thought you were smarter than that."

I give him an impatient stare, daring him to get on with it.

"When Sophie Meyers shows up at your office, you know she's digging for something. For Sophie Meyers to show up at your office two days in a row, then the bitch thinks she's found a story," Christian informs me, narrowing his eyes on mine. "You know, I was going to let it go until Aimee's planner went missing. You see, she doesn't misplace things. I make sure of it. So, I looked up our surveillance footage, and you wouldn't believe what I saw, or in fact, *who* I saw stealing her planner. And it got me wondering about the suspicious timing of the evacuation. So I rewound the footage just a little further, and to my surprise, there's Sophie Meyers impersonating my PA and breaking into my office to steal private and confidential documents."

I swallow back a lump in my throat. Shit. He's clearly not thrilled about the fact that I'm onto him. Though I'm sure that's because he knows I never fail. "It could have been anyone," I say, as his muscle men both start creeping forward.

My eyes flick between them, anxiety and fear pounding through my body, my heart racing with unease. He knows I know, and now he needs to tie up loose ends.

And I just happen to be the loose end.

FUCK.

Where the hell is Dani?

Christian lets out a booming laugh. "You don't think my surveillance has facial recognition software?" he says as he gets to his feet. "I'm a motherfucking tycoon, Sophie. The biggest name in the industry. You don't think I'm out here protecting my interests?"

My heart pounds as the men continue getting closer, and I start to back up. "You need to leave," I demand, my hands shaking at my sides.

"In due time," Christian says with a sick smirk.

Fuck.

I take off like a bat out of hell. If only I can make it to the door, I'll be able to call for help.

My feet pound against the tiles, racing through my home as fear rocks through me. I grip my stomach as I fear for my baby's life, certain that this is the end for both of us. Christian isn't going to let this go with a slap on the wrist. He's coming for blood.

I see the door down the end of the long hallway, but a hand latches around my forearm and yanks me back with an incredible force, pulling me right up off my feet.

Screams tear from my throat as I'm thrown down to the cold tiles flat on my stomach. Pain grips me, but I don't have time to focus on it as fingers curl around my ankles and begin dragging me back into the living room.

I claw at the floor, trying to find purchase on anything to try and get out of his vicious hold. My stomach aches, but I can't allow myself to think about it yet. I need to get out of here, need to make sure my baby is okay. A hand grips into the back of my hair and I'm yanked to my feet as I try my hardest to fight against his hold, but it's no use. My strength has nothing on his.

Christian Baxter stands in front of me with his two henchmen at either of my sides. "Consider this your one and final warning," he says before turning his back and walking away.

His men turn on me with sick smirks, and I see the decision in their eyes as they back me into a corner.

"Please, no," I cry before a fist comes pummeling forward in an uppercut to my stomach. I scream in agony, desperate to cradle my stomach, but with my arms locked in this stranger's firm grip, I have no choice but to suffer through the pain. Tears stream down my face, fearing for my little boy.

I beg over and over again for them to leave me and my baby alone.

To finish their assault and let me be. But it goes on and on until every inch of my skin has thoroughly been beaten and my bones broken.

After what feels like a lifetime, they finally leave me in a heap on the ground with my blood spilled throughout the room. I consider trying to move across the room to call an ambulance, but I simply don't have the energy. Curling myself into a ball with my arms protectively wrapped around my stomach, I weep in agony, wishing for the pain to go away.

My consciousness starts to slip away and I concentrate on my stomach, waiting to feel his little movements inside me as fear claims me, sending my world into darkness.

CHAPTER 9

TANK

Today has been one hell of a long fucking day, and it's not even lunchtime yet. I've been a jittery mess of nerves waiting for this damn meeting. I shouldn't be though, and that pisses me off. I should be confident. I'm the best damn player on this team. I've been here for five years, and about to embark on my sixth. I deserve it. Everyone knows it. Yet there's this tiny seed of doubt in my mind.

It shouldn't be there, but it is.

Nearly all the boys have shown up for this morning's training session, taking advantage of the ice since we all have to be present for this compulsory meeting. It's half past noon when the boys and I get off the ice, and I head into the locker room, stripping off my training gear before heading into the showers.

After cleaning up, I put a little extra effort into getting dressed. After all, if this is going to be my big shot, then at the risk of sounding like a pansy-ass motherfucker, I want it to be special.

I'm just finishing up when Miller joins me. "You ready for this, man?" he asks as he collects his phone from his locker.

"Fucking born ready."

Miller gives me a goofy-ass grin, and I have to look away to avoid smirking back at him like a moron.

I jam my phone, keys, and wallet into my pockets as Coach Larsden comes striding into the locker room. "Conference room. Now," he demands before turning away and stalking back out of the room without another word.

"You heard the man," Miller murmurs as we make our way out.

As one, we all stride into the conference room, and I'm pleasantly surprised to see the place decked out with a wide variety of lunch arrangements, buffet style. The rest of the guys are as well, and we all beeline straight for the food.

With plates piled high, we take our seats and let Coach get the meeting underway.

He starts with the usual housekeeping stuff. How things are going to work, who our biggest competition is this season, and the general plan for how we're going to succeed. He goes over our training schedule and his expectations for the season before finally getting to the good stuff.

"Alright, guys," he starts. "I've kept you long enough so we'll get right down to what you really want to know."

The boys holler and cheer as I feel my phone vibrating in my pocket. I slide my hand into my pocket and quickly pull it out before Coach gets started. I see Dani's name flash across the screen, and I quickly look to Miller who looks none the wiser. Maybe she's been trying to get a hold of him and thought she'd try me. Either way, she's going to have to wait. Now really isn't a great time.

I silence the call, slip my phone back into my pocket, and pay full attention to Coach Larsden. "Alright, we'll start with vice-captain," Coach says as my phone starts up for the second time. I silence it again, hoping no one else can hear the soft vibration buzzing through the room. Not that anyone would care, but it looks bad. "Congratulations, Cameron. The job is all yours."

The boys cheer for Cameron, who looks at Coach with a proud smile and nods, and I realize at some point, I'm going to have to whip this motherfucker's ass into gear. He's not the vice-captain I would have chosen, but the decision is out of my hands.

"Okay, now for this season's captain," Coach says. My eyes flick to Miller, who I know has been waiting for this moment just as much as I have, but my phone starts up again.

For fuck's sake, Dani. Not now.

I concentrate on Coach as I silence the call again. "Your new captain has shown incredible dedication over the five years he has been a part of this team, and he is long overdue for the position. Congratulations Tank. You're the new captain of the LA Storm."

Pride surges through me. I don't even know how to describe the feeling within me. Excitement? Happiness? I don't fucking know, but what I do know is that this day will forever be right up there with the day I met Sophie and our wedding day. It's everything I've worked for since I was a kid learning how to skate, and here it is. All the hard work has finally paid off.

Well, I guess you could say the hard work is just getting started. Now I have to prove I belong here each and every day. I need to be the best damn captain these boys have ever seen, and I'll be damned if I don't lead this team to victory.

Fuck. The only thing missing right now is Sophie. What I wouldn't give to have her in my arms right now. I can't fucking wait to get out of his meeting and give her a call. I can just imagine what she's going to say. She probably has something extra special planned for tonight, and I'm sure it's going to blow my mind.

The boys give their congratulations in the form of whoops and hollers. Miller jumps out of his chair with a massive "Yes," followed up by a fist pump while I grin like a fucking idiot. Coach catches my eye and gives me a proud smile. He comes forward and holds out his hand, and quickly I take it, giving a firm shake. "You deserve it, kid," he says.

"Thanks, Coach. I won't let you down," I say, knowing just how much he hates being thanked, but fuck it, I'm thanking the bastard whether he likes it or not.

The boys finally settle down and Coach calls us to attention. "Okay, now that's over, you may as well eat the rest of this shit. I don't want it going to waste. Give yourselves a quick break, then I want you in the gym." He's just wrapping up his dismissal when his phone comes screeching to life on the table before him.

He looks down at the caller ID before glancing up at Miller. A strange feeling settles in the pit of my stomach. If that's Dani, it must be damn important for her to call Coach, especially when she knows we're in a meeting like this. Coach hits answer and holds the phone up to his ear while his eyes remain locked on Miller, who I notice is looking back at him in confusion, clearly wondering why Coach has him in his sights.

"Dani? What's up?" he asks.

"Dani?" Miller questions with a grunt, getting to his feet, but my attention is on the squawking that's heard through the line, so loud I can hear her clear as day despite not being on speakerphone.

"Where's Tank? It's Sophie, she's been hurt."

"What?" Coach Larsden's eyes instantly flick to mine, but I'm already out of my chair reaching for his phone, snatching the fucker right out of his hands.

"Dani? What's wrong?" I rush out as Miller hovers by my side.

"I called an ambulance. She's been beaten," she starts. "I . . . I . . ."

"What?" I cut in as I take off out of the room.

"A home invasion maybe," she cries, heavy sobs making it almost impossible to make out what she's saying. "You need to hurry. She's lost a lot of blood."

Fuck.

I end the call and throw myself into my truck, Miller already beside me. Kicking over the engine, I slam my foot on the gas and peel out of the parking lot, not giving a fuck about the oncoming traffic. "Head to the hospital," Miller says as he sees me about to take the turn for home.

"She said she called an ambulance. It'll be quicker to meet her there."

Shit. Of course.

I break every fucking traffic law as I try to get to my wife as fast as possible, the thoughts going through my head leaving me crippled and unable to breathe. What the hell did Dani mean she had been beaten? And how much blood had she lost? Was she conscious? Talking? Breathing? What about my son?

Question after question fills my mind and has me pushing my truck to its absolute limits, desperate to get to her.

I pull up outside the emergency ward, half hanging over the curb, and leave my truck in the ambulance bay with the engine still running. They can move it themselves if they need to. Fuck! They can tow it for all I care. I just need to get to my wife.

I run straight in and find Dani bawling her eyes out as Mia screams in her arms. "Where is she?" I roar as Miller takes the baby from Dani, neither of them in a state to be caring for her right now.

Dani gets up instantly and rushes toward me, her eyes red-rimmed and puffy. "They've taken her straight into emergency surgery," she cries. "It's . . . I don't think it's looking good."

"Surgery?" I question in a panic, wondering just how fucking bad she was beat.

Dani lets out a sob. "There was too much blood. It was everywhere, and I . . . I didn't know how to help her."

Fuck. Fuck. FUCK!

I bypass Dani and head straight for the nurse at the check-in desk. "My wife, Sophie Meyers. She was brought in not long ago. I need to see her."

The nurse quickly scans her computer before looking up at me. "I'm sorry, sir. Your wife has been taken into surgery for extensive injuries. You'll need to take a seat in the waiting area. We'll update you when we have any news."

"Fuck," I curse, pacing in front of her desk before whipping back to look at the woman. "Just tell me she's okay," I beg. "Please. Is she still breathing?"

"Sir, I'm sorry. I do not have that information. She came through the doors and went straight into surgery. I should not make any assumptions, but I would presume she is in a very serious state," she says, being straightforward with me.

"And my son?" I ask.

"Son?" she questions as she looks furiously at her screen. "I'm sorry," she says, shaking her head ever so slightly as panic settles over her features. "Only one patient was brought in. There is no mention of a child."

"My son. Sophie's pregnant," I confirm.

She double-checks her screen. "There's no mention here of a pregnancy."

"What?" I shout. "She's five months pregnant. How could they not know? You're telling me my wife is in surgery and the doctors don't know she's pregnant?" My voice gets louder and louder by the second, and suddenly Dani is standing at my side with a hand on my forearm.

"It's okay," she murmurs in a soothing voice. "I told the paramedics. They said it was obvious, and I heard them mention it when they called it in."

I nod my head and let out a deep breath. I turn my back and take a seat in the waiting area with nothing but my own torturous thoughts streaming through my head.

Dani takes a seat next to me with a bunch of papers, clutching onto them tightly. "The nurse asked if you could fill this out," she says, not bothering to hand it to me, already knowing what my answer is going to be.

"What happened?" I ask softly.

She lets out a breath as silent tears slide down her face. "I got to your place just after one. The front gate was open and the door was left cracked as if someone had left in a hurry. I found Sophie on the floor. She was in the corner of the living room in a heap of blood." Dani takes a breath, needing to recompose herself as the images start flashing in my mind. "Her face is badly bruised and cut up. She has a broken arm and there was a lot of blood staining through her jeans. I . . . I couldn't tell if she'd been cut or hurt on her thighs or . . . or if she was bleeding internally."

I hang my head.

I refuse to believe that. Sophie is strong and so is our son. I've felt him kick. I've felt how strong he is. They'll both pull through. They'll be okay. Sophie's just in there getting a few stitches and a cast for a broken arm. Everything is going to be okay.

I repeat the thoughts over and over again.

The next few hours drag by, so when the doctor comes through the door and calls out Sophie's name, I fly to my feet, dashing toward him in pure desperation. "Sophie's my wife," I confirm, so he can get started on the details.

The doctor's eyes bulge out in surprise, and I realize he's a fan, but now isn't the time. He lets out a small cringe before he schools his features, being professional. "Sophie's out of surgery. She's doing okay considering her injuries. However, she will be asleep for a while longer," he tells me. "She'll be taken to the recovery wing within the next half an hour where you'll be able to sit with her."

I nod my head. While he's told me all good things, he hasn't said a damn thing about her injuries. "How is she?" I prompt.

He lets out a sigh. "I'm not going to sugarcoat it. She's in a bad way. Whoever did this set out with the intention to harm her. You'll have to prepare yourself before you see her. There is a lot of swelling and cuts to her face. Her arm was broken in two places and is currently held together with pins. She also has three broken ribs. It will be a lengthy healing process for her, but nothing she shouldn't fully recover from," he explains. "Internally, there was a lot of bleeding," he adds with a different tone of voice as he places a comforting hand on my shoulder. He takes a deep breath before continuing. "There was not a lot we could do for the baby. Unfortunately, the trauma Sophie suffered was just far too great."

"No. No," I say, shaking my head, refusing to believe it as the grief grips hold of my chest and refuses to release me. "What are you saying? My son is dead?"

My whole world comes crashing down around me as the doctor looks at me with regret in his eyes. "I'm sorry, but yes. The baby did not survive the attack on your wife."

I drop to my knees, my head falling into my hands.

I don't hear a damn thing the doctor says following that. I don't notice when Dani and Miller try to offer their condolences. I don't even take notice as a car crash victim gets pushed through the double doors and straight through the other side. The only words I hear are when I'm told I can see my wife.

Dani and Miller stay behind despite their numerous objections, but I don't have it in me to share this time I have with Sophie. I need to be alone with my wife, need to hold her, need to feel her hand in mine. Need to fucking tell her that our son is gone.

The nurse leads me to her room, and I'm in shock as I take in her broken body. I fall into the chair beside her bed and start sobbing as I take her unconscious hand in mine. "Who the hell did this to you?"

I could have stayed there for minutes or hours, but eventually my tears dry up. Finally coming to terms with everything, I give myself a chance to properly look her over. The doctor was right. I should have prepared myself for this, but how could I? It's not something I ever thought I'd have to see.

Her skin is a collage of deep blues and purples, and her beautiful blonde hair is matted with dried blood, making me furious that the nurses didn't spend more time on her. There are cuts covering her body, her arm is . . . pure devastation, and her swollen belly . . . fuck. There's still a bump, but it's different . . . deflated.

My heart continues to shatter with every second that passes.

I never fully understood the pain of losing a child that hadn't been born into the world, but now I know. It's nothing but pure agony. A feeling of complete and utter loss, a helplessness that there was nothing I could have done to protect him.

The grief claims me as I think of all the things he's going to miss. All the experiences and adventures he won't be able to take. The life he won't live.

I look at my wife and realize all the things that we as parents will never be able to experience with our little boy. The fights over who's going to change his dirty diapers, the cuts and bruises Sophie will never get to kiss better, the monsters in his closet that I won't be able to scare away. The bath times, the tantrums, the good night stories, and teaching him to skate.

The list goes on and on, but mostly, the love of being a family and raising a child, the chance of being a father . . . all torn away in an instant.

CHAPTER 10

SOPHIE

A big hand twitches in mine, and due to its sheer size and texture, I know it's Tank. Mmmm, my man. I don't know why he's still home, though. He usually leaves ages before I get up.

I open my eyes, or at least I try to, but it seems a lot harder than usual. Ouch, why does it hurt so much?

I let out a pained groan as my eyes register the sudden brightness of the room. Why the hell does Tank have the blinds open at this time of day? And why is it making my head hurt so bad?

Crap, I must be getting sick. Perfect. Just what I need. I'll have to schedule an appointment with the doctor just to make sure there's no harm to my little guy.

My eyes finally start adjusting to the room when I realize things are off. Way freaking off. The faint beeping in the background is my first giveaway. Then the clinical hospital room with my husband slouched in the chair beside me.

I try to squeeze my hand in his, but it feels too heavy. What the hell?

"Tank," I say, though it comes out as the smallest whisper. My throat burns, but it gets the job done.

Tank flies out of his chair with wide eyes, searching for some kind of threat before his eyes come down on mine. Relief washes over his features as he takes me in. "Babe?" he questions, sadness shining through his red-rimmed eyes. "How are you feeling?"

My brows furrow, taking him in. What's the matter? Tank doesn't cry. This isn't right. He's the strongest man I've ever met.

I try to answer, but my throat is hurting too much, and knowing me so well, Tank reaches for a cup of water on the side table. I try to follow his movements, but it makes the pain behind my eyes get worse. He brings the cup up and guides the straw into my mouth and I take small sips, the cool water instantly soothing my throat so I can talk.

"I'll call the doctor," Tank says as he puts the cup back down.

"Wait," I whisper. His eyes come back to me with concern. "What's . . . what's going on? What happened? Why am I here?"

Regret fills his features as he takes his seat and gently takes my hand in his once again. "You don't remember?" he starts in a soothing voice, looking at me as though his whole world has burned to ashes at his feet, making my heart start to race in fear. I slowly shake my head, the movement causing a heavy thumping inside my skull as I try to remember anything about how I got here. "You were attacked."

The second the words are out of his mouth, it all comes rushing back with a force greater than a freight train. I suck in a loud gasp.

Christian Baxter. The men. The heavy blows. Their twisted laughter.

My baby.

I let out a gasp, but Tank continues. "We think it was a home invasion. Miller checked out our place, and it's been trashed. The cameras were wiped and unless you remember what he looked like, we've got no fucking way to identify the asshole," he explains. "But I don't want you worrying about it, okay? Whoever this fucker is, I'll make sure he gets what's coming for him, no matter what. I'll make sure he pays for what he's done to you."

Shaking my head as tears begin to fall, I try sitting up, but Tank is right there, pushing me back down. "No, you need to stay still," he tells me as I start to notice just how sore my body really is. "You've been through a lot. Internal stitches and a broken arm. You can't move, okay? Promise me you won't move."

"No," I cry as I try to lift my hands to my stomach, but they just won't move. Why won't they move? "Our son?" I question, heartbreak brimming in his dark eyes. "I can't . . . I can't feel him move."

Tank's eyes fill with sorrow as he looks at me and he starts to shake his head, almost as though too afraid to say what needs to be said. I can feel the next words that are about to come out of his mouth, but I don't want to hear it. I can't. "No," I cry, a thick lump forming in my throat and making it impossible to breathe. "No."

"Sophie," he whispers as he reaches forward and wipes a tear from my eye. "He didn't make it."

My whole world comes crashing down around me, burning to ashes. I feel numb, unable to believe what I'm hearing, but I know it's true. I remember the punches, remember the blows and the way they dropped me to my stomach.

Tears come streaming down my face as the sobs begin, my chest shattering into a million tiny pieces as the overwhelming grief and loss begins to cripple me. Tank leans forward and takes my face in his big hands, desperately trying to ease my grief, but there's nothing he can do to settle the agony tearing through my chest.

I failed. I had one job as his mother to protect him, and I failed.

How could my little boy be gone? My sweet angel, stolen from me before I've even held him in my arms, even given the chance to live. To fight.

My heart shatters, completely broken and falling apart. My whole world has been taken from me in the blink of an eye and I know that I will never be able to live past this. Never move on from this heart-wrenching agony. How am I supposed to go on from here? How do I live? How do I go about my day acting as though everything is okay when I'm nothing but a broken shell?

It's my fault. I insisted on investigating Baxter, and look where that got me. Tank begged me not to, warned me that my job was too dangerous, and I didn't listen. And now . . . my son is gone.

But it's not just me who's grieving. My failures and selfishness have lost Tank his only son, too. I took that from him, destroyed him. How will he ever forgive me? He thinks it was a home invasion, but when he realizes it was Christian Baxter's thugs, he will know it was me. My fault. My carelessness. When he realizes the truth, he will hate me. And if he doesn't, he should. The very sight of me should repulse him.

Hell, I'm repulsed by myself.

How will he ever love me again?

If only I had listened. If only I'd backed off when he asked me to. But no, I had to chase another damn story for my own selfish desires. I should have been concentrating on my son, on making sure he was developing correctly, making sure I was eating the right things, getting enough sleep, and exercising. Focusing on becoming a new mother.

But no, that will never happen now. I'll never get the chance to be the mom I want to be, and what's worse is that I have robbed Tank of the chance to become the father he has always craved to be. Our sweet little angel, gone.

What the hell have I done?

There's a light rap at the door before a doctor makes his way into the room, giving me a sad smile before grabbing the chart off the end of my bed. "Ahh, good," he says in a soothing tone. "You're awake."

Tank pulls back from me to allow the doctor to come forward, and he does a quick examination before jumping into a recap of my injuries. To tell the truth, I don't hear a word he says. It means nothing to me. What does it matter anyway? I'm nothing without my son.

The doctor asks me how I'm feeling, but he doesn't get a response. Instead, he looks at Tank for clarification, who lets the doctor know he has just told me the extent of my injuries. In other words, he already broke the news to me that I killed my baby.

The doctor gives him an understanding nod before upping my morphine and exiting the room.

Tank and I sit silently in the hospital room with my hand firmly in his, his thumb moving back and forth across the back of my hand. The morphine makes me feel sleepy, but I need to tell him first. I need to admit this was my fault and hopefully, he'll be able to forgive me. But I know, deep in my shattered heart, that he should leave me. I've taken his world from him. How will we ever be the same?

He should find someone worthy of him. Someone who would be able to give him a child without risking its precious life. Someone who is content with living the housewife role that he's always secretly wanted for me. He deserves someone who's nothing like me.

Letting out a deep breath, I turn my gaze to his, preparing to ruin our marriage. As much as I wish it weren't true, I just don't see how he will ever forgive me for this. "I have to tell you something," I whisper as the shattered pieces of my already broken heart start to quiver. I know that as the father of our child, he deserves to know every bit of truth I can offer, no matter how much it kills me.

Tank looks up at me with concern as he gives my hand a gentle squeeze. "What is it?" he asks, noticing the fear that laces my voice. He reaches forward, bushing his fingers over the side of my face, trying to wipe away my stray tears.

My stare drops to our joined hands, unable to stomach looking into his eyes, despite knowing just how badly he deserves it. "It wasn't a home invasion," I tell him, my voice breaking on the words.

"What do you mean?" he questions, sitting forward and searching my face for answers.

At this, I finally look up at him and my world crumbles all over again. "It wasn't a home invasion," I repeat. "It was Christian Baxter."

His brows furrow in confusion, shaking his head, not understanding how they could possibly be connected. "Christian Baxter?"

I nod ever so slightly. "I'm sorry," I cry, heavy sobs tearing from my chest as I try to get the words out. "He buzzed the gate, and I didn't look before I pressed the button. Then he was at the front door with two men, and they just . . . they barged their way in. Christian said he knew what I was doing, what I was investigating." The tears sail down my face as I watch his heart break in front of my eyes. "This was my warning to stop."

Tank releases my hand, and I watch the array of emotions rocking through this stare. Heartache, agony, fury, devastation. One after another until finally, those eyes that I love so much are cold and dead.

Tank gets up from his chair and starts pacing the room, his whole body shaking with rage when he stops and looks back at me, his lips pressing into a hard line. Unshed tears well in his eyes, staring at me with a fierce betrayal. "Fuck, Sophie," he breathes, barely able to hold onto his will to keep going. "I told you to stop. To forget it. *I begged you.*"

The tears pool in my eyes, not able to find the words that could ever make this okay. "I'm sorry," I breathe, the very last remnants of my soul burning into ashes.

Tank shakes his head at my pathetic excuse for an apology, still trying to process as he realizes that this is all on me. My actions took our son. He doesn't say another word, and we're left sitting in a heavy, broken silence. Though this silence feels different, painful . . . final.

It could be minutes or hours, but when a soft knock sounds at the door and Dani's face appears in my room, I instantly burst into tears. Dani comes rushing in, desperately trying to hand Mia off to Miller. She climbs on the side of my bed as best she can and holds me as we both cry for my son.

"Sophie," Tank's voice says over the fogginess of my nightmare, my body flinching as I relive their violent attack in my unconscious mind.

My eyes spring open to find Tank hovering above me, but he isn't alone. Detective Andrews stands by his side, trying to look as intimidating as ever, but I've known the guy for years. He just can't pull it off. Well, not with me anyway.

"What's he doing here?" I question Tank. After all, he knows just how much I hate this guy.

From the look on Tank's face, I already know what he's going to say. "You're going to hand over your investigation to Detective Andrews. You have no place looking into this further."

"But—" I start.

"No, Sophie," Tank cuts in. "There are no buts here. We've already lost our child. You'd be a fool to pursue this any further. I'm not going to let you risk your life for this asshole. I'm not losing you too."

I hear what he's saying, and I completely get where he's coming from, but now this thing with Baxter is personal. He came into my home. He ordered those men to touch me. He was the one who put me in this hospital and caused the death of my son.

The second I woke up in this room, the need within me to continue this case instantly tripled. I want nothing more than to nail this bastard. I want to be the one who puts him away. I want to watch as his scrawny ass is handcuffed and put behind bars, and I want him to know that I was the one who took it all away from him. That I was the one who nailed him. That I was the one who took away everything he cares about, just as he has done to me.

I look up at my husband with tears in my eyes. "I can't," I whisper. "I need to see him put away."

"I'm sorry, Soph," he says, his heart breaking right in front of me. "There's no choice here. I've watched you do this job against my better judgment, and now look at you. You need to let this one go. Let the cops do their job. They'll get him."

I know he's right, but coming to terms with it tears at my already crippled chest. I let out a breath and slowly nod my head as my eyes leave Tank's and look down at my broken body.

How many pieces of myself do I need to lose?

"Hey, Sophie," Detective Andrews says, stepping forward and carefully sitting on the edge of my bed. "What have you got?"

With a sigh, I let it all out. "Christian Baxter was behind the deaths of Marco Cincinnati, Phillip McDonald, and Andrew Taylor. All his major competitors."

"That's a big claim," he tells me. "All their deaths were officially ruled as either natural causes or substance abuse. You've got evidence to back this up?"

"Bits and pieces," I tell him. "I might have broken into his office and found contracts hidden in the locked portion of his desk. There are five leading construction companies in the city. Baxter Corporation and four others, and I have proof that Christian anonymously purchased shares in each of the four remaining companies, each contract with hidden clauses that in the case of the death of the founder or owner, the shares will go to him. Now all of a sudden three of these CEOs are dead, leaving Christian the major shareholder in each of their companies, giving him power to control the competition. Tell me that's not motive."

Detective Andrews looks surprised, and his brows shoot right up into his hairline. "Wow," he murmurs. "That's good, but it doesn't actually pin him to the crime."

"I know. I have his secretary's planner as well, which puts him in the city on each occasion with no alibi."

"Ahh, see *that* I can work with," he says.

I give him a curt nod and tell him exactly where he can find the information in my home. He thanks me as he gets up off the bed and Tank hands him the alarm code and keys to our home, trusting him enough to go in and get the information for himself.

He's just making his way out the door when I call out for him.

"Andrews."

He turns at my voice with a raised questioning brow. "I want him to go down for all of this," I say, indicating down my body. "He took my son from me, and if you don't pull through, I'll do it myself and I don't care who has to go down in the process."

"You know it's not that easy," he reminds me. "Do you have sufficient evidence?"

I look at Tank. "There's the surveillance, right?"

He shakes his head ever so slightly. "It was wiped," he tells me.

"What about the backup? Doesn't the company we use keep the footage for thirty days?" I ask as I remember a specific dirty joke I'd made when we first got it put in. We had it installed because of Tank's crazy fans. Who would have ever thought that this would be the reason it was used.

"It's possible. I'll give them a call," he says.

At that, he nods toward Detective Andrews who makes his way out of the room, leaving me feeling completely empty. First, my son is taken from me, then my husband hates me, and now my job is gone, too.

I know I have Dani, Miller, and my family, but even with Tank in this very room, I have never felt more alone in my life.

Tank clears his throat to gain my attention. "I'm going to go organize home care," he tells me, hardly managing to meet my eyes.

"Okay," I murmur as he walks toward the door.

Tank stops and looks back at me, a tightening in his eye. "I made captain, by the way," he says with a sadness underlying his voice. With that, he walks through the door and leaves me with nothing but the reminders of everything I've lost.

Fuck. I really am the most selfish bitch around.

CHAPTER 11

TANK

Sophie has been home for a week, and to say things have changed is an understatement. She's nothing but a shell of the woman she used to be. She doesn't eat, she doesn't sleep, and she hasn't said a single fucking word. She just lays in our bed looking at the wall as Gretchen, the home care nurse, fusses around her.

I've walked in a few times to catch her crying as she cradles her empty stomach, grieving the loss of our once growing son. The sight tears me apart each time, but there isn't a lot I can do about it. The anger boiling inside me has kept me away from her. I don't trust myself not to lose my shit, and I know that's the last thing she needs from me.

She hasn't come out and said it, but I know she thinks I blame her. I'm not going to lie, I'm furious that she decided to take on this case during her pregnancy, especially after I asked her not to. She should have been home, preparing to be a mother, not chasing down criminals. But asking her to stop is like asking her not to be herself. It was selfish for me to ask her to change in the first place, and I should have known she would say no. I just can't stop thinking about the what-ifs.

Being an investigative journalist is her passion. It's one of the things I love about her, and despite my better judgment, I hope she has it in her to get back out there and fight for what's right one day. Hell, it's the same as if she had asked me not to step foot on the ice ever again. I simply couldn't do it, just as she could never give up what she loves.

The reason for my anger lies with Christian Baxter.

That bastard caused my family the worst heartache imaginable, and I'm sure he's caused the same for many others. It was his crimes that started this. It was by his word that my wife was beaten within an inch of her life, and it was his doing that caused my son to die before he even had a chance to live.

Making Sophie hand over her investigation was one of the hardest things I've ever done. Watching her take Baxter down would have been the sweetest revenge, right along with me getting my hands on him, but I knew deep down that I needed to do what was right for her. I know she doesn't see it that way. She looked at me as if I was taking something away from her, and maybe I was. Maybe I'm being selfish, but the thought of identifying her in the morgue doesn't sit well with me.

That man will never take another thing from me again. Not if I have anything to do with it.

My hope for Detective Andrews to nail the bastard has started dwindling . . . a lot. He called me the day after the hospital visit to say that all the evidence Sophie had collected was taken from our home, the paperwork she had printed, her computer, her phone, and any electronic device that may have held the information. Gone. He then went on to say they visited her office, which had also been ransacked. Not one ounce of information on Christian Baxter was there, not even her phony article.

Detective Andrews has been unable to do a damn thing. He can't get a search warrant for Baxter's office as he doesn't have any evidence to back it up. He then interviewed his PA, Aimee, who confirmed he had an alibi for everything, including the time frame when he was at my home, taking my son's life.

Hell, the fucking city needs someone like Sophie digging into this shit, because Detective Andrews clearly isn't qualified for his job.

We were able to recover the footage of Baxter barging his way into my home, which confirms Aimee lied about Baxter's alibi, but it doesn't help them to nail the charges on him since there's no footage from inside the house. That means it's Sophie's word against his. It also showed that Sophie had opened the gate for them when they buzzed the intercom, and that she voluntarily opened the door to them.

As Baxter's dodgy as fuck lawyers stated, there's no evidence to show that other occupants weren't already in the house, which is cause for reasonable doubt. So naturally, the fucker is getting away with it.

Though after a few words from me, Detective Andrews promised he won't give up. After all, he knows Sophie's success rate, and he knows she's always right about this shit, so he doesn't want to lose out on the glory of nailing the guy.

I'm getting myself ready for the first official training session of the season, though I'm not exactly that pumped about it. I know I should be since this is my first training session as captain, but I just can't bring myself to the level of excitement that's required.

I know things haven't been great between Sophie and me. My anger, mixed with the different ways we're each dealing with our grief, has put a huge barrier between us. Now that the cops are digging into Baxter, I'm petrified that something could happen to her. That he might come back and finish the job, blaming her for passing the information on. Fuck, the thought of him coming when I wasn't here to kick that motherfucker's ass has haunted me day in and day out. I've been fucking terrified to leave her.

Heading into our bedroom, I gently sit on the edge of the bed, being careful not to jostle Sophie. Even though she won't admit it, I know she's still in a great deal of pain. It's almost like she thinks she deserves this, which is fucking ridiculous. As she feels me beside her, she slowly opens her eyes, and I lean down and press a kiss to her forehead, though all that does is make her look away.

I let out a sigh. "I have to go to training," I tell her.

She gives the slightest nod of her head. "Okay," she murmurs, giving me nothing else.

Damn. I was hoping that might have pulled at least a smile from her, but she needs more time. She's still grieving and will be for a while, and I fear that me alone is not enough to get her through this.

"Alright. Well, I'll see you later."

Sophie gives another nod as her eyes focus on the wall behind me, right where they always stay whenever I'm around.

I get up and make my way to the bedroom door, turning back when I'm nearly at the threshold. "I love you, Sophie," I remind her, my gaze resting on her face.

At that, she finally looks up, and I see tears pooling in her red-rimmed eyes. That beautiful gaze of hers lands heavily on me, and the darkness within her stare almost brings me to my knees. "You shouldn't."

Pain rocks through my chest and I shake my head, her words tearing at me like never before. "Don't fucking say that," I beg as I walk back into the room and drop to my knees beside the bed, taking her good hand in mine. "I love you, Sophie," I repeat. "I don't blame you for what happened. You must know that."

She doesn't answer, just lays there with tears in her eyes. Leaning forward, I press my lips to hers and wait, terrified that she won't come back to me, but after a few agonizing seconds her lips press back against mine. I bring my hand up and run my fingers down the side of her face. "I have to go," I murmur. "If you need me, I'll come straight home, okay?"

She nods her head, and I wipe the tears from her eyes. "I won't be long," I say, getting up and heading out of the room.

I make my way around the house, collecting all my hockey gear before coming to the front door. My heart shatters as I close it behind me. I want nothing more than to be home with Sophie, grieving with her and making things better. But unfortunately, this is just a requirement of being a professional athlete. I have no choice unless I want to lose my contract. Don't get me wrong, Coach Larsden has given me what little time he could, but there's only so far he can push the limits of my contract.

Getting in my truck, I sit in silence before finally starting her up and getting my ass to the ice rink. I drive as slow as possible, trying to prolong the inevitable. Pulling up in the athletes' private parking lot, I'm not surprised to see the ocean of fans waiting outside the doors, trying to get a good look at their favorite player on the first official day of training.

I lug my training gear out of my truck and walk up the sidewalk, listening to the throng of people calling out my name and requesting autographs. Usually I would stop, but today it doesn't feel right.

I notice a few people calling over the crowd, asking about Sophie, but I try my best to ignore it. I can't have the replay of Sophie's injuries and our loss floating around in my mind while I'm training. I need to focus. Need to keep my head in the game.

As I make my way through the throng of people, I notice Crazy Jill reaching out to touch me, but I don't have it in me to show her any kind of attention. I push past her, but what does she expect? She takes it too far. Sure, I'm pleased she's such an avid fan and comes out to support us, but the messages and phone calls? I can't deal with it today.

I finally break through the crowd and into the silence of the closed ice rink. Well, mostly silence. The figure skaters are finishing up their session, so the place is filled with feminine gossip and chatter while the Zamboni putts around the ice, creating a smooth, slick surface for me and my boys.

I head past the girls, who are just getting started on their off-ice workouts, and I'm thankful that they seem to be getting shit done in a timely manner today. My boys don't need the distraction of a bunch of chicks ogling them while they're trying to train.

Pushing my way through the heavy door of the locker room, I instantly feel the pitying stares of my teammates on me, and I do what I can to tune them out. I go about my business, trying my best to ignore them when Cameron finally speaks up for the group.

"Hey, man," he starts, a slight hesitation in his tone. "How's our girl doing?"

Our girl? She's *my* fucking girl, bastard.

I turn to face him, not really wanting to talk about it, but I know this is different. I notice I have every single eye in the room on me, including Miller's, but these guys sincerely want to know how she's doing, unlike the prying, curious minds of the fans from outside. These guys are my teammates, my friends, and more importantly, they're my family. These boys are always ready and willing to support one another when it's needed, so I shouldn't have expected anything different.

"She's not doing so well," I tell them truthfully. I get a few cringes from the guys. Sophie's just as much a part of the Storm family as I am. In fact, these bastards probably like her more than they like me. "Physically, she's healing just as expected. She still has a long way to go, but the morphine is making it easier for her. Emotionally . . ." I say with a sigh, "she's not coping at all."

I hear and see the brokenness coming from the guys as their thoughts lie with Sophie. To be honest, I thought talking about it would have been the hardest thing I'd have to do today, but now that they know, it makes it just that bit easier to breathe.

I hear a familiar voice cut through the silence of the room. "What about you?" My eyes cut to Miller and narrow on him. What's he doing? He knows I'm not handling it. He's been there every fucking day, slowly taking bits and pieces of the nursery apart and removing it before Sophie can manage to walk and see it for herself.

He raises a brow, daring me to answer, knowing just how much I hate talking about myself or my feelings. But something inside me tells me he's doing this for my own well-being. After all, he lost his sister a few years ago, and that was the hardest thing he's ever been through. Yet somehow, he made it out the other end.

Maybe it's possible the fucker knows what's best for me right now. With a sigh, I let the boys have it. "To be honest, I'm not coping at all. Sophie and I have barely spoken over the past week. I have so much anger. I'm scared I'm going to say something I might regret while Sophie lies in bed each day, holding her empty stomach and crying for our son."

Miller gives me a nod before getting back to tying his skates, while the boys somewhat do the same. Some offer me their condolences, others offer me any kind of help and support that's needed.

I realize Miller was right to make me admit it. Being strong in front of the boys has always been a motto of mine. I never show weakness, not if I don't have to, but this is different. This is life and death. This is my child.

Having the boys know that shit isn't okay right now is somehow a blessing. I don't know how, but as a team, it makes us stronger. Knowing how each and every member of this team is doing physically as well as emotionally makes us perform better as a group. And if it takes me admitting that I'm struggling with the loss of my son to help me move forward, then I'm damn glad I've taken that step.

But also knowing these boys will be here when shit gets hard is a blessing in itself.

The second the boys notice the testosterone in the room is running dangerously low, we get our shit together. I pull my gear on and take my seat beside Miller. "I fucking hate you for making me do that, but I think I needed it," I murmur.

"No problem, man," he replies. "Dealing with loss isn't easy."

He couldn't be more right. Before my son, I had never lost a single soul, and now that I have, the grief I suffer from is something I never thought possible. It eats you alive until it has completely consumed you, yet somehow you need to find a way to push through. It's like being under water, looking up at the surface, desperate for oxygen, but no matter how fast you swim, how fast you kick your legs, you can never reach the top.

I try my hardest to push the thoughts of Sophie and my son away from my mind. I came here to train, and that's exactly what I intend to do.

I lead the boys out of the locker room and they instantly fall in line. We step onto the ice while two guys head off to grab the nets and the newbie breaks away to grab the pucks.

We run a few warm-up drills followed by some torturous sprints before Coach takes the ice and pushes us to our limits.

We exit the rink a few hours later, dripping with sweat.

I'm in the middle of getting out of my hockey gear when Coach enters the locker room. "Tank," he calls.

I turn immediately and give him my full attention. "Yes, Coach?"

He meets my stare and I see the familiar tightening in his eyes, something I've become accustomed to over the past week. "Get yourself dressed and meet me in my office in ten."

I give him a quick nod before he disappears, and I rush through a shower before pulling my clothes on. I quickly check my phone to make sure Sophie hasn't been looking for me, but it's not like she would actually call. She's more of a suffer-in-silence type now—something I intend to change. Besides, as far as I know, she hasn't even bothered to set up the new phone and other devices I got her.

After saying goodbye to the boys, I make my way to Coach Larsden's office, and gently rap on the door before pushing my way through and taking a seat. "Thanks for joining me, Tank," Coach says, fondly.

"No problem. What can I do for you?" I ask, getting straight into it as I'm anxious to get home to Sophie.

"Look, I won't keep you long, but I need to know how things are going at home?" he asks with a cringe, knowing I hate talking about myself.

I let out a sigh, hating that I'm repeating this conversation for the second time today. "Not great, Coach. It's hard, but we're slowly getting there."

"I understand," he says. "You're not going to like this, but legally I have to remind you of your options to utilize our team counselor and therapist. I know it's not *your thing*, but they can do wonders for teaching people how to best recognize and deal with their grief." I give Coach a hard stare and he holds his hands up in surrender. "Hey, I had no choice in the matter."

"Thank you, but I'm going to have to respectfully decline," I tell him. "But if I'm being honest, being out on the ice with the boys seems to have helped a lot."

"Good, I'm glad," he says. "How's that woman of yours doing?"

I let out a pained sigh. "She's not coping with it, and I'm running out of ideas on how to help her. She's blaming herself for what those bastards did to her, and I can't pull her out of it. She won't even talk to me," I tell him. "Maybe I could use the counselor for her?"

"It's not a bad idea," Coach says. "I hate that she isn't the bright, beaming woman I'm so used to seeing around here."

"You and me both, Coach."

"Look, you know my door is always open if you need anything," he reminds me.

I give a curt nod before forcing a smile across my face. "Thanks," I say before getting up out of my chair.

"Tank," he calls after me. I turn to face him and notice the cringe sitting squarely across his face. "I hate to say it, but you must know that if there is any decline in your skating or off-ice duties, you'll have to do mandatory grief counseling."

I nod my head in understanding. "It won't come to that," I say with confidence.

"Excellent," he smiles, clearly happy to have this conversation over and done with. "Now get home to your woman."

"Will do."

CHAPTER 12

SOPHIE

It's Tank's first game of the season, and I feel like an absolute bitch. I've been up and walking around for at least a week now. It's hard, but it's manageable. Going to his game would have been challenging, but I would have had Dani there to help me. So when he asked if I was feeling up to it, I gave him the same response I've been giving him since the attack.

I declined.

Not once in the time that I've been with him have I missed a game, except for maybe once in college when I was still denying that there was anything between us. I feel terrible, but at the same time, how can I allow myself to go out and enjoy my life when I've killed my child?

It's not fair to him, and it's certainly not fair to Tank.

I should be miserable.

He should hate me.

Things between us have certainly been rough, and quite frankly, I don't know what he's still doing here. Why hasn't he left yet? He tells me every day that he loves me, and I believe him. I just don't understand how he could.

He deserves so much better than that. He deserves a woman who's going to treat him like the king that he is, the way I used to. I so desperately want to be that woman for him, to have the old me back, but how could I? After my selfish actions took our son away and almost took my own life?

I see the tortured look in his eyes every time he sees me. He will stare into my eyes with love, which gives me hope that maybe he can forgive me, but then his eyes travel down my body, and that love turns to rage. The second he's reminded that I bear no child in my womb, there's nothing but pure heartache on his face.

How could a man be happy in a relationship when every time he looks at his wife, he's reminded of what was taken from him?

God, I'm so desperately in love with him that this whole situation tears me up inside. Why didn't I just leave the Baxter case alone? The fucker has gotten away with it, so it was all for nothing anyway.

I've ruined our lives for nothing.

My gaze travels down to the rings on my finger, and my heart begins to ache. The thought of leaving has circled my mind over the past couple of weeks, purely for the fact that Tank deserves better. The idea of leaving him destroys me, but I need to do it. I need to get away, and I need to give him space to move forward.

He's been so consumed with anger, and he needs to let it go, but in order for him to do that, I need to be gone. The anger will stay as long as he's looking at me every day. I'm the constant reminder of what he's lost.

It's selfish of me to stay, yet it's selfish for me to go.

No matter what I do, I can't win. But then again, I don't deserve to win.

With a sigh, I call out for Gretchen and let her know that I'm going to bed for the night so she can leave early. She gives me a grateful smile before making sure I have everything I could possibly need at my bedside.

The moment I hear the door close behind her, I push back the blankets and find my suitcase. I finish packing a few things, grab my keys, and make my way to the garage door before thinking better of it and backtrack to the kitchen.

With tears in my eyes, I grab a piece of paper and write the only thing I can think of that he might possibly understand.

I'm sorry. I love you.

A tear drops onto the paper as I slip my rings from my finger and place them down on the note.

The emptiness consumes me, but I know it's the right thing to do. I may never move on and heal from this, but at least Tank will have a chance.

I get in my car with tears streaming down my face while I struggle to catch a full breath. Sobs rip through me as I drive to the airport, my ribs screaming in protest with each gasping breath. It's only a twenty-minute drive, but it feels as though it takes a lifetime, and to be honest, with my arm still casted and the rest of me still healing, I probably should have ordered an Uber.

Pulling into the long-term parking lot, I hand my keys over to the valet. He helps me grab my suitcase and gives me a sympathetic smile as he notices my red-rimmed eyes and the state of my injured body.

I thank him and head into the airport. Luckily, I only have to wait an hour before the next scheduled flight leaves for Denver.

I sit at the gate, waiting for my flight, and notice the only entertainment the airport has to offer is Tank's game. Excellent. That's just what I need. Another reminder of the great man I just left behind.

With nothing left to do and my curiosity piquing, I turn my gaze to the screen. As the game goes on with the Storm in the lead, as per usual, the commentators announce Tank as the new captain for the season. They start listing off his stats and achievements, which I have to admit are extremely impressive, and they far surpass those of other players.

The feeling that I'm missing out on a massive day in Tank's career doesn't sit well with me, and I bet he's probably feeling it too. He has always loved it when I go to his games. He even has his little tradition of blowing me a kiss at the start of every game. I feel absolutely tormented that during his first game as captain, those traditions are missed, and it's entirely my fault.

My flight is called, and I make my way onto the plane, struggling to hold back the tears. I take my seat and close my eyes, and a little over two hours later, the plane touches down in Denver. After wiping away a stray tear, I make my way off the plane, find my luggage, and drop down into an Uber.

Not long after, I find myself walking up the old, familiar driveway, dragging my suitcase behind me. Letting out a broken sigh, I raise my hand and gently knock on the door, waiting patiently for someone to answer it.

"Who the hell would be knocking on the door at this hour?" my dad's stern voice comes booming from within.

"Oh, I don't know, honey. Can you answer it? I'm in my nightgown," replies my mother.

"What?" my father grunts. "Over my dead body. I just sat down."

I grin to myself, hearing that familiar banter once again. I hear my mother's groan as her feet carry her across the old wooden floorboards. "I swear, Robert. One of these days you're going to find yourself without a woman, and you won't know how to scratch your own ass," she murmurs as the locks on the door slide out of place.

The door opens slowly, and standing before me is my mother. Her jaw drops, taking me in, shock sparking in her eyes before finally managing to shake it off. "Sophie?" she asks. "My God, what are you doing here?" She flies toward me and pulls me into a deep hug. The second her arms close around me, the overwhelming grief of the past few weeks comes up and consumes me as I sob into my mother's shoulder.

Her hands slowly rub up and down my back, holding me tight.

"It's going to be okay," she promises me. "I know you don't see it yet, but one day, you're going to be able to breathe again, and it'll get easier."

She pulls me back into the house so the neighbors don't have to hear my sobbing, and while still holding onto me, manages to pull in my suitcase before closing the door behind me.

I hear my father from across the room. "Soph?"

He gets up from the couch and scurries across to me, pulling me right out of my mother's arms and into his, holding me tight as the sobs run their course.

"Be careful, Robert," my mother murmurs. "She's injured."

"What?" my father questions as he drops his arms away then steps back to look over me. "Still? That was weeks ago. She looks fine to me."

I roll my eyes at my father as I hastily try to wipe the tears off my face, a smile pulling at the corners of my lips and feeling foreign on my face. He can see the faded bruises and scars as clear as day, but he's trying his best to make me feel better about it. "Am I going to stand in the doorway all night or can I come in?"

"Oh, of course, dear," my mother says, leading me deeper into my childhood home.

I grab my suitcase and follow her, hating how wrong this all feels. I love coming home to my family and visiting, but knowing what Tank will be coming home to tonight . . . fuck. "Where's that hunky man of yours?" my mother asks, still as smitten as ever with Tank.

I let out a heavy sigh as I look at her, and she sees it in my eyes. Just like that, I don't have to explain myself. She understands, just as she always has. "Oh, honey. It will be okay," she murmurs in that motherly voice that makes me burst into tears once again.

Mom pulls me into her arms once more as I hear my father grunting behind us. "What the fuck did I just miss?" he asks, making the smallest smile come over my face.

"Oh, Robert. Watch your language," Mom scolds as what sounds like a herd of elephants rushes down the stairs.

"What's all the commotion down here?" my little brother, Zac, asks as he takes me in. "Ahhh, fuck. It's you."

With a smile, I walk straight up to the loser and wrap my arms around him, making sure to knock him in the back of the head with my cast. "It's nice to see you, too, loser."

"Ugh," he groans as he wraps me up in a tight hug. "Get off me."

I have to roll my eyes at the kid. We've always had a love-hate relationship, which usually consists of me messing with him as he tries to throw it back at me, but he simply doesn't have the skill for it. He tries though, and I have to give him credit for that.

Stepping out of Zac's arms, I wave toward my suitcase. "Be a darl and take my bag up to my room," I tell him.

"In your dreams," he scoffs. "I'm not one of your maids in your fancy, gated McMansion. Do it yourself."

I narrow my eyes at him before turning on my father with puppy-dog eyes, cradling my broken arm to my chest. "Please, Daddy. I'm so tired, and my arms are so sore."

He lets out a huff but does it anyway. "I don't know how you do it, Sophie," Mom says in awe as she takes me by the arm and pulls me toward the kitchen. "Are you hungry? How did you get here? Why didn't you call? You know your father would have picked you up from the airport."

On and on it goes.

Half an hour later, Mom has finally given up on the questions, but only because I promised to answer everything tomorrow. Once she's finished fussing about my room, she sends me off to bed with one of her famous hot chocolates, and I'm finally left alone.

I go through my luggage and decide it's probably best I take a quick shower. After washing off the day, careful to avoid getting my cast soaked, I pull on one of Tank's old shirts and get comfortable in bed. A soft knock at the door catches my attention, and my brother pokes his head in. "What do you want, assface?" I question.

He leans against the door frame as he studies me. "What are you really doing here, Soph?" he asks.

I look at my brother and realize that he really has grown up. Though I don't know why I'm surprised, he's nearly twenty-four. "It's my fault," I say, not needing to clarify what I'm talking about.

"That's the biggest load of bullshit I've ever heard," he says, looking me firmly in the eyes.

"I pursued the case. If I hadn't, my son would still be here," I argue.

"No, you're looking at it wrong. You're blaming yourself for something that was out of your control. Christian Baxter is the one who ordered those men to beat you. He's at fault, not you. He *stole* your baby. You didn't *lose* him."

I get up out of bed and cross the room before pulling him into a tight hug, not having realized just how much I'd missed his stupid face. It's been way too long. "Thanks, kid. But you don't understand," I whisper, refusing to let him go as the tears threaten to spill again.

"You're being an idiot," he tells me. I can practically hear him rolling his eyes as he hugs me back. He makes it quick before finally dropping his arms away. "Goodnight, Soph. Try to get some sleep." With that, he gives me an encouraging smile before backing out of my room, gently closing the door as he goes.

With a sigh, I take my pain meds and squish my head into my pillow. As a lone tear falls from my eye, I realize just how big and empty being alone in my bed really feels. I stretch my hand out over to the other side, the place that, up until tonight, would have been occupied by my husband, while wondering if I've really made the right decision.

I allow myself to drift into a dreamless sleep, wishing things could be different. Wishing I hadn't made such piss-poor decisions, and wishing my son was still safely cradled in my arms beneath my skin.

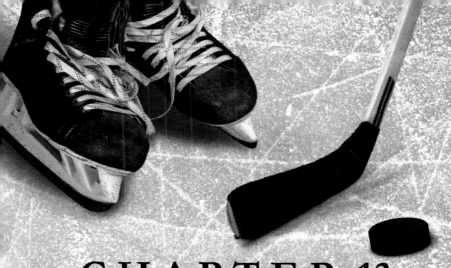

CHAPTER 13

TANK

I step off the ice after the first game of the season. We absolutely annihilated the other team, and to say gaining my first win as captain was fucking epic would be a big fucking understatement. But no matter how good it was, it didn't feel right without Soph sitting up in the crowd, cheering me on. I looked up so many times during the game out of habit, only to see the empty spot beside Dani.

With a sigh, I get on with the after-game duties and go through a quick interview to please the media before making my way past the fans and signing a few jerseys that are thrust into my face. Once I make it down into the locker room with the boys, I can finally relax. Well, sort of. The guys are on one hell of a high. Backs are being slapped, crude jokes are thrown around the room, and asses are being whipped with wet towels. You know, the usual locker room bullshit.

I strip out of my gear as the boys decide we need to head out and party tonight. I reluctantly agree, only to set a good example for the boys, but they know I won't be staying long. Not with Sophie at home alone, needing me.

I rush through a shower and gather my things before Miller and I make our way out of the locker room and meet up with Dani.

She instantly jumps up into Miller's arms and kisses him like they've been separated for the past four years. The sight makes me groan, but mostly it just reminds me that Sophie isn't here. Usually, she'd be the one throwing herself at me, but my girl doesn't have the same self-control as Dani. Sophie would have bulldozed her way through the crowd, past security, and into the locker room to try and jump me in front of the boys. I fucking love it.

I miss my Sophie. I miss her smile and her heart. Lately, I feel like I don't even have that. I don't want to lose her. I can't. Without her, I'll crumble.

Miller looks down at Dani with adoration in his pussy-whipped eyes. "Are you up to party with the boys tonight?" he questions.

"No, actually," she sighs with a slight cringe. "I'm actually kind of tired. I thought I'd let the babysitter go home early."

"Okay," he murmurs. "I won't stay out too late," he adds, but it isn't because he doesn't want to celebrate. We all know it's because Mia isn't sleeping great at night, which means the fucker is exhausted. He doesn't want to go out tonight just as much as I don't, only he doesn't have a great excuse.

"Alright," she says, giving him a quick kiss. "I'll see you guys later," she adds before turning away.

"Hey," I call out to her, watching as she turns back. "Could you check in with Sophie?"

"Sure," she says with sadness in her eyes. "But you know, she's kind of been avoiding me."

"I know," I sigh, feeling that same ache that Sophie does every time Miller and Dani are around. "Don't take it personally. She just finds it hard to see you with Mia. It reminds her of . . . you know."

"Yeah," she says with a sympathetic smile. "I'll let you know how she's doing."

"Okay, thanks," I say, finally letting her go.

The boys and I head out shortly after, and we've only been gone for half an hour when I get a text from Dani.

Dani - Tried calling the home phone, there was no answer, so tried Gretchen. Soph sent her home early. She was really tired and wanted to call it a night. I'll try her again in the morning.

Tank - K. Thanks.

I hang out with the guys for a little while longer, but something doesn't sit right with me about Dani's text. Sophie has never sent Gretchen home early. Even when she's tired, she just goes to sleep and lets Gretchen work silently around her.

I decide it's probably best to head home and make sure she's okay. I'm probably the last person she wants to see, but she's been alone in that big house for who knows how long, and too many bad thoughts circle my mind. The last time she was left alone . . . Shit.

"Hey," I announce to the guys, standing up. "I'm going to head home and check on Sophie."

They all nod their heads and say their goodbyes before Miller stands up with me. "I might head off too. Dani's been taking the night shift and could use a break."

They all give him comments about being soft and a pussy, just as I knew they would, but he shakes it off and follows me out the door, knowing damn well where his priorities lie.

I drop him home before making my way through my front door and dumping my shit just inside. I'm freaking exhausted, and I can't wait to crash beside my girl. Hell, maybe even tonight she might let me pull her into my arms and hold her while I sleep. Don't get me wrong, she always ends up there, but it's done out of habit while she's asleep. That's not what I need from her.

Fuck. I see her every day, try to hold her every day, kiss her every fucking day, and yet I've never missed her so goddamn much.

Our home is dead quiet, so I try to keep it that way. The last thing I want is to wake her, especially since she hasn't been sleeping well. The nightmares have a chokehold on her, forcing her to relive the worst day of her life over and over again.

Kicking off my shoes at the front door, I head into the kitchen for a drink and cut across to the fridge, not bothering to find a cup. Grabbing the milk, I uncap the lid and go to lift it to my lips when I see a note on the counter, illuminated by the refrigerator light. I don't think anything of it, considering it's probably just an update from Gretchen about Sophie's night, but as I tilt my head back to take a swig from the bottle, a subtle sparkle catches my eye.

My brows furrow and my stomach sinks. They're Sophie's rings.

Discarding the milk, I dart across the kitchen and turn on the light before racing back to the counter and picking up her rings between my fingers. I hold them tightly as my eyes scan over the note a million times, my world fucking world burning to ashes at my feet.

I'm sorry. I love you.

Over my dead fucking body.

Slipping her rings onto my pinky fingers, I grab my shit before running straight back out the door. I'm in my truck in no time, the engine roaring back to life before I screech out of the driveway and groan at just how fucking slowly the gate creeps open.

I rush down the highway, the road flying by beneath me, and I'm pulling up at the airport in no time. I don't know how I know, but my gut is telling me she went home to Denver. If that's where she feels she needs to be right now, then that's exactly where I'll be.

Hurrying through the airport, I buy my ticket before waiting the agonizing two hours for the next scheduled flight.

I try to get some rest, but I can't turn off. My mind keeps spinning, and I do everything in my power not to send myself into a downward spiral. What would have driven her to the point of leaving in the middle of the night? She knows she can always talk to me, whenever or wherever. I will always have time for her. I know she blames herself for losing our son, and I have told her a million times that I don't, but she never listens. Maybe all she needs is to just hear me for once. Let go of the grief and just hear me. Let me in and allow me to love her the way she deserves to be loved.

The thought of losing Sophie kills me, but right now, losing her isn't an option. She hasn't truly left me. She's just confused about what she needs. She's still so broken, but she should be leaning on me instead of trying to push me away. I know for damn sure I need her. She's the love of my life, and I'll be damned if I let her get away. Not now, not ever.

There are about thirty minutes left until the flight, and my ass is starting to cramp on these damn chairs. It's well past the middle of the night, but I don't care. I'm going to get to her tonight, even if it kills me.

My phone vibrates in my pocket, and I pull it out to see her father's name on the caller ID.

"Robert," I say as I answer the phone.

"Hi, son. Just thought you should know she's here. She's safe," he tells me.

"I know," I say. "I'm on my way."

"I know you are. She's a stubborn fool like her old man, but she needs you," he says, a broken tone in his voice, hating to see his baby girl hurting like this. Fuck, I hate it too. I'd give anything to take away her pain. "I'll leave the key under the mat."

"Thank you," I say and with that, he cuts the line.

I let out a breath of relief. I knew she was there, but to hear it confirmed and to hear that she's safe is just what I needed. Especially after what she's been through. I have to admit, the thought of her being taken by Christian Baxter is always popping into my head, and it drives me insane knowing it's a very real possibility. Just that knowledge alone makes me want to be by her side twenty-four-seven.

A few hours later, the plane touches down in Denver, and I rush out of the airport, eager to get to Sophie.

Not wanting to wait for an Uber, I jump straight into the back of a taxi and tell the driver to step on it. Within twenty minutes, the taxi pulls up at Sophie's childhood home, and I soon find myself digging under the mat, using the flashlight on my phone, desperately searching for the damn key.

I get inside and silence the need to find her and get straight into our issues. It's nearly sunrise, and I'm fucking exhausted. I make my way up to Sophie's room and find her curled in a ball on the bed, wearing one of my old shirts. I'm furious at her for wanting to take the easy way out, but at the same time, I'm so deeply in love with her that I can simply let it go—at least for tonight.

As I make my way to the bed, I strip off my jeans and shirt, letting them clatter to the floor before climbing in beside her. I instantly reach out for her, desperate to have her in my arms. I hold her against me, the way we used to before Baxter stole all we held precious.

As soon as I have her back up against my chest, she lets out a deep, satisfied sigh, which answers one of my million questions. She didn't want to leave. She still loves me, and she needs me just as much as I need her.

With my woman safely in my arms, I finally fall into a deep sleep.

I wake to the feel of my wife's nails running through my hair, down the side of my face, and into the coarse hairs of my stubbled jaw. My eyes open slowly as I take her in. She lays right by my side with her eyes trained on my jawline, looking as beautiful as the day I met her.

With my arms still wrapped around her, I pull her in tighter, being careful not to jostle her injuries. Her eyes snap up to mine at the movement, but I'm thankful she doesn't try to escape. "You're here?" she questions with pain in her eyes.

"There's no place else I'd rather be," I murmur as I press a gentle kiss to her temple.

Her eyes close as she takes satisfaction in my kiss then nuzzles her head under my chin and up against my chest. "I love you," she tells me. "It wasn't my intention to hurt you."

Hearing her say those three little words for the first time in so long brings a piece of me home, healing something deep inside of me. "I know, Soph," I say. "I love you, too."

I drift back off to sleep and wake later to Sophie climbing out of bed. "Where are you going?" I question as I groggily sit up in bed.

"Nowhere, just getting up," she tells me, still shaky on her feet. "It's past eleven."

Shit. I guess sleeping the morning away is what happens when you play a massive game of pro hockey, catch a red-eye flight, and stay up until five in the morning. But seeing as though we're at Sophie's parents' place, I should probably get up.

I crawl out of bed and walk around to Sophie's side before sitting on the edge. "Babe," I say as she turns and gives me a nervous look, hesitation in her beautiful eyes. "Come here."

She slowly walks over to me, and I take hold of her hips between my legs. "Talk to me. What's going on?"

Her eyes fall from mine as a broken sigh escapes her lips. "You deserve better," she says over a lump in her throat as tears well in her eyes. "It's my fault. All of it. If it weren't for me pursuing that story, we'd still have our baby. My actions are what led to his death. I don't know how you can even stand to be around me. Every time you look at me, I see it in your eyes. You're just as broken as I am, and I can't even be there for you because I'm so fucking destroyed. How could you ever love me when I'll never be able to love myself?"

Her words tear at the broken pieces of my fractured heart as red-hot fury burns through my veins. "You're running away, after everything we've been through. Leaving some bullshit note on the counter for me to find after my game, and running home with a shitty excuse like that?"

"It's not an excuse," she argues.

I let out a sigh, trying not to lose my shit at her as I hold onto her tighter, terrified she might disappear. I stand up and back her against the wall, making sure she only has me to focus on. "It is. What happened to you is not your fault. Yes, you fucked up. You shouldn't have taken the case, especially when I asked you not to. But that does not mean *it's your fault*. Not for one second have I ever blamed you, and I wish for once that you would just hear me," I tell her. "I fucking love you, Sophie, and I refuse to let you leave over this. *I need you*. Without our son, you are all I have left in this world, and I will not live in it without you."

The tears in her eyes fall over her lashes and leave streaks down her beautiful face as she looks up at me, a world of pain behind her eyes.

I swipe my thumb across her cheek, wiping away the tears as I press myself closer to her, the overwhelming grief clear in both of our eyes. "Christian Baxter is the man who did this to you, *to us*. He's the one to blame, and he's the one who is going to pay."

Those eyes focus heavily on mine. "You really feel that way?" she asks with hope. "You don't blame me?"

"Not even for a second," I breathe. "I have never lied to you, Sophie, and I'm not about to start now. You're my world, my whole fucking life. You always have been, since the very first day in the campus gym. I swore I was never going to let you slip through my fingers, so if you really want to leave, you better be fucking prepared to fight for it, because I'm not about to let you just walk out the door. I want this. You and me. I'm not about to let you give up on us. I understand that you're broken and that the pain is just . . . you don't know how to deal with it, and I get it. I can't fucking breathe when I think about everything we lost, all the things we'll never be able to experience with our son. It brings me to my knees, but I need you, Sophie. I'm fucking trying to hold it together for you, be strong for you, but I can't keep holding on without you."

Tears flow from her eyes as she throws her good arm around my neck, pulling me in as her lips fuse to mine. I kiss her deeply, having so desperately missed this connection with her. I taste her tears in our kiss but I don't fucking care as I hold onto her with everything that I am. "I'm sorry," she murmurs through our kiss. "I'm so fucking sorry."

After pulling back, I rest my forehead against hers. "I should have been there more. You're hurting so much, and I feel like I'm failing you. Every time I look at you, it kills me that I can't take your pain away."

She pulls me in again, and I wrap my arms around her as she nuzzles her face into my chest, her tears falls from her cheeks onto my chest. "This is helping," she murmurs. "I feel like I'm coming home."

My eyes close as I hear those sweet, sweet words. Nothing in this world has ever felt better. Sophie relaxes into me, and I pull us back to the bed, sitting on the edge as she curls up in my lap.

"I can't stop thinking about him," she tells me, opening up about our son for the first time since losing him. "It hurts so much. I just . . . I don't know what to do. When I think about him, I can't . . ."

"Tell me about it," I whisper, desperately trying to hold myself together, terrified of breaking. "The things you think about."

"I . . . I don't think I can," she cries.

"Please, baby. I'm missing him, too."

She nods her head, realizing I need this just as much as she does. "I wanted to call him Tyler," she says with a small smile. "After you."

"Yeah?" I question, my whole fucking heart falling out of my chest and crumbling at our feet.

"Yeah," she says. "I always pictured him just like you. Your own little mini me, with your dark hair and kind eyes. He would have given me hell but I would have loved every second of it. I wanted him to have a piece of you, and seeing as though you don't use the name, I thought he could."

Unshed tears start to fill my eyes. Hearing about how she wanted to give our son my name fucking destroys me. I'd never thought about his name, but now that the words have come out of her mouth, it feels so fucking right.

"Tyler Meyers Jr," I whisper, reaching up and curling my fingers around the back of her neck, my thumb brushing across her jaw. "But you're dead wrong. He was going to be like you. Blonde hair, blue eyes, and just as stubborn as you. Trust me, we were going to struggle to keep up with him."

"No way," she says, shaking her head with a fond smile that melts my heart. "He was going to be an easy baby. He'd breastfeed perfectly and sleep all night. I bet he would have had your dimples as well."

"I don't have dimples," I argue.

"Yeah, you do," she smiles, the tears silently tracking down her cheeks and splashing against her collarbone. "He would have been perfect, and I would have loved being his mommy. Singing him songs and watching as he fell asleep in my arms. I mean, I didn't even get a chance to hear his little voice or feel the way his little hand would clutch onto my finger," she cries. "I just wish I had a chance to hold him. Just once."

"I know, Sophie," I whisper, my lips moving against her temple. "I'd give my life if it meant giving him back to you."

Sophie shuffles around on my lap, straddling me so that she can better wrap herself around me, holding on tight as she nuzzles her face into my neck. She silently breathes me in as we each sit with heavy thoughts.

A few moment pass when I finally find the courage to go on. I know she isn't going to want to hear this, but it needs to be said. I don't know if it's going to hurt her more or help her to move forward, but I need to try. "Soph?" I question.

"Yeah?" she sighs as she grabs the blanket from the bed and uses it to dry her eyes.

"For the rest of our lives, every time we think back to him, it's going to suck, and it's going to be hard. That's what grief is. But I'd like to believe that he's looking down on us, and I want him to see us shine. I want him to be proud of the lives we're living. I want him to be boasting to all his little friends up there that his mommy and daddy are rocking it down here. But mostly, I want him to know that everything we do is for him," I tell her. "I don't want him looking down on us to see us broken and falling apart. He's our fucking star, Sophie. He's shining down on us, lighting our way like a guardian angel. And if he has the strength to light up the whole fucking sky, then the least we can do is live every day to the fullest for him, loving and shining, just the way he would have wanted."

Sophie's tears only flow faster as she holds onto me. "You're right," she says, her voice breaking with agonizing pain. "I want to live for him," she says, sitting up a little taller. "My sweet Tyler. I want him to be proud of me."

"He will be," I tell her, clinging to her with everything that I am. "And so will I."

CHAPTER 14

SOPHIE

I don't know how the hell he did it, but somehow Tank has managed to heal a bit of the pain that resides in my heart. He helped me to see a future where my baby won't be around, and despite that being the hardest realization I've ever had to come to, it's the only way for me to learn how to move forward. Just because I don't get to hold him or experience life with him by my side, doesn't mean that I have to forget him.

I sit here curled in Tank's strong arms, thankful that he had enough fight in him for the both of us. That he had what it took to come after me and prove to me that I was wrong. That I belong with him. That there's still a bright and long future for us ahead.

I hate myself for putting him through the pain of the last twenty-four hours, but in the end, it needed to happen. Without his push, I'd still be sitting in my bed, day in and day out, sobbing for my son and wishing there was a way out.

"Thank you," I murmur as I wipe my eyes on the blanket once again, lifting my head to meet his eyes. It's time to accept the fact that just because we lost what was most important to us, doesn't mean we don't deserve to be loved.

"I would have done it a million times over, Sophie. You're my whole fucking world, and I intend for you to stay that way. Even if it means you need a good kick up the ass every now and then," he tells me.

A stupid smile pulls at my lips as he scoops me off his lap and places me down on the edge of the bed before dropping down on one knee before me. He slides my wedding rings off his pinky finger before holding them out to me. "What do you say to a new start?" he asks as he takes my hand in his and gently slides my rings back into place, right where they always belonged. "I fucking love you so much."

I lean forward and catch his lips in mine. "A new start," I say, thinking it over, but decide to word it better. "A new start with an angel looking down on us."

He smiles against my lips. "It's perfect," he whispers as I scoot myself off the bed and drop onto his lap to straddle him.

"Careful," he warns me, still cautious of my injuries.

"Shut up," I tell him, needing to feel him wrap his strong arms around me and hold me tight. "I need you to kiss me."

Without another word, my man obliges.

My hands find purchase on his sculpted back and my nails dig into his strong muscles, telling him I need more. He lifts my shirt up over my head and drops it on the floor. After weeks of constantly being covered up, feeling my skin against his again is absolute magic. Goosebumps sail over my body and Tank lifts me up onto the bed, hovering above me.

I slip my thong down my thighs, opening my legs and feeling his erection heavy against my hip. His lips come down on mine and he kisses me with every ounce of love he possesses before guiding his cock to my entrance.

He slowly pushes inside me, filling me to the brim before starting to move, and I let out a gasp as he makes the sweetest love to me, each of us so desperate to feel this closeness.

I hold onto him as he moves in and out of me, his thumb rolling slow circles over my clit as tears remain in my eyes, feeling as though we're turning a new page together. Tank kisses my tears away before meeting my eyes, making sure I'm okay. And honestly, I don't think I'm ever going to be okay, but the least I can do is try.

We come together with our lips firmly locked, and I feel my heart mending, pulling the broken pieces back together one by one. "I've missed you," I murmur, not ready to let him go.

Tank smiles down at me. "Never again am I going that long without being inside you," he tells me . . . or maybe it's more of a warning. But either way, I completely agree. Some couples talk, some couples touch, but Tank and I, we explode. Despite how much I've always loved staying up until three in the morning, curled in his arms and talking shit, it's nothing compared to when we're physically together. Sex is our love language. It always has been and always will be.

Tank eventually pulls out of me, and we decide it's best to show our faces to the world. I'm sure my parents are dying to check in on me and make sure we're doing okay.

Tank pulls his jeans on as I get myself dressed, still needing to take my time. Tank helps me pull my shirt over my head before following me out of my childhood bedroom and down the hallway. He's just raising his arms to pull his shirt on as my mother appears from the opposite direction.

"Oh, my," she gasps with a hand across her chest as she takes him in and starts to swoon. "You just keep getting bigger and bigger every time I see you."

Oh, geez.

Tank scoffs a laugh but reaches down and pulls her into a tight hug. "It's good to see you," he says, and she looks at me over his shoulder and winks as she pretends to fan herself.

"Put your fucking shirt on before the old bat has a heart attack," I hear my father scolding from the end of the hallway.

"Thank you," I announce. "I couldn't have said it better myself."

We all make our way down the hallway and into the kitchen where Dad and Zac are busy fussing over lunch. And by fussing, I mean Zac is telling Dad how to do it, while Dad huffs and whines about doing it in the first place.

I take over for Dad, needing to keep myself busy as Tank settles in to catch up with my family.

Zac starts dishing out lunch and adds an extra plate to the table, and I'm about to ask the moron if he knows how to count when a knock sounds at the door. "I'll get it," I groan, noticing that Mom is nowhere to be seen, and Dad is busy questioning Tank about last night's game. Even though we all know he watched every second of it.

Making my way to the door, I open it to find some girl staring back at me, and I narrow my eyes as I look her up and down. She must only be around twenty-two or twenty-three, and my guess is she is here to see my dimwit brother. "Can I help you?" I question as I hold the door close to my body, not allowing her entry, while also using the door as a cover to hide the majority of my injuries.

Her eyes go wide as she takes me in. "Holy shit. You must be Sophie," she says.

"Yes, I'm well aware of who I am," I say, enjoying making her squirm. "What I don't know is who the hell are you?"

"Shit, of course . . . um, I'm MJ, or Emma Jane or um . . . I guess you can call me whatever you like," she stutters out, leaving that comment wide open. I give her a pointed stare and wait for her to continue, watching as she visibly swallows. "I'm Zac's girlfriend."

"Girlfriend, hey?" I say with interest, glancing back to raise my brow at my brother. He certainly forgot to mention he had a girlfriend.

"Yeah," she smiles. "It's only been a few months. Though, I hear congratulations are in order. Zac mentioned that you're pregnant," she says as her gaze travels down to where there's no bump, her comment making me absentmindedly clutch at my empty womb.

I clench my jaw, feeling as though I'm about to break all over again, suddenly not enjoying the way she squirms. Hell, I just want her to run for the fucking hills. "My baby died."

Her eyes widen in horror, and I watch as her face turns white, looking as though she's about to be sick. "Holy shit. I'm so fucking sorry," she breathes, her chest heaving with heavy breaths. "Please forgive me. I'm so nervous to meet you. I'm all sweaty, and when I'm nervous I don't think. I just . . . I was racking my brain for something to talk to you about and it slipped my mind."

"Wow, it just *slipped your mind* that my baby was murdered," I say, more than unimpressed with the girl.

She groans as I sense a mountain of a man come up behind me. I watch as MJ's face rises to meet Tank's. Her eyes bulge out, though this time it's obvious she's gawking at the pure size of him. Usually when I see women react like that, it's because they're hockey fans and are wondering if he's the kind of guy they could get into bed. "Stop interrogating the girl," he tells me, his hand at my waist. "Let her in."

I roll my eyes but do as he says before opening the door wider. If only he knew.

Stepping out of the doorway, I wave her in and watch as she scurries past me and beelines straight for Zac, who only just notices her arrival now. He looks at her and notices her freaked-out expression before looking back at me through narrowed eyes. But all I can do is stare in return.

Watching me a second longer, he realizes that whatever must have passed between us was serious enough to really get under my skin. He presses his lips together but finally decides to let it go. Besides, what are big sisters for? I need to get rid of the weak ones, and this one, I don't think she's gonna make the cut.

After quickly finishing up my lunch preparations, we all sit around the table, and it's a flurry of chatter. "So, do you have to go straight back?" my mother asks us, glancing between me and Tank with a hopeful stare. "Or do you have some time? We rarely get to see you both now."

I look at Tank, guilty that I have no idea what his training schedule is like at the moment. "Nah, we're good," he says, taking the reins. "We can head home in the morning."

I raise my brow at him in question. "Are you sure?"

"Yeah. I'll have to call Coach this afternoon to explain why I missed today's session, but he'll be fine. The next game's not for another week, and besides, I think you need a little time at home," he says as he reaches under the table and laces his fingers through mine.

"Thank you," I mouth to him, grateful that he always seems to know exactly what I need.

"I don't know if you're up for it, but the Dragons have their first game of the season tonight. Did you want to go to that?" he asks.

My face brightens as a huge smile takes over. "Can we go to Micky's after?" I question, thinking about his famous burgers. The thought instantly sends me into a downward spiral, remembering how that was my one craving throughout my pregnancy.

"Anything you want," Tank says with emotion heavy in his eyes, almost as if he had missed this easy conversation between us, but I can't blame him. I've missed it too, and while we both still have so far to go, I'm so damn happy to have it back.

Tank squeezes my hand under the table before leaning across and planting a kiss on my lips.

"Ugh," Zac whines. "Do you really need to do that at the table?"

I can't help but smirk at my little brother. "You think that's bad? You should see what he made me do on my kitchen counter."

"Shit, Sophie," Dad scolds as Zac's face scrunches up in disgust. "I don't want to hear this while I'm trying to eat."

"I'm with Dad," Zac says.

"Oh, come on. It's not like you've never done it," I say.

"Actually," Tank says, his gaze narrowing with thick curiosity as he considers my brother. "I don't think he's that adventurous."

"Hmm," I say, really thinking about it. "Maybe you're right."

"What?" Zac says, his eyes widening as my mother rolls her eyes, probably wishing she weren't so used to conversations like this. "I'm plenty adventurous."

"Eh," MJ says with a shrug while Zac looks at her, horrified.

"You should take some lessons from Tank," I grin. "He knows how to show a woman a real good time."

Tank grins in approval as Dad demands the conversation to come to an end, and I can't help but laugh. The sound feels so alien on my tongue. We get back to lunch and manage to finish our meal without any further talk of Tank's good deeds in the bedroom.

After lunch, Tank disappears to call his coach while I spend the afternoon with Mom, who insists on taking me through her own version of a counseling session just to make sure I'm doing okay. But since Tank's kick up the ass this morning, I seem to be coping much better.

That afternoon, we head over to Tank's family's home and have an early dinner with them before finding ourselves at the first Denver Dragons game of the season. Hell, the first Denver Dragons game I've been to in well over five years.

As we step through the doors, a wave of memories come rushing back, reminding me of my final year at college. The smell, the atmosphere, the laughter. Hell, the way I fell madly in love with Tank Meyers after Dani and I unofficially became their PR team for the season.

As we head deeper into the ice rink, we notice the place is a sea of Dragons fans with stalls upon stalls of merchandise. Tank walks up to a table and grabs a stuffed dragon wearing hockey skates and holding a little hockey stick before grinning at me. "And to think all this shit started with you and Dani," he mutters, though all I can think about is how I would have loved to buy something like that for my little man.

I force myself to laugh. There's no denying that he's right, and I'm about to make a sarcastic comment about it when a certain calendar catches my eye. "Are you kidding?" I ask, my eyes lighting up as I point it out. "I'm gonna need that."

Tank follows my eye line and groans when he figures out what I want. "Seriously? You're going to make me ask this chick for a calendar full of naked dudes?"

"Uhh . . . yeah," I say. "My calendar at home is getting a little worn out. I need some fresh material."

He rolls his eyes, but does it anyway, then surprises me when he buys me a large foam finger and a Dragons blanket to keep me warm during the game. I reach up on my tippy-toes and plant a quick kiss on his lips before we search out our seats.

"Do you think we could screw in the locker room like we used to?" I ask as we climb the grandstand.

"Might be a bit weird seeing as though we don't know any of the players anymore," he comments as though the suggestion had actual merit. Though, I guess it did. We have certainly had our way with each other in much weirder places.

"What might be weird?" a deep voice asks from behind us.

We turn around and find a grinning Jaxon leading his wife, Cassie, up the stairs. Tank's face lights up as he comes down a step and I can't help but feel like shit after not having made enough time to see them recently. Hell, it's been ages since my husband tried using their son as a human football. "Hey, man," he smiles, the two big assholes blocking the walkway. "Sophie wants to screw in the locker rooms."

"Ahh," Jaxon laughs. "Some things never change."

I roll my eyes but yeah, he's right. "Don't get me started on you," I warn him, remembering way too many things about this guy. Hell, he was more of a sex-crazed whore than I was in college, and that's certainly a big achievement.

Jaxon holds both his hands up in surrender and starts to make a snide comment when a throat clears from lower on the stairs.

"Come on," Cassie says. "We've got to keep moving. We're holding up the line."

"Yeah," Jaxon agrees. "We'll catch up with you guys after the game?" he questions. "Maybe Micky's?"

"We'll be there," Tank says as he takes my hand and starts leading me back up the grandstand. We find our seats and I get myself comfortable for what should be one hell of a great game.

After pulling my new blanket on and placing my foam finger on my lap to slip on when the time comes, I'm ready to cheer for my team. As we wait for the game to start, Tank busily texts Miller, making him fully aware of where we are with a selfie, while I open up my new calendar to see what goodies lie within.

CHAPTER 15

TANK

Fuck, it's good to be here.

    While the circumstances surrounding how I got here were hard, it's still great to be back in the place that started it all.

Six years ago, I never would have dreamed that I'd be sitting in this very grandstand, next to my incredible wife, as captain of the LA Storm, cheering on the still undefeated Denver Dragons.

Fucking dream come true right here, and at the risk of sounding like a damn pussy, I'm on cloud fucking nine. This right here is home.

The game finishes, and I'm not surprised to see they took out the win. Their team is fucking good, maybe even stronger than when Miller and I were there. Hell, there's some kids in here that I'll be talking to Larsden about once I'm back in LA. What did surprise me was when the team came out of the hole with Coach Harris bringing up the rear, and Shorty right by his side.

After the game, I grab Sophie and lead her straight into the locker room, only getting through because it's the same security that used to work here back when I skated for the team, and he learned really fucking fast not to deny Sophie when she wants to get through.

Sophie grins as we enter the locker room, and she does what she does best, making herself well-known to the team. I roll my eyes as she has the whole team eating out of her hand within seconds, her wide smile making me so goddamn happy.

"Tank," the old man says fondly.

I turn and find Coach Harris beaming at me as he makes his way across the locker room. He pulls me into a warm hug and my arms instantly fly around him. "Hey, Coach. How's it going?"

"Not too bad, kid," he smiles. "What about you?" he asks as his eyes quickly flick toward Sophie across the locker room, talking with his players. "I heard you guys have been going through a bit of a rough time."

"Yeah," I say, taken aback by how hard it is to talk with him about this, feeling my chest constrict with emotion. Coach Harris was a mentor to me. His opinion always mattered, and unloading my burden makes me feel like that freshman kid again, desperately seeking his guidance. "It's been pretty shit, but we're coming out the other end."

"That's good to hear, son. How's Sophie, though? She's all healed?" he questions, still so fond of Dani and Sophie after all these years.

"Mostly," I tell him. "Her ribs are still giving her a hard time, but she won't admit it."

He shakes his head in exasperation. "She's always been so damn stubborn," Coach Harris murmurs.

"Ain't that the fucking truth," I reply as an ear-shattering squeal is heard from behind me. I turn just in time to see Sophie flying across the locker room and into the arms of Shorty. "What's this numbskull doing beside you in the coaches box?" I question.

"Haven't you heard?" he says, a stupid grin on his face. "I'm retiring at the end of the season. Shorty's taking over as Head Coach."

"No shit?" I ask, pride surging through me as I glance at the little dipshit who's currently trying to peel my wife off him.

"Mmhmm," Coach confirms. "I'm too old to be running around after dickheads like you for much longer, and Shorty's a great fit. The boys love him."

Well, of course the boys love him. Shorty is just that kind of guy.

Knowing Coach Harris needs to wrap things up with his players, I say my goodbyes and make my way over to Shorty just as Jaxon appears in the doorway. "You fuckers hanging around here all night or are we going out to party?" he questions.

"Fuck yeah," Shorty grins as Sophie looks at me with a beaming smile.

"Let's get out of here," I say, taking my wife by the hand and leading her out the door behind Jaxon and Shorty, more than ready for the trip down memory lane for the second time tonight.

S tepping off the plane the following afternoon, Sophie and I head around to luggage claim and grab Sophie's suitcase before making our way out to the parking lot.

"You know, as much as I love visiting the family, it's good to be home," I tell her with a gentle squeeze of her hand.

"I know," she sighs. "I'll miss them though, especially Zac. He's so different now that he's older. I feel like I need to get to know him all over again."

"Really?" I tease. "I don't think you're missing much."

Soph rolls her eyes as I see my truck coming into view, and I lead her toward it, but she tugs on my hand. "What are you doing?" I question.

"My car is over there," she says with a flick of her head.

"So? Mine's over here," I tell her.

"So?" she repeats in disbelief as she comes to a standstill in the middle of the walkway with her hands on her slim hips, making the people behind us have to detour around. "I'm not leaving my car here."

"Well, I'm not about to let you out of my sight, especially not at an airport," I scoff as I reach out for her hand. "I'll organize for it to be brought home."

She gapes at me. "You can do that?" she questions with wide eyes as she happily takes my hand and allows me to lead her to my truck.

I grin wide, making Sophie roll her eyes before I've even said a word. "Of course, I can. I'm Tank fucking Meyers. Captain of the LA Storm. I'm a fucking celebrity, babe. Gotta reap the fucking benefits while I still can."

We get to my truck, and I help her up into it before jumping into the driver's seat. "How are you feeling? The plane didn't mess with your ribs?" I question as we pull out of the parking lot.

"A little," she admits with a small cringe, "but it'll be fine. We'll be home soon, and I can dig my pain meds out of my suitcase."

"Okay," I murmur, satisfied with her answer, though my foot twitches to hit the brake and search through her bag now.

"It's probably time I set up my new phone and other devices," she comments, knowing damn well she should have done it ages ago. That distance from the online world was probably good for her, though. Hell, I don't wanna know just how fucked up it would have been had she been receiving the same condolence texts from random assholes from her past the same way I was. Like, how the fuck did these assholes even find out about it? It's not like I was splashing my wife's attack all over the news.

"Ya think?" I grunt with sarcasm heavy in my voice. "Do you know how annoying it was waiting at the airport knowing I couldn't just call you?"

"I know," she sighs. "I'm sorry. But on the bright side, I won't be taking off on you like that again."

"You better not be, or I'm going to have to chain your ass to the couch," I tell her.

She grins at me with mischief in her eyes. "Not the bed?"

I glance across at her and wink. "It'll be a long chain. After all, I like taking you all over the house."

She lets out a laugh, and it's music to my ears. A sound that I will never take for granted again, especially after not hearing it for so long. I've made myself a promise to make her laugh as much as I possibly can. Every fucking minute of every fucking day.

"Babe . . ." I start, waiting for her to look over at me.

"Yeah?" she questions in a small voice.

"Speaking of things you need to do when you get home . . ."

A nervousness flickers in her eyes and she hesitantly responds. "What?"

"You need to make things right with Dani. She misses her best friend, and I'm sure Mia misses you, too," I tell her. "You know, Dani is going through a hard time as well. Her best friend went through something traumatic and she wasn't able to be there for you the way she needed to be."

"I know," she sighs. "It's just hard seeing her with Mia, knowing I won't get to have that. But I've been thinking about it a lot actually, and I hate that she's disappointed in me."

"She's not disappointed in you. She's disappointed that she doesn't get to be *with* you," I say reaching across the center console and taking her hand in mine. She intertwines our fingers before running her thumb across the coarse skin of my hand. "But as for Mia, think of her as your adoptive daughter. That kid needs her crazy aunt just as much as you need her innocence. You balance each other out. Don't shut her out just because it's hard."

"I won't. I promise," she says, and I glance over at her to see nothing but a fierce determination in her eyes. "I'm feeling much better, and while it's always going to be hard, I think I'm ready to be my old self again."

"Babe, no matter what, you will never be your old self again," I tell her, not sugarcoating it. "Neither of us will, but I'm glad you're trying to find a new normal where you can move forward and have happiness in your life."

She gives me a tight smile as we pull up to our gate and I hang my arm out the window before thumbing in the code. Soon enough, we're at the top of our driveway and I'm helping Sophie out of the cab.

We walk to the front door, hand in hand, and the sudden need to carry her bridal style over the threshold takes over me. After all, I just got my wife back in our home, which to me is definitely cause to celebrate.

I scoop her up into my arms and she lets out a surprised squeal, but it's quickly muffled by my lips crashing down on hers. "I'm so fucking happy you're home," I murmur against her lips. "You've got no idea."

Her hand comes up, and she runs her nails across my jaw, feeling the coarse hairs of my stubble beneath her fingers. "Me too," she whispers with her heart in her eyes.

I adjust her so I'm taking her weight in one hand as I reach for the door handle, but what I find has me frozen on the spot.

"What is it?" Sophie asks, alarmed.

"Shhh," I whisper as I gently set her on her feet. I push her behind me as I take in the cracked door. "Stay here," I warn her as I pull my phone from my pocket and hand it back to her. "Call the police."

"What?" she practically shrieks as she tries to keep quiet. "Why?"

"There's someone here," I tell her.

Fear takes over her face, and I know without a doubt she's remembering the last time someone intruded into our home. I give her a gentle kiss on the forehead, feeling the way her hands violently shake. I remind her to make the call before I silently push the door open and creep into the house. It's killing me to separate from her, but there's no way in hell I'm about to bring her in here.

I'm halfway down the hallway when I notice someone behind me, and I whip around, ready to end this motherfucker when I find Sophie desperately trying to catch up to me, her eyes wide with fear. "What the fuck are you doing?" I whisper yell.

"I just . . . I couldn't . . . I'm fucking scared, okay? You can't leave me out there alone," she pleads.

"What, and you think being in here is better for you?" I ask with a groan.

"No, being with *you* is what's best for me," she says with a sharp bite in her tone, suggesting that this is non-negotiable.

"Fine," I grunt, knowing a losing battle when I see one. Besides, we don't have the luxury of fighting it out right now. "But you need to stay right behind me, where I can keep you safe."

She nods and practically glues herself to my back before clenching her hand into the fabric of my shirt. It makes it harder to sneak into the house, but at the same time, I can't say that I'm not grateful she feels safer with me. At least this way I'm not wondering if she's okay.

We creep past the kitchen when Sophie points toward the sink, and I look over to notice a few dishes have been left unwashed. My brows furrow in confusion. I certainly didn't leave them there the night of the game. What kind of weirdo breaks into a home and decides to cook up a fucking feast?

We continue deeper into our home, noticing small details that put us on edge. The remotes for the TV are scattered across the couch, and the bathroom door is left wide open. We've been gone for a day and a half. We couldn't possibly have inherited squatters already.

We hear a noise that sounds like someone moving around the house and Sophie's hand instantly tightens in my shirt.

"Our bedroom," I tell her.

She nods her head in agreement before we make our way down to our room, and we pause at the door, glancing at one another. There's fear in her eyes, but she looks as though she's about ready to face down the whole fucking world. Letting out a breath, knowing just what's on the line, I gently push the door open just wide enough for us to slip through.

We come to a screeching halt, my eyes widening in horror as I take in the sick scene before me.

A very naked Crazy Jill is lying dead center on our rose petal-covered bed, legs wide open as she helps herself to Sophie's toys out of her bedside table, all but squirting across our bed.

WHAT THE ACTUAL FUCK?

Her eyes widen in surprise as she sees me before her, and a beaming smile rips across her face. "Baby, I've been waiting for you," she purrs as her hand continues. "Why don't you come and joi—"

Her words are cut off as her eyes narrow to angry slits, realizing my wife is right behind me, poking her head around my side to take in the scene. "What the fuck is she doing here?" Jill questions as she presses the little button to stop the buzzing of Sophie's favorite vibrator.

At that, the real Sophie comes alive, and I let her fly like the fucking queen she is.

Taking the reins, Sophie steps out from behind me. "What the fuck am I doing here?" she questions. "What about you, you crazy fucking stalker? I'm his wife, you know, the woman who actually married this fucker," she says, hooking her thumb in my direction. "Now, let me spell it out for you. HE'S NOT FUCKING INTERESTED. And besides, from the pathetic display I just saw, you definitely don't have what it takes to keep this machine satisfied. Now get your shit and get the fuck out of our home, so I can start burning it down."

"No," I say, intervening. Jill's face lights up with a smug expression, which I cut down just as fast as it appeared. "This shit has gone on long enough. Call the cops," I tell Sophie. "I want this dealt with and a fucking restraining order."

"But . . ." Jill starts, panic flashing in her eyes.

"No fucking buts," I tell her as I grab what must be her clothes off the floor and throw them at her. "You and I are not a thing. Never have been and certainly never will be. You're a crazy fucking bitch, and you need to leave me alone, you hear me? This shit ends now."

"You're just saying that because she's here," Jill says as she gives Sophie a nasty look.

"No, I'm saying that because it's fucking true. Now get your dirty ass dressed," I say, taking Sophie's hand and slamming the bedroom door behind us.

We sit on the couch as we wait for the cops to show up, and seeing as they're big hockey fans, they're here in no time. I let them in and tell them where to find Jill, warning them what state she might be in when they enter. They bring her out in cuffs moments later, and I notice her tear-streaked face.

"I love you, Tank," she cries as the cops lead her out of my house.

"Ugh," Sophie groans as she looks at me. "I know you're happy to have me home and all, but I'm not staying here tonight. This whole place needs to be disinfected." Her eyes suddenly go wide as she gasps. "What if she fucked herself on our couch?"

We both get to our feet, not taking the risk.

"Yeah, good point," I say as I pull out my phone and text Miller.

Tank - Dude, long fucking story. We're crashing at your place tonight.
Miller - No problem.

An officer comes and talks to us and I give him the rundown of just how long this has been going on. Exactly what she does, how often, and what is said. It's then that Sophie pipes up and admits that Jill has been sending her messages for the past two years, telling her that she isn't good enough and to back off her man. So naturally, Sophie responded to each and every message.

The cops leave with a promise to set up the papers for a restraining order, and I tell them I'll be down in the morning to get it sorted out.

The second the door closes behind them, I look at Sophie.

"What?" she questions.

"How could you not tell me she's been messaging you?"

"How could you bring me home and not remember stashing a naked woman in our bed?" she quips.

"Sophie," I warn. "This is no time to make jokes."

"Fine," she mutters, rolling her eyes as though I'm the unreasonable one in this situation. "I just didn't want to worry you. It was the same shit that she sends you. No threats or anything, just empty messages saying she loves you and that you should be together."

I let out a sigh as I take two steps to get to her before dropping my hands to her hips and pulling her into me. "And you didn't think it was necessary to tell me?" I murmur as I press my lips to the soft skin of her neck.

"Not at all," she replies as she readjusts herself so her lips are firmly against mine. I kiss her deeply as I lift her off the floor, and her legs automatically wrap around my waist. I press her into the wall when she pulls her head back and gives me a stupid grin. "What does this mean for naked cooking night?" she questions, her brows furrowing with a deep curiosity. "It better be fucking good after that."

"Don't worry, baby. I got you covered," I promise her, and with that, I crush my lips to hers and show her just how good it gets.

CHAPTER 16

SOPHIE

An idea hits me as Tank and I go about the house, throwing our shit into an overnight bag to spend the night at Miller and Dani's place. He looks up at me with a suspicious stare as he grabs the high heels I just tossed in the bag. "What the fuck do you need these for?" he questions.

"None of your goddamn business," I grin as I carry on.

I grab the phone and tablet that still sit in their packaging on my bedside table and decide I should probably bring those along with me too. You know, I might have a little downtime between my crazy planning.

As soon as the cleaners show up, I give them strict, extremely specific instructions on what to do and what to burn before we make our way out of the house. "Are you sure they'll do a good job?" I ask Tank as we get in his truck.

"Fucking better for what I'm paying them."

I roll my eyes, but it's true. If you want the best, you've got to pay for the best. But it'll be worth it . . . hopefully.

We pull up at Dani and Miller's place a minute later. Which is no surprise, we basically live on the same street. When we barge our way through the door, we find them screwing on the kitchen counter.

Dani squeals as Miller grins, not bothering to cover himself, though it's nothing we all haven't seen a million times before. These two fuck like bunnies, no matter where they are.

I don't want to, but out of respect for my girl, I turn away until they can get themself fixed up. I mean, they are both fucking hot. Miller, Tank, and I all have questionable pasts when it comes to what we were willing to do between the sheets. And I must say, after a night of heavy drinking, the idea of the four of us has entered my mind on a few occasions. But since being married, Tank went caveman on my ass, no longer interested in those games, and Miller is that way too. Dani has always been a one-man kind of girl, but she really doesn't know what she's missing out on.

I look up at Tank, and from the look he's giving me in return, he knows exactly what I've just been thinking about. He gives a slight shake of his head. "Not going to happen," he murmurs.

I shrug my shoulders and give him a grin. "At least they seem to be getting the hang of naked cooking night."

"Nah, they don't quite do it like we do," Tank says with a knowing grin.

"Very true," I laugh.

"Ahhh . . . Do you guys mind?" Miller asks, drawing our attention back to the kitchen counter.

"Not at all," Tank says. "Carry on. We'll wait."

Dani squeals once again and attempts to cover up as best she can when she realizes we're happy to stay and watch. "Come on," Miller groans. "Can a guy get a break around here?"

"Fine," I grunt. "But if you're going to make us wait, at least give it to her good. My girl deserves to be thrown over the counter and fucked hard while having her ass spanked like the naughty little girl she is."

Dani squeals with embarrassment as Tank grabs my hand and leads me down the hall to their spare bedroom, but I speak no lies. Besides, I know all about how they used to fuck in college. This shit is tame compared to that.

Twenty minutes later, I'm grinning ear to ear, hearing Dani scream as the sound of her ass being spanked echoes through the big house, and after their big finale, we get the all-clear to exit the spare room.

As we walk down the hallway, I hear Mia stirring in her room, and without thinking, I turn on my heel and walk into the nursery, greeting her with a big smile. The precious little girl beams up at me, and I scoop her into my arms. "Did you have a good snooze?" I ask the cuddly little gem in my arms.

She lets out a nice big fart, and I take that as a big whopping yes. Taking her over to her changing table, I get her a fresh diaper before coming out to the kitchen where I find Tank shoving disinfectant into Miller's chest, and demanding he gives the kitchen counter a good scrub, especially if we're eating dinner here tonight.

Dani turns as she sees us joining them in the kitchen, and a relief-filled smile spreads over her face as she sees me holding her sweet baby. "Are you okay?" she questions. "Do you need me to take her?"

Tank looks at me with her question, but I ignore his curious gaze. "No," I tell her, more content than I ever thought I could be. "I think I'm alright. I mean, it's definitely pulling at the heartstrings, but I'm not turning into a sobbing mess on the floor."

Dani comes over and wraps her arms around both me and Mia. "You have no idea how happy I am to hear you say that," she murmurs in my ear.

"I know," I tell her. "I'm sorry I've been such a stranger. It's just been hard, especially with Mia."

"It's okay, you don't need to explain," she murmurs. "You handled it as best you could."

My eyes start welling with tears, and I do what I can to try and blink them back. "Shit, Dani," I scoff. "Laying it on thick. I didn't handle it at all."

"Well, no. You didn't," she agrees with a laugh, the sound making life seem just that little bit easier. "Now, what do you guys want for dinner?"

"We're not eating here," I inform her.

"What?" Tank asks with a groan. "You don't really feel like going out?"

I turn to Tank with a grin. "Let me clarify," I say. "Dani and I are going out for dinner while you two stay home and look after Mia."

"Oh, really?" Dani says with excitement as Tank lets out another groan, remembering the heels in our bag.

"Hell yeah," I grin. "And then we're getting shit-faced and Tank is going to come pick us up at God knows what hour of the morning."

"A girls' night? Holy shit, you have no idea how desperate I am for one of our girls' nights."

"But—" Miller starts.

"No," Dani says, turning on him. "I need this and so does Sophie. Don't ruin this for us."

Miller holds both hands up in surrender, always one to cave to his wife's every need. "I was just going to remind you to pump first. I think we're all out of breastmilk."

"Oh," she says with an embarrassed smirk. "I can do that."

"So, it's settled then," Tank says. "Miller and I will be Mia's bitches for the night while you two go out and enjoy yourselves."

I walk into his arms and give him a big kiss. "And you'll be happy to pick us up?"

"Always," he murmurs against my lips as he takes Mia out of my arms and holds her close to his chest. "One condition though," he says.

"And what's that?" I ask with suspicion as I pull back to look at him clearly.

"You need to set up your phone first. I don't want you out there with no way to contact you."

"Fine," I mutter with a heavy sigh. I wasn't really planning on spending the time to do that right now, but it's the least I can do to make sure Tank feels comfortable about all of this. I don't blame him though, had the roles been reversed and he'd been hurt like I was, I'd be keeping tabs on him every minute of the day. "I'll set it up while Dani milks herself."

I make myself comfortable on the couch, setting up my new phone as Dani sits on the opposite side with some weird contraption attached to her tits. I watch with a strange fascination as the thing sucks her nipple in, drains her of milk, and fills up a bottle connected at the bottom.

"Can you stop looking at me like that?" she asks.

"I can't help it," I tell her honestly. "I don't know whether to be impressed or disgusted."

She rolls her eyes and carries on with her task, while I try my best to concentrate on mine.

Two hours later, we're dressed and ready for our night. Though I have to say, having this stupid cast is really not doing wonders for my outfit. My husband reluctantly drops us off at a cocktail bar, reminding us to eat something before we hit the drinks, and we practically skip inside. We find ourselves a table and order the barman to keep the cocktails flowing.

Following dinner, we decide the cocktails just aren't doing it anymore, and we start hitting the hard stuff. The dance floor calls to us, and I'm pretty sure we're making a menace of ourselves, but I simply don't care. I'm having the time of my life, and to be honest,

I really needed this. Hell, after the shit I've been through, I freaking deserve it.

Dani starts huffing and puffing on the dance floor and demands we take a break from ass shaking. She loops her arm through mine and together we stumble to the bar and take a seat. "Holy shit, this is such a great night," she slurs as she slaps a hand down on the bar to gain the bartender's attention. "You-hoo, Mr. Barman," she yells over the sound of the raging music.

The bartender looks down the bar and gives Dani a quick nod followed by a wink. "Shit, did you see that?" she asks me. "I push a fucking watermelon out my vag, and I can still reel them in. My husband is one hell of a lucky guy."

"Amen to that, sister," I laugh as the bartender comes down and pours us each a shot. We clink our teeny-weeny little glasses together and down them in seconds. From there, our night quickly spirals out of control, but I do my best to take as many selfies as possible so we can remember the fun we had for years to come.

After being told to get off the tables, Dani and I drag ourselves back to the bar for our eighth, ninth, or tenth shot of the night. The room spins for both of us, but as far as I know, we're both going strong.

I laugh as we take our seats between a bunch of guys and a group of skanky chicks, but as Dani drops her ass to the chair, she slips straight off the side and falls to the ground instead. I wobble as I bend down to try and help the klutz to her feet, but my uncontrollable laughter means she has to manage by herself.

"Shit," I say as the laughter finally settles down. "I'm pretty sure I just peed a little."

"Yeah, well, I've got a sore ass," she giggles. "Even worse than the time I let Miller have it. That fucking hurt."

"Dani," I laugh. "Are you serious? You should have told me you were going to do that. I could have given you some pointers."

"Well, I would have been fine if Miller didn't have such a big dick."

I burst out laughing and am about to get started on my pointers when the conversation coming from the skank-ass bitches behind me catches my attention.

"The Storm fucking sucks. That new captain is going to destroy them. I'm placing my bets on the Wolves," the chick sitting behind me says.

My back stiffens, meeting Dani's stare, knowing without a doubt how this is about to go down. "Oh, no she didn't," I gasp, electricity pulsing through my veins, itching to put this bitch in her place. No one talks about my man like that.

"Oh, she fucking did," Dani says, always down to get messy. Though, let's be honest, she'll stand back and watch like a little bitch, while pretending that she's getting messy.

"I agree," someone shouts. "It's about time the *Dream Team* moved the fuck over and took their asses back to Denver."

"Shit's about to get real," I warn Dani as I get up from my seat and start taking out my hoop earrings. I shove them down my bra as Dani does exactly the same thing, which honestly surprises me. If she hadn't been drinking, she'd be trying to drag me away, but tonight, she's right there by my side.

"Hey," I shout, getting in the girls' faces as Dani puts her hands on her hips beside me, trying to look intimidating, but she's like a little fluffy penguin. "What's your problem with Tank and Miller?"

The girl who's sitting right beside me grins at my question, clearly thinking we're some dumb, obsessed fans. "They're shit. They're just a bunch of muscle the Storm hired to make them look good for the media. You'll see. With Tank as captain, they'll be a sinking ship."

"Excuse you," Dani says, stepping forward. "Tank and Miller are the best on the team. They're taking out the championship, just like they have for the past five years."

Another girl scoffs. "Shit, look how fucking desperate you are for them. Are you chicks puck bunnies? Going around, trying to fuck the whole team behind the Zamboni?"

"Don't waste your time," someone else says. "Tank and Miller are both hitched to some whores. I caught them outside the rink the other night after their game. I offered them a threesome, but the little bitches didn't have the balls to go for it."

At that, Dani's face goes bright red in anger, but I beat her to the punch line as my fist comes hurtling through the air and knocking the bitch into the bar.

Her friends jump in, but I have a fuming Dani right beside me, and when someone crosses her man, the little she-devil turns into the Energizer Bunny, ready to go all fucking night. And with that, we hold our own until our bitch asses are being hauled away in cuffs.

Dani and I are led through the police station, past the interrogation room, and through to the holding cells. The cop unlocks the heavy metal door before taking our cuffs off and sending us in.

Dani takes one look around and notices a chick sitting on the bench. "Shit," she gasps. "I'm too innocent for this. I don't want to be her bitch."

I let out a sigh as I study the woman. I mean, she isn't that bad. Bit rough around the edges, but still hot. "Don't stress," I tell her. "As long as she's willing to give what she gets, then I'll take one for the team."

Dani visibly relaxes as she follows me into the cell and sits down next to me on the bench. I introduce us to the woman, and we instantly hit it off. Her name is Marge and apparently, she loves cats. On her days off, she likes to ride her Harley around the streets of LA while picking up chicks at random biker bars. Just beautiful.

We're barely into her life story when a cop unlocks our cell and tells me I can make a call.

Nervousness drums through me when I get to the phone and dial Tank's number, waiting as it rings at least three times before he answers. "Soph, is that you?" he asks into the phone, and from the sound of his voice, it's clear he was fast asleep.

"Um yeah," I slur. "Who else are you expecting to be calling you at three in the morning? Some skank whore looking for a threesome? Or how about a crazy stalker bitch who wants to fuck you with my toys—OH GOD! I need to buy new toys."

"Fucking hell," he mutters under his breath before getting back on track. "Whose phone are you calling from? It came through on a weird number. But I'm taking it you girls are ready to come home?"

"Yep," I declare, popping the *p*.

"It's about fucking time," he murmurs. "Are you still at that cocktail bar?"

"Um . . . nooooooooo," I grin into the phone, for some reason extremely proud of our adventures. Hell, I'm busting to get back in my cell and find out all about Marge's third wife, Rochelle. "We're at the police station."

"What?" he questions, suddenly sounding wide awake. "What the fuck are you doing there?"

"Well . . . It's kind of a long story," I giggle before hiccuping. "But Dani and I sort of got into a bar fight, and now I need you to bail us out. But for the record, she totally spurred me on."

"Fuck, babe," he groans, but I hear the amusement in his voice. "I'll be there soon."

"Love you," I remind him as I hang up the phone and join Dani in the cell. The cop asks her to make her call, but she doesn't bother. She knows Tank's got her back, and she wouldn't want Miller to drag Mia out at this time of the night anyway.

Forty-five minutes later, I'm faced with a grinning Tank as he watches Dani and me being released from the cell, making sure to record the whole thing so Miller doesn't miss a single second. He hands me my purse, and I quickly pull my phone out to make sure we get a good selfie with Marge in our cell. You know, it's important to celebrate our wins.

Marge happily obliges, and we quickly make our way out of the station.

We practically chat Tank's ears off as we recap our night and tell him exactly how we ended up in there. Though Tank wasn't too impressed about the whole fighting thing, considering my body is still healing from the last one, but honestly, those chicks needed to be put in their place. And besides, I had enough alcohol pulsing through my system not to feel a damn thing. Something tells me I'll be sore come tomorrow.

I mean, that woman tried to get both our husbands into bed at the same time. Nu-uh. That shit ain't going to fly with either of us. Unless it's the four of us in bed, but apparently that shit ain't flying either.

We finally make it back to Dani's place, and Tank helps us both inside before forcing a glass of water down each of our throats. He drags me down to our room and attempts to help me get undressed, but the second he pulls the zipper down on my dress, I'm instantly jumping into action. As usual, my husband is not one to disappoint.

I wake the next morning with a killer headache and smile at the painkillers and glass of water Tank has left on my bedside table. I down the pills and groggily make my way out of bed and down the hallway, following the smell of bacon and eggs. I greedily take my seat at the table, patiently waiting for Miller to stop burning the bacon.

"Mmm," I moan as my breakfast makes its way to my stomach.

I distantly notice conversation around me, but we all know I won't be participating until the pills have kicked in, breakfast is happily situated in my stomach, and a coffee has washed it all down.

Half an hour later, I join Dani on the couch, finally starting to feel like myself again. She is in the middle of recapping the story of our night while she gives Mia a bottle, and I grab my phone and start flicking through our photos, making sure to show Tank and Miller all the good ones. I'm busy scrolling when I notice a shitload of photos that definitely shouldn't be there.

"Holy shit," I gasp as I start flicking through them.

"What is it, babe?" Tank questions as he gets up and comes around the back of the couch to peer over my shoulder.

"It's all the photos of the documents I had on Baxter. They must have saved in the cloud thingy and downloaded when I connected it all yesterday."

"Fuck. Seriously?" he questions as he takes the phone from my hand and begins zooming in on the contract pages.

"Yeah, it's all there."

"That's awesome," Dani says from beside me.

"Sure fucking is," Tank murmurs with a satisfied grin. "It's one step closer to nailing the bastard."

With that, I make quick work of calling Detective Andrews and emailing through all the documents. The thought of reopening this case sends a shiver sailing down my spine, considering the risk behind it all. I just hope now that I'm in a good place, Baxter doesn't come after me for supplying evidence. But whatever happens will happen, and I'll be ready if he comes . . . Well, I have no idea how I'll be ready, but I know for damn sure the fucker won't be putting me in the hospital again.

By the afternoon, Tank and I are heading back to our place when I turn to him with a thought. "Maybe I should start working again," I tell him.

His whole face drops as he looks at me like I've gone crazy. "You're not seriously thinking of picking up the Baxter investigation again?"

My eyes widen at his comment. "God, no," I quickly rush out. "As much as I want to see him go down for everything, I want to stay away. Especially now things are good again," I explain. "What I meant was going back into the office and taking on little cases, like petty things. Just something to keep my mind busy during the day. I'll work back up to the good stuff when I'm ready."

He looks at me, knowing damn well I won't be able to resist jumping straight into the deep end the second I'm back in the office. "I don't know, babe," he says, thinking it over.

"What if I promised to talk to you about each case before I accept it? That way you know what I'm working on all the time. And if I need to leave the office, I'll let you know."

He's quiet for a while and sits still in the driver's seat, even after we've pulled into the driveway. "I'll make a deal with you," he starts. I look at him and wait for whatever genius plan he's come up with. "I'll be happy for you to go back to work if it's only minor cases, like nailing the dickhead who keeps running the red light on Main Street, and if you literally have no contact at all with the suspect. You've got to do it all undercover without the guy knowing you're writing the story."

I think it over for a bit before holding my hand out. He puts his hand in mine and shakes on the deal, both of us knowing that this isn't something that will keep me satisfied in the long run, but it's still something we can both agree on for now. "You realize you've just made my job a million times harder," I tell him.

"Yep," he declares.

"And you also know that the extra challenge is going to push me more," I warn him.

"I know," he sighs. "That's the part I'm worried about."

"Good," I smile. "Then you've got yourself a deal, big guy."

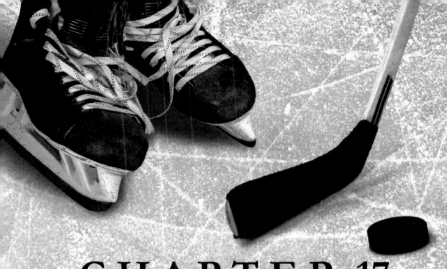

CHAPTER 17

TANK

I push the boys as hard as they can go. We're a few games into the season, and while we're still undefeated, I know we can do better. After all, those chicks that Sophie decided to beat up think I'm not good enough, so I'm going to bust my ass until I prove them wrong. Not just those bitches, but every last fucker who doubts me will soon learn who owns this fucking season.

Tank fucking Meyers is here to lead the LA Storm to victory, and come the end of the season, not one person will doubt me again. This'll be the best season the LA Storm will ever see.

I push myself to the limit as I put the boys through some sprints. I shoot up the length of the rink, keeping my puck firmly in sight before my blades cut through the ice and create an avalanche of shavings as

I come to a sudden stop, only to turn and push myself back up the other end.

My strides push me ahead of the other guys, and I hear their desperation as their blades cut through the ice, desperately trying to keep up with me. Miller included.

"Alright, boys. Bring it in," Coach finally says.

We all come into the center of the ice and drop down to one knee. The rink is silent apart from the boys' heavy panting as they try to catch their breaths. I look around the circle of guys, and see they are all a ragged mess of sweat. That's when I realize that I need to be pushing them harder in their cardio. They're all above where they need to be in their weights training, but they all fucking hate cardio.

Well, that shit is about to change. Cardio is about to become their bitch.

The LA Storm won't just be unbeatable. We're going to be the team that people think about when they think of the best. Coaches all over the world will be showing our plays to their teams because we're just that damn good. We'll be the fucking benchmark for success. We'll be the team that kids dream to be a part of, and those very same kids will work their asses off to make their dream come true and continue the great name of the LA Storm, just like I know my son would have.

I quit dreaming of the bright future this team has and concentrate on Coach Larsden as he gets stuck into today's plan. He splits us into two teams, placing myself and Miller as the leaders, wanting us to go over our new plays during a mock game.

I grin over at my best friend and see the challenge written in his eyes. The fucker thinks he's got this, and it's going to be pretty fucking amazing taking it from him.

Two newbies get the nets and place them in position at either end of the rink as a few of the guys collect the pucks scattered over the ice. A few minutes later, the timer is set and the whistle blows.

Two hours later, after one of the craziest training sessions we've ever had, I stand with Miller in the locker room, stripping off my training gear. "That last shot was a fluke," Miller says as he sits to untie his skates.

"Bullshit," I scoff, knowing damn well he's right, but I'm not about to admit that shit. "I'm too fucking good for a fluke. You're just out of sorts because you can't beat me anymore."

"Whatever," he mutters. "It was definitely a fluke."

I roll my eyes and quickly get myself showered and dressed before heading out to the parking lot with Miller. I'm telling him all about Sophie's deal for returning to work when he cuts me off.

"Holy shit, dude," he says as he gawks at the parking lot.

I look up and follow his line of sight straight to my truck, and my jaw drops. The shock of what I'm seeing quickly wears off, and morphs into red-hot fury.

The whole thing is trashed, and I don't mean someone backed into it trying to park. I mean that it's trashed in the Carrie Underwood "Think Before He Cheats" kind of way. All four tires slashed, and it looks like someone took a baseball bat to the windows and bodywork before finishing it off with a can of spray paint.

"Who the fuck would have done this?" Miller asks as we rush over to my truck to inspect the damage.

"I have no fucking idea, but whoever it was is going to pay," I tell him.

Miller looks over the spray paint, reading the words out loud. "Liar. Cheater. Dickhead," he says. "Dude, it sounds like a jealous girlfriend or something. Maybe the bitch got the wrong truck."

"Maybe," I grunt, taking in the damage to the grill.

"Fuck, man," Cameron says as he comes to look at my truck with a few of the other guys. "You've been up to no good, aye?" he questions with a smirk. "Got a side chick we don't know about?"

At that, I grab him by his shirt and slam him against the side of my fucked-up truck. "You ever suggest that I've been unfaithful to my wife again, and I'll kick your ass so hard that you'll never walk again."

"Shit, dude. I was just messing with you," he says, holding his hands up in surrender. "I know you wouldn't mess around on Sophie."

I narrow my eyes on the dickhead and see the sincerity in his eyes before letting him go. "Good," I grunt, as he takes two big steps away from me.

"Who do you think did it?" he questions.

"No clue," I say, as I notice nearly half the team has formed a semi-circle around the truck.

"Go check the surveillance. There's a camera pointing right at the team parking," Miller says.

Why the fuck didn't I think about that? I take off with Miller by my side because, let's face it, the fucker isn't going anywhere. He's now my ride home.

We make our way to the security section of the building and get them to pull up the footage. It doesn't take long before I see Crazy Jill appear on the screen carrying a bag and a baseball bat.

I cringe as I watch her approach my truck and start rubbing her body all over it, and from this angle, I'm pretty sure she just got off on my truck, squirting all over the fucking hood. Then, things change. She grabs the bag and bends down as she searches through it. She pulls out a knife and gets to work slashing the tires as if it is the most casual thing in the world.

Next comes the baseball bat, which honestly makes me look away. My stomach starts to turn as I then watch her go to town with the spray paint before climbing up in the bed. My brows furrow, unsure of what she's doing before she pulls her pants down and takes a massive shit right in the back.

"Ahh, fuck no," I groan, not even bothering to try and save it now.

"That bitch is fucking crazy," Miller mutters.

Damn straight. First, it's the constant calls and messages to me and Sophie, then she intrudes in our home and defiles it, and now she trashes my truck and takes a dump in the bed. Fucking hell. This shit has got to stop. I'm fucking over it.

Not to mention, I'll be putting in a complaint to the head of security at the rink. I mean, what the fuck have they been doing all afternoon while this shit was going down? How do they miss a crazy bitch swinging a bat and backing one out in the back of a fucking lifted truck?

We step out of the surveillance room and head back out to the parking lot as I call the police and get them to come and document the damage. They arrive in no time, and after I've given a statement, my beautiful truck is towed away, shit and all.

They explain as it's Crazy Jill's first offense against the restraining order, that she'll only be given a warning, and will obviously be lumped with the charges of the repairs to my truck. But come to think of it, I don't want a repaired truck. I want a brand-new one. One that isn't tainted by Crazy Jill.

Shortly after, Miller gives me a ride home, and I soon find myself spread out on the couch with Sophie on top of me as I tell her all about my afternoon.

"I swear, if I ever see that crazy as shit woman again, I'm going to give her the beat down of her life," Sophie vows with that gorgeous little crease between her eyebrows, suddenly thinking she's some kind of professional MMA fighter after her bar brawl.

"Calm down, woman. You gave a beat down a few days ago and got yourself locked up. I don't want you getting a reputation."

"What?" she shrieks. "I was defending your honor."

"I know, babe," I laugh. "But my honor doesn't need defending. Trust me, nothing is going to knock me down."

A grin creeps over my wife's face, and I know exactly what she's thinking. "You know, you're damn sexy when you talk like that."

"You mean when I talk with my ego?" I grin.

"Mmhmm," she murmurs as her lips come down to mine. "It's just that your ego is so damn big."

I let out a laugh as I hold my wife close to my body. "Fuck, I love you."

"I know," she smiles. "I'm just so damn loveable."

We lay silently on the couch, taking comfort in being in each other's arms, when Sophie lets out the softest sigh, and I run my hands down her back. "What is it, babe?" I question.

"Hmmm?" she murmurs as she raises her head to look at me.

"You're thinking about something."

"Oh," she says with another sigh. "I don't know. Dani kind of mentioned something today, and I don't know if it's a good idea or not."

"What's that?"

"That we should hold a little memorial for Tyler," she says.

"Why wouldn't it be a good idea?" I question, already completely on board and mentally running through all the things we could do to celebrate his short existence in our lives.

She shrugs her shoulders as she looks at me. "I guess because I was only five months pregnant. I mean . . . it's not like he was born yet. I don't know, maybe it's silly."

I sit up on the couch and bring Sophie up with me so she straddles my lap. "It's not silly. He was our son and he deserves a memorial just as much as any other person would. Just because he didn't get the chance to be born into this world, doesn't make him any less real."

"You think?" she asks. "I thought it would be a nice way to send him off and celebrate him. I wouldn't want it to be like a black-tie event where everyone is mourning and sad or anything like that."

"No, we'll make it special for him."

Sophie gives me a sad smile as she lets out a breath of relief. "And no one can wear black. That's a rule."

"Okay. I'll make sure everyone knows."

"No, not everyone," she says with a sudden shake of her head. "Just the closest people. Like the ones he would have called aunty or uncle."

"You got it, babe," I say, wrapping her up in my arms and pulling her in tight.

She rests her head on my shoulder. "I almost don't want to do it. It just . . . it makes it so final."

"Consider this his official send-off," I tell her. "But you also need to remember he's looking down on us, so it's never really goodbye."

I feel her head move against my shoulder as she gives a slight nod. "You know, if he was looking down on us when I was whooping that bitch's ass, he would have been so proud of his momma."

I can't help but laugh as I roam my fingers over her shoulder. "Damn straight he would have been."

Later that night, we settle into our usual routine as Sophie gets up to make dinner, and I watch her as she moves around the kitchen. Every last thing she does in there is completely wrong, and I know without a doubt that dinner is going to be awful. But she wanted to cook, so I'm rolling with it.

After watching her set the oven way too high, I decide it's time to intervene. I get up off the couch and make my way across the kitchen, and reach around her to lower the temperature on the oven as her body folds into mine.

"I hope you're not trying to take over the kitchen," she accuses in a sultry voice.

"No, just keeping it from burning down," I murmur into her ear as my hands travel down her body. Hell, she was in a nasty house fire during college and I'm not looking for any repeat performances of that night.

Sophie lets out a moan as she grips the kitchen counter and presses her body harder into mine. My hands come to the hem of her dress, and I slowly slide it up her legs before finding her underwear.

My hand snakes around the front of her body and slides down into the front of her panties to find her ready for me. "I wanted to wash up some of the dishes while dinner was cooking," she moans as she grinds her sweet pussy against my hand.

"Not a chance," I tell her, just as my fingers plunge deep into her cunt.

She lets out a surprised gasp, which quickly turns into another moan, and I watch as her grip on the counter tightens, her knuckles turning white. Then pulling my hand out of her panties, I grab her by the waist, quickly spin her around, and lift her onto the counter.

Sophie's hands greedily reach for my jeans and she makes quick work of freeing me, while I pull her dress up over her body and tear those panties right off.

As my jeans fall to the ground, I quickly step out of them and allow Sophie to pull my shirt over my head. As usual, her hand dives for my chest and abs while the other snakes around the back of my neck, holding on as her nails dig into my back. My cock trails through her wetness and we both groan, and as the need becomes too much, I thrust deep, plunging into her tight cunt, listening to the sweet sounds of her needy cries.

Not getting the angle I want, I lift her off the counter and press her up against the fridge. She lets out a squeal as the cool metal assaults her skin, but that doesn't stop her from holding on tighter and going along for the ride.

I fuck her hard and raw, both of us drowning in a sea of undeniable pleasure when she calls out for me to stop. "Seriously?" I question, stopping immediately.

"Oh, yeah. It's my turn," she says, and instructs me to take her to the couch where she can straddle me. The second she comes down on me, she forces me deeper, and I let out a groan, her tight cunt clenching around me. I raise my hips to meet her thrusts, but she pushes me back down. "Don't even think about it, big guy. This is my show now."

Fuck. I'm in trouble.

I halt my movements and watch as my wife rides me, unable to glance down between us, loving the way she takes all of me. I'm desperate for a release, but I know it won't come until Sophie decides she's good and ready, so I guess now it's my turn to hold on for the ride.

My hands roam over her perfect body, and I soon find my fingers dipping down to circle her clit. "Fuck," she screams. Knowing I can't possibly last much longer, I press down a little harder on her clit, which is just what she needs to go flying right over the edge.

Her body explodes around me as she clenches down on my

cock, allowing me to finally find that sweet release. I come hard as she continues riding out her orgasm, but I find myself paralyzed with pleasure as I pour myself into her, shooting hot spurts of cum deep into her pussy.

"Holy shit," she pants, as her head drops to my shoulder.

"You can say that again," I murmur, my hand curling around her back.

With a grin, she looks up at me, and I see those beautiful eyes sparkling with mirth. "I think dinner might have burned," she says, noticing the smell that's been filling the house for the last ten minutes.

"I know," I tell her, smirking up at her and taking in those dazzling blue eyes. "Don't stress. I watched you cooking it. It was going to be shit anyway. I ordered Chinese."

"What?" she shrieks, purposefully clenching around my cock and making me groan, her tight hold almost enough to drop a motherfucker.

"Yeah," I say, leaning forward and unlocking my phone to check the time. "It should be here soon, actually."

Soph lets out a huff as she climbs off my lap and heads into the bathroom to clean herself up. I get up and turn off the oven, retrieving our clothes from the kitchen floor in the process. I pull the oven door slightly ajar and peer in, wondering what the hell I'm supposed to do with the mess in the oven.

"I'm not eating your stupid Chinese," Sophie tells me as she comes striding back into the kitchen, finding her clothes on the counter. "You should have more faith in my cooking skills."

I pull open the oven door further so she can see the charred remains of her dinner perfectly, and a wicked grin crosses my face as her own falls flat. "Fuck," she groans. "I just want to get it right, just once."

"Babe," I say, slamming the door back into place and stepping into her arms. "Just face it. You can't cook. You've never been able to in the six years I've known you."

She lets out a huff. "I'm not ready to accept it yet."

"Well, you better hurry up. There's only so much more I can take of it."

"What do you mean? You eat my dinners all the time," she questions.

"Only because I love you," I tell her as the buzzer for the gate sounds. I press a gentle kiss to her forehead and excuse myself to make dinner like a real man. I press the buzzer and wait by the door for the delivery guy, and shortly after, I'm dishing up real food for a very grumpy, but starving, wife.

CHAPTER 18

SOPHIE

I wake up on Monday morning, more than ready for my new start. Today, I go back to work and get my shit together. The cast is gone, my ribs are healed, and my faith in myself is restored. I will no longer be the moping, grieving housewife. I'm a strong, independent woman, and while my heart still aches for my son, I need to keep moving forward.

After finishing in the shower, I pull on my blouse and skirt, the ones I know my husband can't resist. Not that it matters right now. He was up and gone for hockey training hours ago.

Heading into the kitchen, I make myself a piece of toast and a cup of coffee before turning and striding back down the long hallway. I sip at my coffee when I pass that one door that has remained closed for the past few months.

I become rooted to the ground, unable to continue as I turn to face the door, my heart racing. Before I realize what I'm doing, my hand falls to the handle. I must be insane right now, or maybe I just enjoy a bit of torture on a Monday morning. But either way, something deep inside is screaming at me that the time has come.

Turning the handle, I find myself stepping over the threshold into what should have been Tyler's nursery. A heaviness settles within my heart, but it's soon replaced with a strange fondness as I take in the empty room.

Tank must have come in here and cleared everything out for this exact reason. He knew I would come in here seeking some kind of comfort, but he would also know that it would remind me of everything I've lost. Had I done this any earlier, it would have killed me.

I step further into the room and sit down in the center of the carpet to finish my coffee. I can't explain it, but being here in this room makes me feel that much closer to my son. Which is ridiculous, right? It's just an empty room. One he didn't even get to use.

I place my mug down beside me and lean back onto my hands as I begin picturing where all the furniture was and how I would have decorated it, when I notice the closet door is slightly ajar.

My curiosity gets the best of me and I get up and make my way toward the closet. I open it up to find a basket filled with all the important things, like the first ultrasound picture, and one of the four positive pregnancy tests I'd taken all those months ago. I smile to myself as I take them in and make a mental note to thank Tank for not getting rid of these.

Searching through the basket, I pull out the very first outfit I bought for my little guy. It was right after the doctor's appointment when we found out we were having a boy. I immediately dragged Tank into the first baby store we came across. He went on and on about how he didn't want to be out baby shopping, but the second I pulled the tiny little outfit from the rack and held it up to him, a massive smile took over his handsome face. That moment will forever be ingrained in my mind, and I'm thankful for it because it was another precious moment I was given by my son.

An idea strikes, and I rush around the house to find a bag before striding straight back into the nursery. I put the ultrasound, the piss stick, and the outfit into the bag, and I place it in the hallway next to my handbag, which is when I realize the time.

I'm going to be late.

Feeling great about my idea, I rush down to my bathroom and get started on drying my hair and putting on a little makeup. A few minutes later, I decide this will have to do, and I slide my heels on.

Grabbing my handbag and the bag of baby things, I go to leave when I remember the photo Dani took of Tank and me when I was about four months pregnant. He had his arms wrapped around me and those big hands resting on my stomach while I looked up at him. Without even a second of hesitation, I dump my bags and run around the house like an idiot searching for the photo.

Finally, I head into the garage, checking and double-checking the house is properly locked up. After all, I just had my house scrubbed clean, I wouldn't want any crazy stalkers coming in and rubbing their nasty pussy juices all over my furniture again. Hell, knowing my luck, the bitch will break in and take a shit in one of my handbags.

After arriving at my office, I push my way through the door for the first time in three months, and I have to say, it kind of feels weird to be back here again. I dump my bag on the floor and take a look around. It's instantly clear that my office is not the way I left it. While everything is neat and tidy, it's also a big mess.

The first thing I notice is the new door and computer. My corkboard has a big crack through it, and my couch is in the wrong spot. On closer inspection, the papers on my desk have all been tossed together into a neat pile, and my desk drawers look as though they've been emptied and someone has thrown the stuff back in. The picture frames of my most daring articles have all been reframed and are back up on the wall . . . in the wrong order.

I consider leaving it the way it is and getting started on a new investigation, but I know better than that. There's no way in hell I'll be able to concentrate until this shit is sorted out.

With a sigh, I get started fixing up my office.

An hour later, I finish perfecting my workspace and boot up my new computer. I'm pleased to find the computer guy must have been in here and worked his magic. Everything is exactly how I had it on my last computer.

I click on my emails and wait as everything from the past three months attempts to load. While the emails slowly trickle in, I head out to the kitchen and start working on another coffee while I catch up with the other girls in the office. We get carried away with our mindless chatter, and I soon have to excuse myself to get back to work.

Pleased to find all my emails downloaded, I take a seat and start sorting through them.

One by one, I go through and unsubscribe from all the mailing lists about healthy babies and fetal development, then I delete them. I go through and remove all the emails from my sources about tips on new cases, not needing the temptation. Well, I only delete the ridiculous ones and the ones that could potentially get me into trouble again. The ones that Tank would deem too dangerous, but the ones I feel really need to be investigated are forwarded to the next best in the business, leaving me with the shitty but super easy ones.

Though I have to say, it won't be that easy now that Tank has demanded I do it all with Harry Potter's invisibility cloak. I have no idea how I'm going to make this work, but I guess I'll have to be creative.

After printing off the few tips that I can actually work with, I start doing a little research on my new scumbags, and by lunch, I've nearly got one solved, and the rest are well underway.

Feeling a bit claustrophobic in my office, I head out for lunch and find a little café to eat at while sitting outside in the warm LA sun. I decide to head to the mall after, pushing my way through the door of Frisky Framing. The little bell above the door chimes as I make my way up to the counter.

The guy behind the counter looks me up and down as an interested grin takes over his face, and I briefly consider walking straight back out the door. I'm not sure I want to trust this guy with my most precious possessions.

I can't help but look him over as he brings his hands down on the counter and leans forward. I start at the top and make my way down, taking in his unwashed, unbrushed man bun, his tanned skin that's also peeling from what must have been a very nasty sunburn, down past the long scrawny body that I'm pretty sure I'd be able to see his ribcage through, and finishing off on the toneless, chicken arms supporting his weight on the counter.

I can't help but groan, knowing he's going to try to hit on me. I can't think why he even thinks he stands a chance. I'm married to a man who's at least four times his size, and has the whole dark, smoldering thing going for him. This guy looks as though he owns one of those hippy vans that breaks down on the highway with a surfboard on top.

I finish making my way toward the counter and begin rifling through my bag, searching for my other bag filled with my baby things while his grin becomes wider and his eyes become hooded.

Ugh. My gaze quickly scans the shop to check if there are any other employees, but just my luck, I'm stuck with Man Bun.

"Hey," he says as he gives me a slight nod. "What brings such a beautiful woman like you into my store?"

I ignore his flirty comments as I dump my little bag on the counter. "I need this stuff arranged into a frame."

"Uhh . . ." he starts as he rips his eyes away from mine and down to the counter. "Sure . . . wait. Is that a . . ."

"A piss stick? Yes," I confirm.

His face scrunches up in disgust. "You can't put that there," he informs me.

"Seriously?" I groan. "You think I'm getting around with dripping piss in my handbag? It's clean. Can you do it or not?"

"Yeah," he sighs. "What were you looking for?"

I rattle off the few ideas I have floating around in my head and leave him with it while also giving him specific instructions on being careful with my things.

I give him a friendly smile before turning away, making my way to the door when he calls out to me.

"Ahh, Sophie, is it?"

I turn back around and look at him, unsure of what he could want. I mean, I've already given him all my ideas and have already paid. "Um, yeah?"

"You, ahh . . . wouldn't fancy going on a date? Maybe dinner tonight?"

Is this guy kidding me? After I just showed him the picture of my husband cradling my baby bump, my piss stick, and an ultrasound, he still wants to ask me out. At least the guy has balls.

"I'd love to go out on a date . . . with my husband," I tell him.

He gives me a tight smile and a nod. "Fair enough," he says before looking away.

I take that as my cue to leave and dash back out of the store, a little too excited about the final product. Hopefully, it doesn't take too long to put together. Though one thing's for sure, I can't wait to surprise Tank with it.

I make my way back to the office and give Dani a quick call, letting her know all about my little project. Soon enough, I find myself back behind my desk, searching for new and improved spyware and bugs that I could use in my new investigative techniques.

By the afternoon, I stumble in through my front door and dump my bag right next to Tank's. I make my way down into the living room and instantly collapse into his lap. "Holy shit, I'm exhausted," I say as he wraps his arms around me and pulls me into his body so I can lay back.

"Big first day back?" he asks.

"You can say that," I grunt. "I've already got three ongoing investigations."

"Three?" he questions. "You never work on more than one at a time."

"I know," I sigh. "But I'm playing by your rules now and only taking the easy ones. The first one's basically done. I just have to put the article together. The other two will be finished by the end of the week. Besides, after taking so much time off, my inbox is crawling with new leads."

His dark eyes narrow on me for a moment before he finally speaks up. "So, how are you solving the cases so quickly?" he questions in a strange, knowing tone.

A grin cuts across my face. "That's for me to know and for you to never find out."

"Really now?"

"Mmhmm," I murmur as I adjust myself on his lap so I can face him properly.

He grins back at me with a sparkle in those sexy eyes. "Interesting."

I narrow my stare on him, his tone suspicious as hell. "What's interesting?" I question as his fingers come up and push a stray lock of hair behind my ear.

"Well, I got a call from the bank today. They informed me that they thought someone was fraudulently using our account to buy a shitload of spyware."

"Really?" I question, feeling like a fucking queen as I somehow manage to keep a straight face. "That is interesting."

Tank rolls his eyes as he pulls me in close to his chest. "Just be careful with that shit," he tells me. "I don't want you getting in trouble with it."

"I will," I say, leaning in and pressing a comforting kiss to his lips before resting my head on his shoulder. His hand starts rubbing up and down the length of my back as he turns the TV to ESPN and finds a game. He turns the volume down, and I soon find myself falling into a deep, well-needed sleep.

CHAPTER 19

TANK

I sit among our closest friends after a beautiful memorial that Sophie and I held for our son. Both our families managed to make the trip here from Denver, which was great. Sophie really needed her mom by her side today. Unfortunately, they've all had to head back home, but it was still great seeing them.

After the service, everyone headed back to our place where I surprised Sophie with a plaque with our son's name and conception date on it. I purposefully left off the day he was taken from us. I'm not sure that reminder would have been good for Soph, especially after the day she's had.

Most of the guys from the team have come and gone, leaving just the few closer ones and of course, Dani and Miller are never far away.

We all sit in our living room, and the girls have hit the liquor hard, while the rest of us hockey guys are taking it easy, seeing as though we're in training.

"Remember when Sophie came busting into the locker room after that game and burst into tears," Cameron smirks as he looks at Sophie.

She grabs a potato chip from the bowl in the center of the coffee table and launches it across the room at him. "Shut up," she grins. "I was hormonal. I couldn't help it."

"You think that's bad," Dani says as she throws back another shot. "I had to be the one to massage her boobs when they were hurting."

"Doesn't sound so bad to me," I murmur with a grin.

"Really?" Dani questions. "I'm sure you'd absolutely love it when she's sobbing and throwing up all over you at the same time?"

I can't help but cringe as I look to my wife for confirmation. "Surely that didn't happen?" I question.

Sophie gives me a guilty, embarrassed smile as the rest of the guys crack up into howling laughter. "That morning sickness really is a bitch," she tells me.

"I second that," Dani pipes up.

"Whatever," Miller grunts to his wife. "You didn't have it that bad."

"Are you kidding me?" Dani shrieks, her brows practically flying through the ceiling.

"Yeah, you threw up a few times. That's it."

Dani's jaw drops to the ground as she stares at her husband in shocked silence, making the rest of us worry that she's about to explode. Thankfully, it never comes because Sophie is quick to defend her best friend. "What would you stupid boys know anyway? Apart from sex, your bodies are practically useless. We have to suffer through ovulation, period pains, and nine months of pregnancy, only to then destroy our bodies by pushing a fucking watermelon through our vaginas. And just when you think the hard work is over and you can finally enjoy your little creation, we're used as a tiny human's personal feed bag."

Sophie finishes up her declaration by taking another shot while Dani gets to her feet beside her. "Fuck, yeah," she exclaims as she fist-pumps the sky.

Miller and the rest of the guys sit in stunned silence as they stare at our girls.

"Are you done, babe?" I ask.

Her fuming eyes turn on me, and the anger instantly dissipates. "Yes, I think I am," she tells me with a grin, turning to Dani with a gleam in her eye that could only be one of mischief. She grabs Dani by the hand and disappears from the room, taking the bottle of tequila with them.

"Ahh, shit," Miller murmurs. "It's going to be a messy night."

"Got that right," I say. "But as much as it goes against everything I know to sit back and watch Sophie annihilate herself, I know she needs it."

"True," he says. "But if they somehow get themselves arrested again, I'm going to bail them out. There's no way in hell I'm missing that shit again."

"Deal," I smirk.

I sit among the boys, and as expected, the conversation quickly turns to hockey.

An hour later, after not hearing a word from the girls, I decide to go check on them to make sure they haven't passed out in a pile of their own vomit.

I follow the sound of giggling and snorts coming from our home office and then round the corner to find both Sophie and Dani sitting on the floor, looking at Sophie's laptop while they listen to what sounds like the conversation the boys and I were having in the living room.

I lean against the door frame and look down on them with a smirk, watching as they continue on with whatever the fuck it is they're doing, having no clue that I'm here.

After they each take another swig from the bottle of tequila, I make my presence known by clearing my throat, and they both look up as their faces drain of color. I raise a questioning brow at my wife. "What the hell are you doing?"

"Nothing," she grins as she fumbles around, trying to close her laptop.

Dani bursts into laughter and is suddenly rolling around on the floor, unable to control herself before she slaps a hand between her legs. "Fuck, I'm going to piss myself," she laughs, which sets off Sophie.

Once the girls have themselves under control, I look down at my wife. "Did you bug our living room with your new spyware?" I ask.

She squishes her lips together as hard as humanly possible as she tries not to smile. "Nope," she lies. I give her a stare as I wait for her to come clean. "Fine," she admits as she crawls across the room and grabs a little device off her desk before dropping it and losing it in the carpet. "I had to make sure these little guys actually worked," she explains.

"Fair enough," I laugh. "What about your laptop?"

She gives me yet another guilty smirk. "Well, I, umm . . . Don't be mad, but I've kind of been learning how to hack into other people's computers."

"What?" I grunt.

A massive grin takes over her face. "I'm in Crazy Jill's computer right now," she tells me as she opens her laptop and turns it to show me.

"Shit, seriously?" I ask, pretty damn impressed with my wife's newest skills. I walk into the office and sit at Sophie's desk while I take the laptop out of her hands and start looking.

"Yeah. She really is crazy obsessed with you," Sophie says. "I looked up her browser history and she has been searching for the Tank Meyers sex tape for weeks," she laughs.

I can't help but grin at that. I mean, it's not like Sophie and I haven't got a sex tape. We actually have quite a few to be honest, but there's no way in hell we're letting that shit go public. Seeing my wife like that is just for me.

I click into her gallery and find nearly every photo is of me. It's not just photos of me that the media have taken, though they're certainly here too. The photos are ones that she's personally taken of me—and not just at games either. There are some of me training in the gym, some where I'm grocery shopping with Soph, there are ones from my few hours of sitting in the airport waiting for my flight to get to Denver, but more importantly, there's one of me sitting by Sophie's bedside in the hospital with my head in my hands as I waited for her to wake from surgery.

My gaze automatically falls to Sophie on the screen, taking in the state Baxter left her in with her half-deflated stomach. The very day our son was taken from us.

Seeing the photo infuriates me. That was a private moment not intended for a single soul to have witnessed, and now this crazy bitch has it documented for the world to see. "Can you delete this shit?" I ask Sophie.

"Yeah, but she will know someone has been in her computer, and knowing how damn crazy she is, she probably has a backup, and a backup for the backup."

I let out a sigh. She's probably right, but at least this is a start. "I don't care. Get rid of it," I tell Soph.

"No," Dani cries out.

We both look at her with questioning stares. "Why the fuck not?" I ask.

"Because it could be evidence if shit ever gets worse. This is the perfect way to document just how fucking crazy she is. It's proof of just how often she's stalking you. Plus, if you keep an eye on it and notice anything new, you'll have proof that she's violated the terms of the restraining order."

"Wow. Who would have known that your brain could still function after having so much tequila," I tease.

"Who cares about her brain," Sophie grunts as she takes her laptop and sits down in my lap. "It's a damn good idea," she informs us as she gets to work.

Dani grins wide, more than proud of herself. "See, not just a pretty face."

Ten minutes later, Sophie has shut down her laptop, and I'm leading the girls back into the living room where Sophie cuts off all conversation of ice hockey and turns the music on. She starts dancing around the house with her bottle of tequila and her best friend, both of them rocking out and having the time of their lives.

Some of the guys join in, but they simply aren't drunk enough to keep up with the girls.

Sophie's soon laying on the cold tiles with her arms and legs spread out, telling the guys how she would have made snow angels with our son before explaining how to make a snow angel. Just in case they've never heard of the concept before.

Dani runs to the pantry and grabs the bag of flour before instructing Sophie to close her eyes before tipping the bag upside down and spinning around, making it snow flour in my living room. The girls crack into laughter once again, and soon enough, the bag of flour is empty and Dani is laying on the ground beside Sophie, making a flour angel of her own.

Miller rolls his eyes as he watches his wife on the floor beside mine, but I see the spark in his eyes. He could never pass up an opportunity to see his wife having the time of her life. "I take it I'm not getting laid tonight," he grunts when Dani suddenly jumps up and runs to the bathroom, covering her mouth.

"That would be a no," I laugh just as Sophie does the exact same thing.

Miller scoffs, far too amused. "Looks like I'm not the only one."

CHAPTER 20

SOPHIE

Fuck me. My head is killing me.

It's first thing on Monday morning, and using all of yesterday to recover from my tequila-filled night was clearly not enough time. I stumble around the house, desperately trying to keep my head attached to my shoulders, when I give up and call work.

Knowing it's too early for anyone to be in the office, I give our receptionist, Jen, a call on her cell. It rings a few times before she picks up in a way-too-cheery voice for so early on a Monday.

"Sophie, hey. How are you?"

"Ugh. Do you need to be so loud?" I whine.

"Geez," she laughs. "I heard you had a big night on Saturday, but I didn't realize just how big."

"Yeah," I sigh. "It was huge."

"So, I'm guessing you're working from home today?" she questions.

"Well, I'm going to try to," I tell her honestly. "Who knows how much work I'll actually get done."

She lets out another laugh. "Okay. Well, let me know if you need anything."

"Thanks, Jen," I say before ending the call and collapsing onto the couch.

Just knowing that I don't have to get my shit together today makes me feel a million times better, but I should at least try to get a little work done. Though, it can wait until I've had a few more hours of sleep.

I head back to bed and climb straight in. My head hits the pillow, and within moments, I'm falling straight back into a well-needed, deep sleep.

I'm woken a few hours later by my phone ringing on the bedside table, and I grab it to find Dani's name on the screen. With a groan, I try my best to sit up and answer the call.

"What do you want?" I mumble into the phone. "I'm trying to sleep."

"I can't handle it today," she whines. "Mia has a temperature, and I haven't quite recovered from Saturday night yet."

"Me either."

"I'm assuming that since you're sleeping, you're home? Can we come around? I'll bring lunch and we can take care of this baby together."

I let out a groan. "Fine, but lunch better be good."

"Thank, fuck," she sighs in relief. "Are you good with hamburgers?" she questions. "I can't be bothered to actually make something."

"Yeah," I say before hanging up the phone and crashing back down on my pillow.

Half an hour later, I hear Dani unlocking my front door and the sound of Mia's cries instantly fill my home.

I pull myself out of bed and slide on my bunny slippers before making my way down the hallway. I find Dani and Mia in the kitchen, and I walk in after them to the smell of my lunch, making my stomach grumble. Mmmmm, that's good.

I take the screaming baby from Dani and curl her in my arms. "What's wrong, my little princess?" I soothe.

She looks up at me with tears in those big blue eyes and the sight breaks my heart.

"She's been like this since the middle of the night," Dani tells me as she searches my cupboards for some plates.

My heart breaks further. Mia's so tiny. It's not fair for her to be suffering from this sort of pain. If there was a way I could take it from her and make the pain my own, I'd do it in a heartbeat. "Have you taken her to the doctor?" I ask as I slowly rock her in my arms.

"Yeah, the home doctor came out during the night. There's not much we can do for her besides letting her rest and waiting it out," she tells me. "She wasn't calming down at home, so I thought I'd try you. She always seems to relax with you."

I smile down at the precious gem in my arms. "That's because I'm your favorite person in the whole wide world," I tell her in my baby voice as I walk her to the couch and take a seat, snuggling her close to my chest.

"No way. She loves her mommy the most. You come in a close second though," Dani says as she brings our lunch over to the couch and sits down beside us. "Maybe her daddy in third."

"I don't know what your mommy's talking about," I tell Mia. "She must have taken a trip to crazy town."

Dani ignores me as she dives into her lunch, and I do the same, struggling with only being able to use one hand. An hour later, after a lot of rocking and soothing, we manage to get Mia settled into a deep sleep.

After placing Mia down in the little makeshift bed Dani made for her, I find Dani spread out on the couch just moments from falling asleep, and a small smile pulls at my lips.

Leaving her be, I go about the house, cleaning up after lunch and collecting all of Mia's toys and pacifiers that are spread out over the living room. Deciding I should at least do a little work today, I make my way into the office and get stuck into my investigations as I allow Dani some time to catch up on her rest.

I'm an hour in when a call comes through on my phone. I look down with a frown, not recognizing the number.

"Hello?" I say with a questioning tone.

"Hi, uhh . . . is this Sophie? It's Luke from Frisky Framing," the voice says.

Understanding dawns instantly. "Oh, hi. Yes, it's me. What can I do for you?"

"I was just calling to let you know your frame is ready," Luke says.

"Already?" I ask in surprise. "I wasn't expecting that for another week or so."

"Yeah, I know," he says sheepishly. "I sort of put a rush order on it."

"Oh," I say, slightly taken aback. "You didn't need to do that."

"Well, yeah, actually, I did. Consider it an apology after I awkwardly hit on you last week when you made it obvious you have a husband and a kid."

I don't want to go into the details of correcting him, so I let it slide. "Thanks," I say. "I have a free afternoon. Can I get it today?"

"Yeah, sure. It's pretty big though," he warns. "You got a big car?"

"Sure do," I smile before ending the call, an excited rush pulsing through my body. I can't wait to see how it turned out. Tank is going to be so surprised, and I know he's going to love it.

Excitement fills me as I try to get back into my work, but I can't concentrate. Deciding to give up for the day, I dash down to my room to get dressed before coming back out to the living room and gently rocking Dani's shoulder. "Mmm?" she questions with her eyes still firmly closed.

"I'm ducking out for a half hour. Are you good here?" I ask, trying to be as quiet as possible as to not wake little Mia. Though, her soft snores let me know she is truly out of it.

"Yeah," Dani mumbles as she adjusts herself on the couch, clearly not very comfortable.

"Why don't you go climb in my bed?" I suggest. "I'll bring Mia in with you. I'm sure you'll both be much more comfortable."

Dani lets out a deep breath as she pushes herself up off the couch, looking as though she has no idea what's going on. "Good idea," she murmurs before sleepily making her way down the hallway, dragging her feet. Carefully scooping up the napping bundle off the ground, I take her down to my bedroom and slide her in beside her momma.

I can't help but gaze at them together, and I'm hit with a wave of grief crashing over me. I back away, unable to take it a second longer. I hurry out the front door, making sure to lock up behind me before I'm in my car and pulling up outside Frisky Framing.

I push through the door of the little store and instantly come to a screeching halt. My frame leans up against the front counter, and my God, it is big. Much bigger than I anticipated. My gaze roams over the piece and I take in the picture of Tank and me that has been blown up and printed in black and white.

The picture perfectly captures the love we have for each other, and also the love we have for our child as Tank cradles my stomach, forever protecting him.

A tear slides down my cheek as I make my way closer to the counter. "Hey, Sophie," the framing guy says. "Do you like it?"

I look up at him with a beaming smile. "It's absolutely perfect," I tell him with complete honesty.

"Excellent."

I look at the pure size of it and realize there's no way I'll be getting this home by myself, so I look up at Luke with my man-eating smile.

"Do you mind helping me get it to the car?" I ask.

I have to stop myself from laughing at the way he stares before he's able to pull himself together. "Oh, um, yeah. Of course," he says as he comes around the front of the counter and helps me lift this bad boy.

We make it outside and he balances the frame against the glass window of the store as I quickly go through my car and put the back seats down.

After a lot of maneuvering and struggling, we finally get it stashed in the back, and I close the door to thank him when I hear a voice calling out from across the street.

"Hey," the angry voice roars, demanding my attention.

I turn around and practically drop my jaw in shock at the person I see storming toward me. Crazy Jill rushes across the road, and doesn't come to a stop until she's right up in my face.

"Umm . . . Can I help you?" I question as I take a step back to give myself a little personal space, but all that does is back me into my car and make me appear scared of the crazy bitch.

"Yeah, you can," Jill says, raising her finger and jabbing me hard in the chest. "You can back the fuck off," she demands.

Ahh, fuck. Here we go with this shit again.

I grab her finger and give it a hard twist away from my chest and use every bit of my willpower not to rub the spot she just jabbed. Regretting my choice of stepping back into my car, I push myself forward, forcing her to take a step away from me. "Back off?" I question. "Look who's talking," I practically laugh at her.

"Tank is mine," she tells me like the crazy bitch she is. "He's wasting his time on you, and now that your kid is dead, you can stop trapping him and he can finally see that he belongs to me."

No. She. Fucking. Didn't.

"Excuse me?" I question as I get in her face and start backing her into the wall of Frisky Framing. "How dare you mention our child."

"Please," she scoffs. "It probably wasn't his anyway. His child wouldn't be weak like yours was. I couldn't have been happier that day. I followed him to the hospital, and it was like all my dreams came true. But I swear, I could have killed you for making him feel that way. I would never do that to him. You don't deserve him."

I see nothing but red as she continues spurting out crap, but a voice to my side pulls me out of my rage-fueled anger. "Ahhh . . . I'll leave you to it, Sophie," Luke says, with both hands raised, letting me know he wants nothing to do with this.

"Yeah, thanks," I grunt as I turn my attention back to Jill, tears of rage filling my eyes, unable to believe that anyone, even this crazy bitch, is so fucking shallow as to say such nasty things about my sweet baby boy.

"Just great. You're fucking cheating on my man," Jill continues as she looks at Luke's retreating form. "How much do you plan on hurting him? I can't believe he's so blind to this shit," she says with a shake of her head.

"You're fucking nuts," I laugh. "Tank. Is. My. Husband. He married me. He made vows. He comes home every day to me. He is mine and will never ever will he be yours. So get the fuck over this crazy obsession you have with my husband and find one of your own because he's not going anywhere. He's not interested in a bat-shit crazy stalker like you," I tell her. "Didn't you get the hint with the restraining order?"

I watch as her face goes bright red and she clenches her jaw together. Jill's hands turn into fists at her side, but I just don't care. This woman spoke ill of my son, so she's going to get every single one of my opinions thrown her way, and if she doesn't shut her mouth, I'll be throwing something a little more substantial at her.

"He's going to leave you. He's in love with me," she yells.

"The day he leaves me would be the day he takes his final breath. I have done literally everything possible to fuck up my marriage, yet he still stands by me," I tell her. "Is that not proof enough? He has had every chance to leave me, yet he doesn't. You know why? Because he fucking loves me, and he shows me every day when he comes home and fucks me until my legs shake."

Reaching her breaking point, she lets out an ear-shattering scream and runs full force into me, slamming us back into my car before we both fall to the ground. She comes down on top of me, and I try my best to push her off, my body still not completely recovered from the attack.

Jill holds on, and suddenly a dull, aching pain cuts through my forearm. My stare drops to my arms to find the bitch fucking biting me. Like what the actual fuck? Is she a fucking toddler? Who the hell bites someone in a fight?

Raging fury rocks through me, and I decide I've had enough. I don't need to be shit-faced this time to start throwing punches. No one gets away with knocking me down in a public street, airing my dirty laundry, and fucking biting me for the world to see.

With my leg squarely between hers, I bring my knee up and nail her in the cooch, which is enough for her to release the death grip her teeth have on my arm. Jill lets out a roaring cry and with the distraction of her aching pussy, I'm able to push her off, but she keeps coming for me, sending a fist flying straight for my face.

I move away as quickly as I can, but I still get nailed in the shoulder, and I hear the distinct sound of people in the street starting to gather around. Some are calling for help while others are letting the world know there's a catfight.

One thing I know for sure is that sooner or later, someone is going to break this shit up, and I refuse to let that happen before I finally have the chance to put this bitch in her place.

As she comes back toward me, I raise my leg and kick it out, smacking the bitch right in the tit and sending her flying back on her ass to the middle of the sidewalk. Not nearly done with her, I scramble up and leap toward her before straddling her waist and letting every bit of my weight come down on top of her. Rearing my arm back, I let my fist fly free. It shoots straight and connects hard against her jaw with a devastating blow. I give her a second and then a third for good measure.

One for me. One for Tank. And one for my son.

"This is your last fucking warning," I tell her. "Tank is not interested in a delusional twat like you. Leave him the fuck alone. Stop harassing him at training. Stop calling him. Stop messaging him. Stop breaking into our home. Stop fucking stalking him everywhere he goes because I swear to you, if you don't, I will fuck you up."

Her eyes open wide, and I see the very moment she understands just how serious I am. Jill doesn't agree, but at least I get the feeling she might back off a bit. For now.

Leaning down, I press my weight against hers as I use her body as a crutch to get to my feet. There are cheers coming from the men standing by, and I cringe as I notice that a few of the people have been recording the whole thing. Great. Just my fucking luck.

Taking a step away from Crazy Jill, I look down at her to make sure she's staying down. Once I'm completely satisfied, I make my way to my car, because this is now the last place on earth I want to be.

I reach for the door handle when an approaching person clears his throat.

What now?

With a groan, I look up to see none other than Detective Andrews staring right at me. "Don't even think about it, Soph," he says, pointing to my car.

"You can't be serious?" I grunt.

"Sorry," he says with a tight smile.

"No," I say, shaking my head and refusing to go with him. "This is all on her," I say pointing to Jill on the ground. "She's the one we have a restraining order against."

"Yes, I realize this, and she's being taken in too, but I can only go by what I've witnessed, and that was you threatening this woman after punching her three times."

"Seriously?" I groan. "You're telling me you missed the rest?"

He nods, giving me a tight smile, though I know he's secretly enjoying this. "Unfortunately."

"Fuck," I mutter before looking around at the crowd and trying to search out one of the dickheads who was filming, but they've all scattered at the sight of the cops.

"Come on," Detective Andrews says. "Let's get this shit over with so you can get home."

"Fine," I murmur, letting out a heavy sigh as I follow him to his car. He reaches for the door handle of the back seat, and I give him a look. "You're seriously going to make me sit in the back like some kind of criminal?"

"Damn straight," he says as a wicked grin stretches wide across his stupid face.

I let out a frustrated groan and climb into the backseat, trying to figure out just how I'm going to explain this one to my husband.

CHAPTER 21

TANK

I finish tying up my skates and am heading for the locker room door when my phone starts buzzing in my locker. My eyes quickly snap to the clock, and I realize that I have all of thirty seconds before Coach is busting my ass to be on the ice.

Ducking back to my locker, I grab the phone, only to realize it's coming from an unknown number. I go to put it down, but after everything that's gone down with Sophie over the past few months, I think better of it and answer the call.

"Hello," I say into my phone, hoping whoever this is can keep it quick.

"Babe," my wife's hesitant voice says through the receiver.

"Soph?" I question. "What's up?"

She lets out a heavy sigh and I prepare myself. "Don't be mad," she warns me.

"Mad?" I grunt, taken aback. "Babe, what's going on? I'm supposed to be on the ice," I tell her, hoping to hurry her along.

"I sort of got myself arrested again," she admits.

"What?" I rush out before quickly glancing around, realizing my tone has caught the attention of a few of the guys. "What the fuck Sophie? What did you do?"

"Hey," she demands as she starts to get defensive. "I told you not to get mad. It's not even my fault. I can't help it that you have a crazy as fuck stalker."

Fuck. That could only mean one thing. I sit down and squish the phone between my shoulder and cheek as I start undoing my skates. "What did that bitch do now?" I question with a sigh.

"It's a long story," she tells me. "Can you come get me? It's fine if you can't. I can call Dani instead, but Mia's not well."

"Yeah, babe," I say. "Hang tight. I'll be there in a bit."

She lets out a breath of relief and ends the calls. I throw my phone back into my locker and rush through the process of getting all my gear off. After getting myself dressed, I grab my phone, keys, and wallet before dashing out to the rink.

"Tank?" Coach hollers across the ice. "Why the fuck are you not on this ice running drills?"

Fuck. I stop in my tracks as I turn to face him, knowing I've already taken enough time off the ice recently. He practically bolts across the ice to get to me, trying to catch me before I get the chance to slip away.

"Sophie got arrested," I tell him. "I need to bail her out."

"Fuck," he grunts in surprise. "What'd she do?"

"Not really sure," I say. "But it has something to do with Crazy Jill."

"Shit. That can't be good. I hope your woman put her in her place," he says before giving me a stern look. "Go get her, then get your ass right back here. We have a game tomorrow night."

"Yes, Coach," I say with a nod before sprinting out the door.

I'm soon pushing my way through the door of the police station and signing all sorts of papers to bail my wife out of jail . . . again.

I'm led down to the cells and find Sophie behind bars, slumped on a bench with her arms crossed over her chest. She looks up the second I walk through the door, and her face instantly lights up, though there's a huge difference from the last time I caught her in here.

A woman in the cell beside hers throws herself to her feet and flies toward the bars, latching on with both hands. I recognize her immediately, and a heavy scowl takes over my face. "Tank," Crazy Jill sighs. "Thank you. I knew you would come for me."

Sophie's scoff from the next cell has my eyes flashing back to her. "Fucking delusional," she mutters, making a smirk cross my face.

I walk up to her cell and she instantly gets to her feet and comes forward. I squeeze my arms through so she can fold into me the best she can. "Are you okay?" I ask as I check her over.

"Yeah," she says. "I just want to get out of here."

"Agreed."

Sophie pulls out of my arms as the cop goes about unlocking the cell.

"What?" Jill shrieks as she bangs her hands against the bars. "What are you doing? Why are you helping her? You're supposed to be here for me. It's my turn, Tank. I love you."

Jesus. When will this shit end with this woman?

Sophie turns to face her, but I put my hand on her shoulder to stop her. This is my fight, not Sophie's, and I should have dealt with it myself rather than letting it fall on her like this. I walk up to the bars, directly in front of Jill, but make sure to keep my distance. The last thing I want is this crazy bitch reaching out and touching me.

I give her a venomous stare and enjoy it as she shrinks away from me. "There is no you and me, Jill. It's all in your messed-up head. I don't love you. In fact, I don't even like you. I never have, and I certainly never will," I tell her. "You need to back the fuck off. I can handle you harassing me, but now you've taken this shit too far. No one touches my wife and gets away with it. Do you fucking understand me?"

I watch as the color drains from her face, and she visibly swallows. She doesn't say a word, so I push her further. "I asked you a question, Jillian," I roar. "You've got three fucking seconds to answer it."

She manages to pull her shit together and hastily nods her head.

I narrow my eyes on her further, just to make sure she's got my point as a soft hand slips into mine, my wife appearing at my side. "Come on, let's go home. It's over now."

I turn to Sophie and put my arm around her shoulder. "Okay," I murmur, as I let her lead me out.

We leave Jill behind us, hopefully never to be seen or heard from again, and make our way back to the main part of the police station. I leave Sophie to grab her things when Detective Andrews approaches us.

Sophie instantly gives him a scowl that has him shrinking back, but it just manages to turn me the fuck on. "Ahh, could I see you both in my office?" he asks. "I have an update on the Baxter case."

The scowl disappears from Sophie's face as she practically runs and drags me into his office. He takes a seat behind his desk while Sophie and I make ourselves comfortable in the stiff chairs opposite his. "What did you find out?" Sophie questions, not skipping a beat.

"Wow, you don't waste a second," Andrews comments, and I'm glad she doesn't. I'm all too aware of the fact I'm supposed to be on the ice right now.

"Don't try to be cute. You're still on my shit list. Just answer my question," Sophie demands.

"Watch it, babe. The bastard might arrest you again," I murmur.

"He wouldn't fucking dare," Sophie grunts as she fixes him with another fierce scowl.

I watch in amusement as Detective Andrews swallows and fixes his tie, before finally recovering enough to get to the reason why we're here. "So, Sophie, the images you managed to recover from your cloud were enough to get us a search warrant, and while that didn't bring up much, we were able to find Baxter's connection with the two men who entered your home. Oliver Jensen and Blake Casey. Jensen was on his third strike and cracked during interrogation, providing us with a signed, full confession, so we have Baxter and his hired help on assault charges. There's no way they won't stick."

Holy shit. That's amazing. I look over at Sophie just as she does the same. The relief is evident on her beautiful face as she reaches out a hand and laces her fingers through mine. I squeeze her hand and she repeats the gesture, squeezing mine right back. "What about the dead CEOs?" she questions.

He gives us a proud smile as he begins his explanation, and I can't help but feel he has good news. "That was the tricky part," Andrews starts. "The evidence you supplied was helpful, but not quite enough to make anything stick, as you would know. However, his receptionist, Aimee, had some holes in her story, mainly regarding Baxter's alibi. It never seemed to quite match up, so we got her into interrogation and she admitted she lied. That left Baxter with no alibi for all three occasions," he tells us.

"So, you were able to place him at the locations?" Sophie asks.

"Sure were. Once there was enough reasonable doubt, we were able to get a warrant for the security footage of the night Marco Cincinnati died at the brothel. The footage showed Baxter at the site, paying off the security guard who disabled the cameras. However, he failed to disable the camcorder feeds in the private rooms, probably because he didn't know they existed. Baxter was seen an hour before Marco's death, handing a stash of drugs and cash to a sex worker before disappearing. The footage then shows the same woman pumping Marco full of drugs all night long. Even if there wasn't such a large array of drugs involved, the sheer quantity was enough to kill him."

"Holy shit," I grunt as I turn to Sophie. "You were right. You got him."

She beams back at me. "Aren't I always right?" she questions with a smug grin, something I've missed seeing from her over the past few months.

"Not even close," I laugh.

Andrews clears his throat to gain our attention, and we reluctantly turn back to him. "With further digging, we've managed to get him on all three murders. Same MO: cutting security feeds and sneaking onto the premises," he tells us. "So, I guess it was all worth it in the end."

"Worth it?" I spit in shock, unable to believe what just came out of the fucker's mouth. "Baxter took our child from us. Killed him while he was still inside my wife's womb. How the hell could it be all worth it?"

Andrews blanches for a moment before accepting his error. "I apologize. I was not thinking. Of course, it could not possibly make up for your loss," he says, fixing Sophie with a look of pure regret.

She nods her head, accepting his apology and letting me know she isn't going to dwell on his comment. "So, you have a warrant for his arrest?" Sophie asks, moving on.

He nods his head. "Just about. The paperwork is being put together now and will be on its way to a judge later today."

"Perfect," Sophie says in a quiet voice, deep within her own thoughts before turning to me. "It's over."

"It sure is, baby," I tell her as we get up and make our way out of the police station. I can't help but notice how Sophie walks with her shoulders held a little higher. It's as if all her worries have finally disappeared. She's her old self again, and I couldn't be prouder. She's come full circle.

Yes, we're missing one, massive, important part of our lives that we'll have to live without until our dying days, but with the knowledge he's in a better place, it makes it that much easier.

Our shining star watching over us, and Sophie's guardian angel.

I kick over the ignition and look at my wife. "I love you," I tell her as she reaches across the center console and takes my hand.

"I love you, too," she says with the most dazzling smile that takes my breath away.

"I can't wait to get you home," I tell her.

"I know, me too. It's going to be one hell of a wild night after the shit Crazy Jill put me through. Maybe I deserve more than just one naked cooking night. Let's make it a weeklong thing," she grins.

I roll my eyes as I pull out into the traffic. "You got yourself a deal, babe."

"Excellent," she laughs before turning to me, a guilty as fuck grin stretching across her lips. "So . . . I know you're probably in shit with Coach Larsden, but could you drop me off at Frisky Framing? I need my car."

I let out a deep breath. I couldn't possibly get in any more trouble than I'm already in. "Sure, babe."

"Thanks, big guy," she says with a wink before leaning forward and turning up the music.

It's game night, and my boys are just as pumped as I am. We all shuffle around each other in the locker room, taking practice shots at the target that's been painted on the wall as we wait for one of the officials to give us the go-ahead.

As usual, I line up my shot just perfectly and watch as it sails straight into the center of the target. I turn and give Miller a smirk as if to say *beat that* and he scoffs as he lines up his shot. His stick rears back before flying forward and the puck sails through the air with incredible speed, and as usual, it finds its mark, except it's just a smidge off-center.

Miller scrunches up his face as he turns back to me, having to declare himself the loser of this little challenge. "Mia was up all night," he says, attempting to excuse his poor efforts. But in all honesty, his shot is still one of the best in the team. Right behind mine, of course.

"Bullshit. Soph called Dani this morning, who said she slept right through," I laugh.

"Fuck," he curses before pushing his way to the front of the line and giving it another go.

I snicker to myself as I make my way across the room and to my locker. I grab my phone to send a quick text to Sophie but find one already waiting. I open up the message from my wife and smirk at the picture attached.

"Fuck me," I groan to myself as I take in my very naked wife in nothing but a pair of heels, sitting in a very suggestive position with the words *Good Luck* written across her tits in my team's colors. I'm one lucky son of a bitch and can't wait to take that woman home and show her just how happy she makes me.

I was wondering what she was doing this afternoon all holed up in our bedroom and refusing to let me come in, but it's certainly worth it now.

Knowing I only have a moment, I type out a quick reply.

Tank - Fuck, babe. I'm going to rock your world when we get home. All. Fucking. Night.

Sophie - I'm counting on it, big guy.

I can just imagine the sexy smirk on her face as she typed out her message. The thought has me grinning like a fucking idiot and growing hard beneath all this gear. And trust me, with the fucking cup I'm wearing, this shit ain't comfortable.

I adjust myself as I put my phone back in my locker while Coach Larsden calls our attention. The boys stop what they're doing and give him their undivided attention because they know exactly what would happen if they didn't.

"Alright boys," he starts. "Tonight is a big one. This determines if we make it to the semifinals. I want each and every one of you on point. No fuckups, you hear me?" he demands. "Cameron, keep on top of your footwork. Jake, no illegal moves. The rest of you, watch out for their defense. They're good, but not as good as us." His speech goes on and soon enough the boys are rowdy and excited.

The game official barges in, letting us know it's go time. We line up with me at the front and soon enough I'm leading the boys out of the hole.

The crowd roars the second we show our faces, and my stare snaps up to my wife sitting in the grandstand, only she isn't sitting. She's up on her feet jumping around like a fucking idiot, but at least she's not alone. Dani is right there by her side, letting the crowd know exactly who they're cheering for.

Twenty minutes later, I'm standing in the center of the ice, facing my opponent as the referee drops the puck. My stick snakes out and we scuffle for a second, fighting for the puck. I come out on top, and as soon as I have that puck safely in my possession, I take off like a bat out of hell.

I push forward with my boys right by my side, defending the puck just as they have been taught. A big fucker from the opposition comes barreling down the ice toward me, and out of all the guys on his team, he's probably the only one big enough to take me out.

I flick the puck across the ice to Cameron, who sends it straight to Miller just as the big fucker reaches me. I see his intention the moment before he makes his move, and I have all of one second to twist this situation in my favor.

He cuts around me and tries to throw me into the barrier, knowing I'm one of the biggest threats in the game and hoping to take me out early. I come to a hard stop and throw my body to the side, and the dickhead completely misses, throwing himself into the walls.

I grin at the fool, but don't have time to dwell on it as he drops to the ice like the sack of shit he is. After all, I have a game to dominate, and I refuse to let losers like this take me down. Besides, my wife is watching.

The crowd is suddenly on their feet cheering, and I search out the game to see Miller is close to shooting the first goal of the night. I take in his position against the opposition, and I know without a doubt he has this in the bag. Well, depending on how good their goalie is, but Miller has always had a talent for reading people.

I watch as his stick shoots forward, sending the puck sliding across the ice. It travels straight through the center and right between the goalie's legs. The buzzer sounds, followed by the sound of the crowd, yet Miller doesn't stop. He loops around the back of the nets and straight for me. I prepare as quickly as I can for the idiot as he leaps into the air and slams his chest into mine, tackling me to the ice.

"You can't say I don't still have it, fucker," he laughs as the rest of the boys pile on top of us.

"Just you wait. The game's still new," I say, trying to shove the moron off me. "I'll step off this ice with twice as many goals as you."

"Is that a challenge?" he asks with an excited twinkle in his eye as the guys start climbing off us.

I get to my feet and pull the dickhead up with me. "Fuck, yeah, it is," I grin.

By the end of the game, I'm proud to say that I whipped Miller's ass. Well, I didn't double his goals, but I sure as fuck beat him. Either way, we were on fire. Hell, the whole fucking team was.

The second we get the media off our heels, we head into the

locker room, and as expected, we've just started dropping our gear when that sexy as fuck voice is heard from the doorway. "Cover up, boys. I'm coming in."

My wife barrels through the door and runs straight for me. She throws herself into the air, and I catch her around the waist. She doesn't waste a single second before her lips are crushing down on mine.

"I swear that woman has a radar for half-naked men," I hear one of the guys mutter.

Sophie pulls back and turns toward the voice. "Correction. I have a radar for when my husband is getting naked. The fact that the rest of you guys are doing the same is just a bonus for me."

"Ugh," Miller grunts. "Please don't tell me I'm included in that bonus?"

"Sure are, hot stuff," she winks.

Miller scrunches up his face as he turns away from us and walks into the showers. "Don't tease him like that," I scold her.

"I thought you liked it when I was a bad girl," she grins.

"Fuck, babe. I gotta get you home. Give me two seconds to shower," I tell her.

"Don't even think about it," she warns me in a low, sultry voice that tells me she's dead serious. "I'm coming with you."

I raise my eyebrow, knowing she doesn't mind the audience as I desperately try to think over the consequences of screwing my woman in the showers. I mean, there's one stall with a door. "Are you sure, babe?"

She licks her lips as her eyes become hooded. "I've never been so sure in my life," she tells me "But make it fast. I need you now."

Fuck me.

I don't need any more convincing than that as I carry my wife into the bathroom and fuck her up against the cold tiles of the locker room showers.

CHAPTER 22

SOPHIE

What an amazing night. Watching my man dominate the ice and then dominate me in the locker room, wow. Since the day I met him, he has rocked my world in every possible way. Even six years later, he still manages to surprise me.

We pull up to our home and he practically jumps out of his truck and rushes around to my side. I open my door and he scoops me out of my chair before throwing me over his shoulder and spanking my ass.

I can't help but giggle at this big goofball as I kick my legs and beg him to let me down. I mean, the guy is ginormous. If I were to fall, it would be a long way down. But on the other hand, there's no way my man would ever let me fall.

He wraps his arm firmly around my body as he uses his other hand to fish his keys out of his pocket. While he's distracted, I slip my hand down the back of his pants and grab a handful of muscled ass, wondering if we'll actually make it to the bedroom.

As I wait for the door to open, my hand gets lower and lower and is dangerously close to somewhere that I know is going to earn me a damn spanking, but I can't help but grin knowing how much he hates it.

He gets the door open, and I'm flying through the air until I find myself wrapped around his torso with my legs twined around his waist and my lips crushed to his. He kicks the door closed with his foot and walks us down the hallway.

We come into the clearing of the living room when his body stiffens and he rips me off him before throwing me to my feet and stepping protectively in front of me. "What the fuck?" I question as I try to move around him, only his arm shoots back, slamming painfully hard against my chest, caging me behind him.

"I think you're lost," Tank says in a chilling tone that sends shivers sailing right down my spine, turning my blood cold.

What the fuck is going on?

My stomach sinks as I peek my head around my husband's side and a swarm of terrifying memories come rushing back. My heart starts to race and my palms begin to sweat, seeing my whole fucking world flashing before my eyes.

Christian Baxter sits in my living room chair, the same one he'd sat in all those months ago, right before he had my sweet baby murdered.

I never imagined in my life that things could ever get worse than what happened that day, and yet here he is again. Only this time, he sits with a gun pointed directly at my husband.

My hand slips into Tank's back pocket and I pull out his phone, discreetly searching for Detective Andrews' number as fast as I can before pressing the call button. Fuck, I hope he answers quickly and gets a damn move on, otherwise, we're fucked. I have no idea how we could possibly come out on top in this situation, but I know I'm not going down without a fight. There's no way I'm letting this lowlife get away with harming my family again. Not if I have anything to do with it.

Christian's chilling voice rings out through the room. "I think I'm exactly where I need to be," he says before directing his cold stare to me. "I warned you, Sophie. But you wanted to play with fire."

Tank subtly moves so that his body hides me from Christian's view. "You need to leave," Tank says in warning.

"Really?" Christian asks with an amused tone in his voice, waving the gun in his hand. "Do you think you're in a position to be making requests?"

I hear the familiar squeak of the couch telling me that he's on his feet. Tank makes slight adjustments and I realize Baxter must be moving about the living room.

Tank ignores Baxter's comments as he takes a small step forward. I glue myself to his back, knowing that's exactly where he wants me. Even though the thought of getting closer to this monster terrifies me, my gut tells me Tank is trying to get as close as possible in the hopes of disarming him.

If Baxter notices Tank's movement, he doesn't mention it. "You know, it's funny," Christian says. "I was out of town when I got the message there was a warrant out for my arrest. My home was raided and then my office."

Tank scoffs. "Must be a strange concept for you."

I almost want to high-five my husband for the amount of balls it must take to make a snide comment to a man wielding a gun, but then at the same time, I want to throat punch him for being so stupid.

Baxter ignores him and Tank takes the opportunity to take another step forward. Once again, I follow as closely as I can, hoping to God that Detective Andrews has answered the phone already.

"None of this would have happened if it weren't for you, Sophie," Baxter says. "Why don't you step forward and take responsibility for your actions, rather than making me go through your husband?"

I don't say a word, knowing that would only piss Tank off. "You're in this situation because you murdered three men and then went after my wife," Tank says as he takes another step forward. "Why don't you take responsibility for your actions and hand yourself in?"

"Why don't you step out of the way so I can deal with your bitch of a wife once and for all," he snaps at Tank.

I can almost hear the smirk in Tank's voice. "You're fucking delusional if you think I'd ever do that."

"Fine by me," Christian says in a tone that sends shivers straight down my spine. Something tells me this is it. That Detective Andrews is too late, and I'm about to lose my husband. In a moment of sheer panic, I step out from behind Tank and notice the gun pointed directly at his chest.

Baxter's gaze follows my movements, but mine follow the mountain of a man who launches himself clear across the room, tackling Baxter to the ground.

A scream tears from my throat as they scuffle on the living room floor. Tank manages to get the gun from Baxter's hand and tosses it across the room.

I run as fast as I can and chase the gun as it slides across the tiled floor. I grab it and turn it on Baxter, but my hands begin to shake. I've never held a gun before, and I can honestly say, it's not something I ever want to do again.

"Stop it," I scream as the two men continue to scuffle on the ground, completely oblivious to the gun in my hand. Either that, or neither of them believe I have the balls to pull the trigger and follow through.

I watch as Tank finally gets through and nails him hard with a punch to the jaw that has Baxter's head flying backward, a sickening *crunch* sounding throughout my living room. The blow looks as though it should have knocked him out, or at least slowed him down, but it's as though he doesn't even notice it.

They continue on, and I watch with fear as tears fall from my eyes. When will this stop?

My husband's pained curse has my eyes widening, focusing harder as Baxter lets out a wicked laugh. My eyes roam over Tank's body, but I don't understand what caused his cry until his body goes limp and he falls to the side clutching his stomach, blood seeping between his fingers.

"NO," I scream.

It's then I notice the knife in Baxter's hand and the evil smirk plastered across his face as he attempts to get to his feet.

My eyes flick back to my husband bleeding out on our living room floor, the greatest fear in his dark eyes. "Run," he yells, but I can't move. I can't fucking breathe.

Baxter begins to stalk me, but my feet remain glued to the floor. Anger burns in Tank's eyes, but surely he must know that I won't ever leave without him. He's all I have left of my heart. I could never turn my back on him.

Baxter takes another step toward me, the knife held steady in his hand as Tank's blood drips from the sharp blade. "I warned you, Sophie," he says before pointing at Tank, who watches on in fear. "Now look what you've done."

"Stop," I demand as I point the gun more firmly at his chest.

Baxter smirks at me as though I'm some misbehaved child playing with something I shouldn't be touching, yet somehow, that's exactly how I feel. He continues stalking me with the blood-stained knife, almost daring me to pull the trigger. "You won't do it," he practically laughs. "Look at you, you're pathetic. You couldn't save your kid, and now because of you, your husband is going to bleed out on the floor. Even with a gun in your hand, you can't save yourself. You don't have the guts. You're weak, Sophie."

I take a hesitant step backward as I begin to question myself. I don't want to pull the trigger, but I have no choice. It's either me or him, and I can guarantee that if he's the survivor in this situation, he won't be saving my husband.

He spins the knife in his hand and the blade catches in the light, displaying just how deadly the weapon truly is as blood spatters across the room. He takes another step, making my stomach clench in fear. "I'm going to finish you, Sophie Meyers. Just like I should have done the first time,"

Tears continue rolling down my face as the nausea hits. This fucker is going to kill me. I back up another step and he follows me, matching my strides like we're in a wicked dance. I see the moment he makes the decision, pure lethalness in his dark eyes.

In a split second, his arm winds back and his knees bend, ready to strike. "NOW, SOPHIE," Tank roars from across the room, using whatever ounce of energy he has left.

I don't hesitate.

The gun rings out and echoes through my head, my arm flinging back with the recoil, pain blasting through my shoulder. Baxter drops to the ground as my ears scream in protest, and I watch with wide eyes as he latches onto his chest, letting out an agonized groan.

He doesn't move, and as he starts gasping for air with blood seeping out onto his shirt, I realize I must have punctured a lung.

Without a second of hesitation, my gaze flicks toward Tank across the room, and my feet are already moving before I've even finished taking him in. "No, no, no, no," I chant, racing toward his limp body, the life draining out of him as the blood pools beneath him.

I drop down at Tank's side and the gun clatters to the floor beside me, my hands violently shaking as I press them to Tank's wound, attempting to stop the bleeding. Panic tears at my chest as the blood seeps through my fingers like an endless stream, unable to be controlled.

I'm going to lose him.

The front door is kicked in and I hear someone call out "Police," but I ignore their advances as Tank's eyes begin to close. "No," I cry. "Stay with me. I can't do this without you."

Sobs begin ripping up my throat as Detective Andrews drops down beside me and places a hand on my shoulder. "Sophie. Let me take over," he demands.

"Where's the ambulance? I need an ambulance!" I yell.

Someone grabs me and moves me out of the way so the police can start first aid, but I don't let them take me far as I hold onto Tank's motionless body. "Don't you dare leave me, Tank," I demand as the sobs completely take over. "Open your eyes. Please, open your eyes."

The paramedics arrive a moment later, and it's a blur of activity as they rush to get Tank into the back of the ambulance and to the hospital. The trip could have taken two minutes or it could have been half an hour. I'll never be sure. All I know is that I haven't taken my eyes off my husband's body. The only type of relief I have is the very slow beep coming from the heart rate monitor telling me that for now, he's still holding on. Still fighting.

The moment we arrive at the hospital, Tank is whisked away, and I'm left behind in the waiting room with nothing but my thoughts. My head drops low into my hands, and soon enough, I'm surrounded by friends and family. I have absolutely no idea how they knew to come. Maybe I called them. Maybe I didn't. I don't know.

I sit in a mess of tears as Dani holds onto my hand with every last ounce of strength she possesses. He can't leave me. He's going to make it. Tank is the strongest man I've ever met. I just know he'll be okay. Otherwise, I don't know how I'm going to survive. I can't help but think that if he were to leave me, at least our little boy could be with his daddy, and the thought gives me some semblance of peace. But I'm not ready for that. Not even close. I'm selfish enough to need to keep him here with me.

My eyes continue looking up at the clock, watching the hours tick by. My nerves get the best of me, and I stand from the chair that I've spent the last five hours sitting in and begin pacing the room. Doctors and nurses come in and out of the room, and each time I hold my breath, waiting for them to call my name.

And then finally . . .

A disheveled doctor comes through the doors, seven hours after arriving, and calls my name. "Mrs. Meyers?" he questions the packed waiting room.

I practically sprint to the doctor, desperate for answers. "You're the wife of Tyler Meyers?" he confirms.

"Yes," I nearly shout at him.

"Why don't you take a seat?" he asks as he motions to the available chairs beside us. I hastily take a seat, trying not to yell at him to get on with it.

I wait impatiently as he lowers his exhausted body into the space beside me. He lets out a breath before getting started. "Your husband is now out of surgery and is doing well." Instant relief takes over me, and I have to force myself to pay attention. "He lost so much blood that we needed to restart his heart three times. However, he's one hell of a strong man, and he had a lot of fight in him."

He goes on to discuss the types of internal injuries that were sustained and how they were rectified. I listen intently so I don't miss a thing, and when he finally says that I can go sit with him, I throw my arms around the good doctor.

"Thank you, so much," I say as I cry onto his shoulder.

"No need to thank me, sweetheart," he says as he gives my shoulder a gentle squeeze before awkwardly trying to move away from me. "It's what I'm here for."

With that, the doctor disappears through the door, and I follow him until I find a nurse who can give me directions to the recovery ward. My head is way too foggy to remember the directions, even after spending enough time here myself.

Pushing my way through his door, I race to his side and collect his big hand in mine, just the way he'd done for me. I'm silently begging him to wake up so I can see those eyes I thought I would never see again.

An hour later, his hand twitches in mine, and my stare snaps to his handsome face. His eyes begin to open, and it feels like all my Christmases have come at once. A tear escapes my eye as I lean in closer to my husband.

"Tank?" I whisper into the quiet room, desperate for this wait to be over.

He turns his head toward me and squeezes my hand with the faintest smile gracing those perfect lips. "Don't cry, baby," he says. "You can't get rid of me that easy."

Tears of joy spring from my eyes as I look at my incredible husband. "Don't you ever do that to me again," I sob.

He lifts his hand out of mine and gently wipes my tears with his thumb. "Are you okay?" he questions, his voice thick with sleep.

"Me?" I nearly shriek, unable to believe he came back to me. "I should be asking you that."

He tries to sit up, but I fly forward and force his big body back down. "Don't move," I warn him. "You have like a million internal stitches."

"Shit," he groans. "I'll be out for the rest of the season."

"Don't worry about that right now," I tell him, knowing how much that must be playing on his mind, hating the thought of letting down his team. "You need to heal first, and then we can sort out how you're going to keep kicking ass."

"Speaking of kicking ass," he says before resting his eyes on mine. "You shot him?"

"Yeah," I sigh before looking away, the reminder making my hands start to shake. "He's apparently a few rooms down, but he has a police escort."

"Are you alright?" he questions.

I look back at him and bite the inside of my cheek as I really think it over. "Um . . . Yes. No. I . . . I really don't know. I haven't really had a chance to think about it. All that mattered was getting to you and making sure you were alright."

He gently shakes his head, everything he isn't saying evident in the way he watches me. "I told you to run."

My mouth drops and I gape at my husband before gripping his hand even tighter and leaning into him. "When I went back to Denver, I told you I was never going to run again. I'm sure as fuck not going to start now. You're my person, Tank. If you're going down, I'm going right down with you."

Tank holds my stare, his eyes shining with overwhelming love. "Get your fucking ass over here and kiss me," he demands.

Even straight after major surgery, he's still a demanding asshat, but I can't possibly resist. I climb up onto the hospital bed and gently wiggle my way in beside him, knowing he must be in excruciating pain. Though I know without a doubt that he isn't going to mention it, and I know better than to ask.

Curling into his side, I look up at him as his arm wraps around my body, holding me tight against him as though he might just die without me. "I thought I was going to lose you," I tell him as another tear streaks down my cheek.

"I know, baby," he murmurs as his fingers trail up and down my arm, desperately trying to soothe me. "I'm not going anywhere."

"I love you so much," I tell him as I reach up and place my forehead against his.

"I love you, too, Sophie," he tells me before inching forward and capturing my lips in his. "It's you and me for the long haul. You, me, and our star shining down on us."

I can't help but smile, finally feeling my heart starting to settle before kissing him once again. I don't have the whole world like I always wanted to have, and there's always going to be a gaping hole in my chest. But as long as I have Tank at my side, I know I'm going to be okay.

"Tank?" I whisper, pulling back from his kiss, a soft smile playing on my lips. "I think we're going to need a new house."

"Hmm," he agrees, trying to grin back at me but not having the energy to force it through. "Somewhere private and hidden away, with armed guards stationed at every entrance point twenty-four-seven."

"Definitely," I tell him. "Imagine all the new places we would have to christen."

He groans low and I feel it rumble right through his chest. "Is that a challenge?"

I shake my head, grinning wide. "No, big guy. It's a fucking promise."

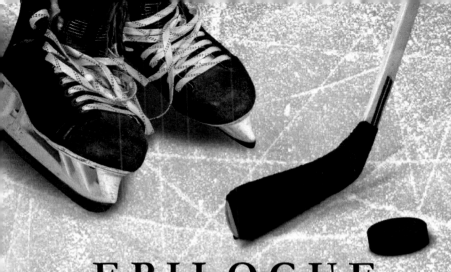

EPILOGUE

SOPHIE

2 YEARS LATER

I stand next to my brother on his wedding day, and I can't believe this day is finally here. It feels like it's been such a long time coming, and so far, it's been absolutely beautiful. Though I would have preferred to have been in one of the shimmering golden dresses the bridesmaids are wearing rather than a black tux like the rest of the groom's party, but I guess that's what happens when you struggle to get along with the bride. On the other hand, Zac let me pimp out my tux, so I must admit, I look damn fine.

Standing here on this day, in my hometown between Zac and Tank, with my parents right before me, there's truly nowhere else I'd rather be. The music begins just as Tank laces his fingers through mine.

It's been a struggle these past few years. We barely survived all the Christian Baxter bullshit and then Tank was put out for the final two games of the season. Coach Larsden gave him another shot at being captain the following season, but it's still a loss that hit Tank hard.

Not to mention, when we finally found ourselves ready to start trying for another baby, we were devastated all over again. Month after month the pregnancy tests would come back negative until we went to get me checked out. And once again, Christian Baxter had taken everything from me.

My injuries from the attack made it impossible for me to carry another baby, and that's something I've been struggling with ever since.

I look up at Tank and give him a beaming smile as the first bridesmaid commences her way down the aisle. Today is not a day to dwell on the horrors of our past, but to welcome more happiness and light into our lives.

One after another, the bridesmaids come down in those stunning dresses, and judging by the perkiness of MJ's sister and the way she keeps eyeing Zac's best friend, that dress will be on the bathroom floor at some point tonight. And when it is, you can bet your ass that dress will be mine.

The music changes and the crowd gets to their feet. "Are you ready for this, baby brother?" I murmur as we wait for MJ to make her appearance.

He turns to me with a smile that I've never quite seen before, and I read the answer in his eyes before the words get a chance to slip through his lips. "Yeah," he says. "I've never been so ready."

A vibration starts in my pocket, and my hand clenches down on Tank's, my eyes widening with horror.

Shit. I forgot to turn off my phone.

Tank looks down at me in concern as I slide my free hand into my pocket and fish my phone out while discreetly stepping behind my brother so the massive crowd won't notice. I go to send the call to voicemail when I glance down at the screen, my eyes widening once again.

"Holy shit," I gasp, my heart kicking into gear.

"What?" Tank questions as he pretends to continue smiling and being the perfect groomsman.

Zac gets wind of our conversation and turns around to find me staring down at my phone, just watching it ring. "Are you shitting me right now? MJ is about to come down the aisle. Put your fucking phone away."

"Too late, little brother," I grin as MJ makes her appearance at the other end, looking absolutely stunning. My comment draws his attention away as he focuses on his beautiful bride, allowing me to focus on the phone call.

I cringe knowing this isn't the best time, but I hit accept on the call anyway, all too aware that my brother will hold this over my head for the rest of our lives. Pulling Tank a step closer to Zac to hide me behind them, I hastily lift the phone to my ear. "Hello?" I whisper.

"Hi, there. Is this Sophie?" The woman on the other end says, sounding a little unsure, probably not able to hear me properly.

"Yes, this is her," I answer as my brother turns around and gapes at me.

"For fucks sake," he mutters before gesturing to Mom and Dad as if they can do something about me.

"Hi, Sophie. It's Suzannah from the LA Adoption Agency. I'm just giving you a call to let you know your birth mother has just gone into labor."

Oh, holy fuck. It's happening.

"Seriously?" I shriek in excitement as my hand clenches down on Tank's once again. Holy crap. I knew it would be soon, but I didn't quite expect it would be today of all days.

Tank turns around and I look up at him with tears brimming in my eyes. "Yes, dear," Suzannah continues, absolute joy in her tone. "It's still very early and the process is coming along slowly, so you have a few hours before you need to be at the hospital. However, you should start making arrangements."

"Okay, we will," I smile as the tears really start streaming down my face. "Thank you, so much."

I'm going to be a mommy. I'm going to be a mommy. Holy fuck, I'm really going to be a mommy.

"No problem. I'll meet you at the hospital with the paperwork," she tells me before ending the call.

"What is it?" Tank questions the second I pull the phone away from my ear.

"Lily's gone into labor," I tell him as I throw my arms around him. "We're going to be parents."

"Holy shit," he says, his body going rigid. "Are you sure?"

Zac turns again with an angry scowl across his handsome face. "What the fuck is going on?" he demands as MJ makes it to his side. She takes his hand, and he looks back at her with an adoring smile. "You look amazing," he tells her. She blushes slightly before zoning in on the fact that something is going on down this end of the aisle.

Tank ignores everyone in the room as his full attention is on me. "Shouldn't we be going?" he questions with urgency.

"No, not yet," I tell him. "We still have a few hours. We can make the end of the ceremony then catch a flight back home. We won't miss it," I promise him.

"What?" Zac demands. "You two aren't going anywhere. I haven't even said my vows yet."

My dad takes this opportunity to step in, followed by my mother right behind him. "What the ever-loving hell is going on over here? I came to see a damn wedding, and all I can see is a bunch of idiots screwing it up," my father demands.

"Our birth mother just went into labor. We're going to have a baby," I tell them all elatedly, while also feeling like a complete douchebag. This is Zac's big day, and here I am, spurting my news as his soon-to-be bride has only just made it down the aisle.

"Ohhh," my mother starts sobbing as she pulls me into a hug, and then grabs Tank to bring him in on the action.

From then on, I can't really recall who says what, but after five minutes, my father manages to pull everything back into order. "Right," he says. "Get your shit together. We have a wedding to get through, so you two can get out of here."

"What? You're not staying for the reception?" Zac whines.

"Sorry, bro," I cringe. "But nature calls."

"Don't worry," MJ intervenes. "It will be fine. We'll fly in tomorrow to meet your beautiful baby and we can tell you all about it. You need to be there for your child."

"Thank you," I smile, thinking I might just like her after all. "Now, let's get you two idiots hitched."

"Holy shit," Tank mutters to himself for what must be the twentieth time.

I grab his hand and hold on tight as our private plane touches down. We had to run from the ceremony to the airport, only to find that every domestic flight from Denver to LA was full, so we did what any other newly expecting parents would have done and booked ourselves a private plane, while thanking the heavens that my husband is raking in cash.

We anxiously wait for the plane to come to a stop before we find ourselves rushing through the airport and trying to get out the front doors.

Tank decides I'm not keeping up well enough and grabs me around my waist, hoisting me over his shoulder, and taking off to his truck.

He throws me in the truck and demands I buckle up before slamming the door and bolting around to his side. The ignition is started and we're peeling out of the airport parking lot within seconds.

"Calm down," I tell him as he drives us to the hospital. "You're going to freak poor Lily out."

"Sorry," he grunts as he pulls into a parking spot. "I can't help it."

"I know," I laugh, jumping out of his truck and meeting him around the front. "Are you ready for this?"

A massive grin takes over his handsome face. "Fuck yeah."

That's enough for me. We take off inside, hand in hand, following the directions to the maternity ward. Soon enough, we're ushered into the room with fifteen-year-old Lily, who is currently going through the worst pain of her life.

She clocks us the second we walk through the door. "Oh, you guys are here," she smiles as a bead of sweat trickles down the side of her face. If she notices the matching tuxes, she doesn't mention it.

"We wouldn't miss it for the world," I tell her before coming right to her side and taking her hand. "How are you doing?"

"Not great," she pants as another contraction comes on. "It hurts so bad."

"I know, sweet girl, but you're doing great so far. Not much longer to go," I soothe her as I order Tank to grab her a damp washcloth. He brings it over, and I instantly press it to her forehead, doing everything we can to make this easier for her.

"Shit, you guys are going to be great parents," she tells me, which has tears springing to my eyes.

"Thank you," I whisper as Tank stands behind me and rests his hands on my shoulders.

"Is there anything you need?" he asks Lily, who's preparing for another contraction. "Water? Ice chips?"

"Drugs?" she questions.

"Sorry, Lily," the doctor says as he comes into the room. "You're too far along now. It's just about time to push."

Her eyes widen as she looks at the doctor in fear. "Oh, shit," she breathes as she latches onto my hand, squeezing so fucking tight I lose feeling in my fingers.

"You'll be okay," I soothe as the doctor moves around the room, preparing Lily for delivery.

A short ten minutes later, her legs are up in the stirrups, and the doctor is telling her to push. With Tank and I on either side, we watch as our beautiful baby is brought into the world.

Tears of joy stream down my face as the doctor places the most gorgeous child in my arms and I instantly fall in love, my world finally feeling complete for the first time in nearly three years. "Congratulations," the doctor says with a proud smile. "It's a girl."

Tank comes and stands by me, looking down at our daughter in awe. "She's beautiful," he breathes as he presses a kiss to my forehead.

I raise my chin and capture his lips in mine. "God, I love you so much," I tell him before looking down at our daughter again, his warm arms circling us both.

"She's absolutely perfect," I whisper before turning to Lily, who's watching us with tears in her eyes. "I don't know how we're ever going to be able to thank you. Nothing will ever be enough."

She wipes her eyes before giving us a sad smile, and I'm sure that this will be the hardest thing she'll ever do. It will be a moment she'll think about every day for the rest of her life. "Just be the best parents you can be to that little girl. That's all I'll ever ask of you."

"We will," I promise her.

"Do you have a name picked out?" she questions, struggling to keep the tears at bay.

I look up at Tank with a proud smile before turning back to Lily. "If it's okay with you, we'd like to name her Lily."

"Really?" she questions, her voice breaking.

"If it weren't for you, we'd never have this child. We owe everything to you," Tank says.

Her sad smile quickly becomes a proud, beaming one as she looks at the child she just gifted us. "Lily is perfect."

We're soon ushered out of the room with our new baby so Lily can go through the recovery process, and I must thank her at least a million times more before we're led away.

We're taken to the maternity ward, where our beautiful little girl is measured and weighed before we have the chance to dress her.

A nurse comes in with a bottle of formula and explains the process of how to make up her bottles while Tank listens intently, terrified of screwing it up, but he won't. He's going to be such an incredible father to this little girl.

Before we know it, our daughter is a few hours old and is fast asleep in her daddy's arms. A knock sounds at the door, and I find a very pregnant Dani pushing her way into the room with Miller and Mia right on her heels, completing our beautiful family.

While they gush and coo, I can't help but think that this little girl is a gift sent to us from above. A gift sent to us by a beautiful little boy, who I have no doubt hasn't stopped looking down on his mommy and daddy with an abundance of happiness.

And I vow, in this very moment, that I will do everything I can to ensure our daughter knows just how loved both she and her big brother are.

Forever and always.

THANKS FOR READING

If you enjoyed reading this book as much as I enjoyed writing it, please consider leaving an Amazon review to let me know. https://www.amazon.com/dp/B0BSDJDLGG

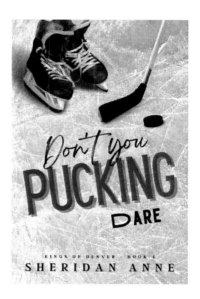

For more information on the Kings of Denver, find me on Facebook –

www.facebook.com/sheridansbookishbabes

STALK ME!

Join me online with the rest of the stalkers!!
I swear, I don't bite. Not unless you say please!

Facebook Reader Group
www.facebook.com/SheridansBookishBabes

Facebook Page
www.facebook.com/sheridan.anne.author1

Instagram
www.instagram.com/Sheridan.Anne.Author

TikTok
www.tiktok.com/@Sheridan.Anne.Author

Subscribe to my Newsletter
https://landing.mailerlite.com/webforms/landing/a8q0y0

MORE BY SHERIDAN ANNE
www.amazon.com/Sheridan-Anne/e/B079TLXN6K

DARK CONTEMPORARY ROMANCE - M/F
Broken Hill High | Haven Falls | Broken Hill Boys | Aston Creek High | Rejects Paradise | Bradford Bastard

DARK CONTEMPORARY ROMANCE - REVERSE HAREM
Boys of Winter | Depraved Sinners | Empire

NEW ADULT SPORTS ROMANCE
Kings of Denver | Denver Royalty | Rebels Advocate

CONTEMPORARY ROMANCE (standalones)
Play With Fire | Until Autumn (Happily Eva Alpha World)

PARANORMAL ROMANCE
Slayer Academy [Pen name - Cassidy Summers]